CAST OF CHARACTERS

Abraham Family

Jason: Patriarch & father of Jeffery & Aaron
Amanda: Matriarch & mother of Jeffery & Aaron
Jeffery: CEO Abracorp & father of JT, Salina & David
Sonia: Professor of Horticulture, mother of JT, Salina & David
John (JT): Captain ECS Valiant

Salina: Marine Biologist
David: Financial controller Abracorp
Aaron: Freebooter Trader, estranged brother of Jeffery

Coalition Space Corps
Skye Wilson: Fleet Admiral
Simon Morris: Rear Admiral, Deputy to Wilson
Sam Grogan: Admiral – Commander Space Corps
Alan Dean: Captain – Adjutant to Admiral Morris
Sol Radchak: Captain – Commander Space Corps training

Crew ECS Valiant
JT Abraham: Captain
Jarad Cross: First Officer
Greg Holgate: Tactical Officer
Amy Rodregas: Chief Engineer
Colin Bryant: Sensor sensor/defence officer Sharon Holm:
Communication officer & linguist Helen Tradeski: Weapons
Officer

Dave Carmelli: Second Weapons Officer
Holly Morgan: Navigation Officer

Freebooter Characters

Freebooter Trade Ship (FTS) Condor

Aaron Abraham: Captain and CEO AA Trading

Petra Mannix: First Officer

Kate Albrecht: Second Officer

Simon Holm: Navigator

David Cross: Tactical Officer

Dianna Holland: Chief Engineer

Colin Anderson: Engineer

William Croker: Sensor Officer

Phillip Harper: Cadet

FTS Albatross

Steve Harris: Captain

Greg Lewis: First Officer

Zab'ata Gollti: Second Officer

Other Freebooter Characters

Henry N'Gabo: Proctor AA Trading

Jacinta N'Gabo: Henry's Wife and Medical Technician

Allen Grainger: Freebooter Prime

Other Characters

Salim Malik: President Earth Coalition of Planets

Silas Greenbach: CEO Greenbach Technology

Kratc Dokad: Admiral – Krell Imperial Navy

Damien Albrecht: CEO Vision Cruise Lines

Eugene Sarclan: Former CEO of Sarcorp (liquidated) – dissident

Anthony Crompton: Director Coalition Intelligence Directorate (CID)

GREG MUTTON

Chronicle of the Twelfth Realm

BOOK 2

SEDITION RISING

Cover design: Gail Rust.
Image: Shutterstock
ISBN: 978-0-909497-02-6 (paperback)
978-0-909497-03-3 (Ebook)
Second Edition 2020
Font Calibri 11.5 pt

Ivan Klastok: General – Commander Coalition Army

Damien Albrect: CEO Vision Cruise Lines

Janice Barker: CID Operative

Dr Anton Alvaris: CEO Omnicron and Security Consultant

Inter Realm Characters

Eldrac-Tar: Senior Eldoran Councillor

Jok-Tar: Son of Eldrac-Tar

Zal-Tar: Daughter of Eldrac-Tar

Mondrac: Eldoran Council Member – half-brother to Eldrac-Tar

Zarof: Leader of Galdor

Nefaris: Queen Regent of Nileros

Tocmal: Admiral – Commander Reglaos armed Forces

ACKNOWLEDGEMENTS

As with the first book in the series, I have many people to thank. The Advance Team I have is invaluable, their contributions make writing very rewarding. They read my work, critique it and make suggestions based on their reading experience. To me this is the most important contribution I can have. Editors, writers and other literary professionals examine from their learned perspectives, but a reader reads the book, and their experience is the most telling review of all.

I can't name all, there are too many, but I thank each and every one of them for their invaluable help and advice.

*At the centre of your being you have the answer,
you know who you are and you know what you want.*

Lau Tzu

At 10:45am on Friday 14th February 2921, a small space ship reinserted into normal space in the twelfth realm, approximately 100,000 kilometres from Jupiter station. The vessel's transponder activated, announcing their presence – the response was immediate.

Unidentified vessel this is Earth Coalition station Jupiter, please verify your identity.

Aaron Abraham smiled and opened the comm channel. 'Jupiter Station this is FTS Condor Junior, requesting transit to Earth.'

FTS Condor Junior, we verify your transponder but we cannot locate you on sensor. Please deactivate your cloaking device.

Aaron chuckled. 'Jupiter Station, we have no cloak.'

Condor Junior, hold your position. We are sending a patrol craft to visually verify.

Aaron shook his head and looked to Petra. 'You heard him... all stop.' And he replied to the comm, 'Jupiter Station, Condor Junior holding position. Do you have an ETA for the patrol vessel?'

Condor Junior, we have requested one to be despatched, ETA your position twenty minutes.

'Twenty minutes, confirm Jupiter Station.'

Twenty minutes, confirmed.

Petra switched the nav system to station keeping and left the pilot's chair. 'Nothing to do but wait, I'll let our guests know.' She patted Aaron on the arm as she left the bridge. Aaron moved to the comm station and quietly dictated a message. When he finished, he sent it via the sub space link.

'A-Bra-Ham, do you expect trouble?' Tocmal asked, seeming a little too enthusiastic.

'Not really, just letting others know we are back, and that we are being delayed here.' He resumed his seat and settled back to wait. The patrol craft arrived twenty five minutes later, and closed to within 20 kilometres before the comm system announced its presence.

FTS Condor Junior, this is Coalition patrol vessel Cambridge. We have visual of your vessel... please state your business in the Solar System.

Aaron sighed and answered, 'Coalition patrol vessel, this is Captain Abraham. We are on a diplomatic mission to the Coalition Council.'

FTS Condor Junior, our sensors have detected two alien life forms not on our data base, and two human life signs in stasis. Please explain this?

'Cambridge, we have on board Ambassador Tocmal of Reglaos and Ambassador Mondrac of the Eldoran Federation, they have urgent business with President Malik. I would suggest you think carefully before starting an interstellar incident. Who is in command?' Aaron's voice was firm.

Lieutenant Commander Considrio; please wait. The mention of a possible incident seemed to have an effect;

they waited while Considrio conferred with his commander. The comm system activated again, this time a different voice.

Captain Abraham, this is Commander Hargraves, commander of Jupiter station. We have no notification of any diplomatic mission and no record of either the Eldoran Federation or this Reglaos you mention. You will, therefore, proceed to the station, under guard, and dock so we can verify these ambassadors' bona fides.

'Commander Hargraves, I am a member of the Freebooter Council of Seniors and, as included in the articles of status with your government, am to be afforded diplomatic immunity. Your demands could be interpreted as a hostile act and I don't think either of us wants that, do we?'

Tocmal was clicking and buzzing furiously; Aaron could only translate a small portion of it but got the impression he didn't like bureaucrats here anymore than he did on his own planet.

'Commander, I suggest you call Admiral Grogan and ask him what you should do, before this situation escalates.'

'A-Bra-Ham, another vessel has just appeared from hyperspace. It is heading this way,' Mondrac called. Mondrac transferred the data feed as Aaron started the recognition program.

Jupiter Station, this is Captain JT Abraham aboard the ECS Valiant... what seems to be the trouble?

Hargraves voice replied, *Captain, that vessel has unidentified alien life forms aboard and refuses to dock so we can verify them... their Captain claims he has diplomatic immunity.*

That's correct, Commander, he does. I'll take this from

here, Valiant out. There was a pause as the comm systems were secured, *Well, Captain Abraham, you certainly know how to make friends.* Aaron could almost hear the smirk he knew JT would now have on his face.

'Thank you Captain, our cup of diplomacy is empty at the moment,' Aaron replied to his nephew.

Roger that, but you need to understand you caused a bit of an uproar when you disappeared last Sunday. Where have you been?

'Long story JT. Get us back to Earth and we can discuss it.'

OK, I've cleared a path, transmitting Displacement data now. I'll clear things with the station and we can leave. Aaron transferred the data to Navigation and activated the system. Their displacement drive opened a worm hole and Junior left Jupiter Station behind.

The arrival in Earth orbit was very different. Junior was met by three patrol vessels and escorted to Perth Space Port, where they were directed to a VIP hangar. Here a delegation including Malik, Wilson and some of the senior Coalition Council members were waiting. Aaron finally grounded the ship, completed the power down sequence and opened the airlock. He turned to his companions. 'Time to face the music I suppose.'

'What is music? It doesn't sound very inviting,' Tocmal questioned.

Aaron and Mondrac laughed. 'Just a figure of speech; actually, music is something very dear to Humans. I'll show you sometime but for now, official duties await... Ambassadors.' He stood to one side and allowed them to leave the bridge first.

As they reached the exit ramp Petra joined them, she was

holding four prototypes of the translator. 'I thought it might be appropriate to have some of these ready... I could only make four.'

'Excellent idea,' Tocmal clicked, 'for this small group that should be enough.' Aaron and Petra left first and stopped either side of the ramp as the others came down. They walked forward to the reception committee.

'President Malik, may I introduce Mondrac, Ambassador of the Eldoran Federation. Mondrac, President Malik of the Earth Coalition of Planets.' Mondrac stepped forward and greeted Malik. Next, Petra stepped forward and handed the translator to Malik, instructing him on its use. 'President Malik, this is Admiral Tocmal, Ambassador of Reglaos.'

'I am pleased to meet you, President Mal-lik. I bring greetings and an offer of friendship from our Mother Queen.' Tocmal spoke and to all but Malik, it sounded like a lot of strange buzzing and clicking, but, thanks to the translator, Malik heard the words in Basic, the standard tongue for the Coalition.

'Ambassador Tocmal, I thank you for your words and offer friendship to the people of Reglaos,' Malik replied. The formalities continued with translators given to Admiral Wilson and Madam Collard, senior council member. The last unit was for Grainger, who accepted it and greeted both Ambassadors on behalf of Argos and Freebooters everywhere. In the brief communication Aaron had had with Grainger, he had requested that his guests be given time to acclimatise before any official duties were required.

He had also contacted Jeff and arranged for them all to spend the weekend at Orange, allowing time for acclimatization and more importantly, time for more translators to be made. However, protocol demanded a reception, and this was held in the conference room adjacent to the hangar. Thankfully, it only lasted for an hour, with each person present being able to talk to, and welcome, both ambassadors.

Finally, Malik called a halt to proceedings and announced that a formal reception would be held at the Presidential Palace the following Tuesday. Protocol now satisfied, Aaron led his entourage back to Junior, with two extras; Grainger and Jeff Abraham had joined them for the trip to Orange.

Once airborne, the comm system again activated.

FTS Condor Junior, this is ECS Valiant. We have been assigned as your security, for the moment, and we will be tailing you to your destination. Strange thing is I can see you, visually, but you do not register on any of our sensors.

'JT, glad to have you on overwatch, can you hang back and call me when you lose visual.'

Wilco!' Aaron took this as his cue to accelerate. It was only a few seconds until JT called.

Condor Junior... I've lost visual. Aaron checked his sensors; 35 kilometres. At the altitude they were flying at, Junior should have been easily visible.

'JT, I'm decelerating... call when you see us again.' While this was a very basic test, it did demonstrate how valuable the Reglaon coating could be.

Junior, I can see you again. Again Aaron checked his sensors; 20 kilometres.

Duly impressed, Aaron hailed Valiant. 'Thanks JT... I'll explain over the weekend.' Tocmal and Mondrac had never seen Earth before and Aaron wanted to give them a good view of the planet.

They headed to the northern hemisphere where the massive ice sheet that now covered almost half the land mass of Earth astounded Tocmal. The inevitable question as to what had happened was answered honestly, much to the dismay of Tocmal who found it difficult to believe that any species could do so much damage for nothing. When asked the motive for such stupidity, the answer was equally unbelievable, to Tocmal.

'You mean that your ancestors caused all this? Almost wiped themselves out for something that didn't actually exist… something that had no real value?'

Aaron understood how this might confuse his friend and tried to explain. 'Back in those days, when the real damage was done, the goal of everyone was wealth. Without money the world, as it was, couldn't function. Money was used for everything: to buy food; to buy a house; to buy clothes… but the worst part was hoarding.

'Success was measured by how much money one could accumulate; how many things one could own. Entire industries sprang and thrived, satisfying the demand for needless requirements; the latest gadget, the latest computer game or application becoming a symbol of ones standing. Eventually people were reduced to the same currency, automation and robotics became cheaper resulting in many humans left without work. Without work there was no money; no money and a person had no value. Thankfully we changed, but not before we all contributed to this devastation.

'We still use a form of currency, though it is not the main driving force now. We just haven't been able to devise a better form of exchange.'

'I am sorry A-Bra-Ham, but that doesn't sound like the

actions of a rational being.' Tocmal shook his head, still gazing at the white desolation before him.

Aaron laughed. 'I never said Humans were rational, my friend. One human on its own may be very rational, but a herd of humans can be totally irrational. But, as I said, we learned our lesson; we now try to live in harmony with the worlds we inhabit.

'When we were at our lowest ebb, there were twelve billion of us on the planet. Now there are a little over three hundred million but, on the colonies, we now number over forty billion, and each colony has its own responsibilities to their planet. I don't think humans will ever repeat this mistake again.'

He changed course and headed back south, flying over central and South America, the scenery here more to Tocmal's taste. Beautiful forests, jungles and sensitive developments were flashing below them. Aaron took them over the Antarctic continent and back to Australia, the last part of their tour at low altitude and slow speed so they could take in the view.

They were off the coast north of Sydney at an altitude of 30 metres when just ahead something leapt out of the water; huge paddle like protrusions attached to its side slapping the water as it landed.

'What was that?' Tocmal clicked as he jumped back from the view screen. Aaron brought Junior into hover mode and switched on more visual sensors.

'That was a whale... a Humpback, quite a large one too,' Jeff answered, almost reverently, 'one of the creatures we almost destroyed. They were actually classed as extinct but recently there have been a number of sightings. I've never seen one alive before… magnificent aren't they?'

As if to prove it was indeed alive the whale breached again and this time, another smaller one followed. 'My daughter is a marine biologist… she'll be able to tell you more.' He consulted the time on his console. 'Time we were heading home.'

Aaron nodded and turned the ship for the coast. With a couple detours over Sydney and the mountains, it took another 50 minutes to reach the compound. Aaron handed control to Petra who brought the ship in for a perfect landing. They parked in the family hangar and were met by Sonia, Jason and Amanda, each wearing one of the new translators.

'I had the first batch shipped here,' Jeff informed the group. 'We can test them and work out any issues before we put them into production.' He then led them down the ramp, where he introduced Mondrac and Tocmal, noting that the translator seemed to be working. Introductions over, they decided to take the walkway, giving the new visitors the opportunity to stretch their limbs.

Grainger held back slightly, indicating to Aaron he wanted to talk. 'What happened? I arrived and you had already vanished. Evidently Space Corps tracked you and your ship simply disappeared.'

'Eldorans… we met Jok-Tar's ship and he transported the yacht into it… must have looked like we met with some mishap.'

'Some?' Grainger smiled. 'Within an hour they had mobilised everything available and started to search the area. When they found no trace… well, you can imagine the response.'

Aaron chuckled. 'Yeah, I can. As soon as our guests are settled, we'll go through what happened. Some of it will be very hard for people to believe.' The conversation ended as they emerged from the walkway and entered the house. Sonia was directing everything, and soon had seating arranged on the terrace. Aaron was pleasantly surprised to see Reglaon seating had been fabricated for Tocmal.

'I hope we got the specifications right,' Jason asked.

Tocmal took his seat, 'An excellent job, considering you have never met a Reglaon before.' Finding the adjustment switch, he altered the configuration. 'The work is very impressive. I thank you for this.'

Sonia entered the conversation. 'Ambassador Tocmal, we have also set up an apartment for you with the specifications that Aaron sent us, I hope you find that equally comfortable. Ambassador Mondrac, we also have an apartment for you, but I had no specific requirements.'

'No problem, I have found the accommodation on A-Bra-Ham's vessel to be most agreeable. Eldorans are very similar in physiology to Humans.'

'Excellent. Now food... what do each of you require for sustenance?' Sonia was at a loss as this was the first time she had accommodated true aliens, and at such short notice.

Tocmal gave one of his chuckles. 'We Reglaons have a wide diet. I am sure we can do very well on human food, especially if you have coffee.'

This caused Aaron to laugh. 'Sonia, Tocmal has developed quite a taste for strong, sweet coffee. Most of the food I have seen Reglaons eat is protein and vegetable based, as is our diet. The only difference is most has been in a pulp form.'

'That is true,' Tocmal added, 'unlike Humans and Eldorans, Reglaons do not have teeth... we need to ingest our sustenance in paste form.'

Aaron was relieved Sonia was here to organise things. He hadn't even thought to discuss these requirements. Sonia left to make the food arrangements as Amanda quietly took Petra aside.

'I thought I should discuss this with you, I've had an apartment set aside for you and Aaron.' She paused to allow Petra to digest the information. 'If you want, we can take a look at it now, before things here get settled. If I'm wrong, or too forward, just say so.'

Petra gave her a grateful smile. 'Thank you... let's have a quick look.' They left the room unnoticed, leaving the men to continue their discussions, in peace. The apartment was on the third floor, and had two bedrooms, a lounge, and separate office area. There was a small, but functional food preparation area for times when they wanted a quiet meal together and a very well appointed bathroom, complete with large spa. 'This is wonderful, but surely you'll need this for company people?'

Amanda shook her head. 'My dear, if I am correct, you're family now... that takes precedent over everything else. Do you think Aaron will approve?'

'I hope so.'

'If he doesn't, then he can sleep on the yacht!' Amanda added, jokingly.

'Who can sleep on the yacht?' Aarons' voice came from the lounge. 'Sonia just told me about our apartment so I thought I should check it out while she settles the others.'

'Well, does it meet with you approval?' Amanda asked her son.

'Yes Mother, it sure does!'

Amanda smiled, her intuition had been right again. They spent the next few minutes inspecting the rooms and the clothing supply. Amanda had taken Petra's measurements and programmed the dispenser in the wardrobe. She had also had it set up a basic wardrobe for Petra to use and they started going through this.

Aaron got that distant look indicating he was in communication with George, Condor's brain. The conversation was kept subliminal, with Aaron nodding and making other expressions, subconsciously. To those who were unaware of the link, he sometimes looked like a person with severe issues.

Finally, his conversation finished, he turned to Petra. 'George says that everyone has been informed of our return. I've decided to extend the vacation time through to next week. Also, he has summoned Henry... evidently his programming also takes issues with the company seriously. He had to assume we had met with foul play and protocol demanded he summon the Proctor.'

Aaron smiled inwardly at the thought, but realised neither of the women was interested in his raving. 'Ok, I'll be downstairs with the others when you two are finished.' He made a hasty retreat out of the room.

Back downstairs, Aaron quickly found his brother and father still on the back veranda watching something in the sky. As he joined them he saw the shape of Valiant hovering overhead. As they stood there, three smaller vessels detached and began to drop to the landing pads. Valiant turned and accelerated away, back to her dock.

'What's going on?' Aaron asked.

'Don't know. JT just called and asked permission to land three shuttles,' Jason answered.

'Shuttles… two are Darts and the other is the new Hawke, and JT has the only one now operational. We'll know soon enough… the pod just left the hangar area,' Jeff replied as he turned and led the way to his study.

It was just after 5:00 pm so he opened the drinks cabinet, poured three measures of his favourite scotch and they all sat down to wait. Ten minutes later, JT walked through the door. His father poured him a glass and indicated for him to sit.

'Ok, what gives with the fighters?' Jeff asked.

'Orders; Malik and Wilson decided our guests must be protected during their visit and, given the events of the last week, I agree. There is also a ground force on the way, should be here in ten minutes… seems that the safety of the two ambassadors is a high priority.'

At that moment, Sonia led the other guests into the room. 'Ambassadors Tocmal and Mondrac, may I introduce my son, Captain Johnathon Thomas Abraham the Fourth.' She beamed as she made the introduction, then, turning to her husband, she asked, 'Jeffery, how many more will be arriving for dinner?'

Jeff shrugged and looked to his son. 'JT, can you answer your mother?'

'Yes, the ground troops will have their own supplies, but I have Sol and four others with me.'

'We can handle that. Luckily the accommodation is mostly empty, at the moment, but a little more notice in future would be appreciated,' she reprimanded as she left the room.

Aaron, noticing the expression on Mondrac's face asked,

'Mondrac, you seem confused. Can I help?'

'Yes, A-Bra-Ham, it seems we have an issue of names. We have always referred to you as A-Bra-Ham but now there are so many, how do we address the others without causing any affront?'

'Mondrac, our culture uses a person's first name or title, if they have one. For example, my brother could be called either Jeffery or Mr Abraham, but that leads to another problem. In this room, three of us would answer to Mr Abraham, so I think this would be a good time to start using our first names.' Aaron smiled. Going around the room, he introduced everyone by their first name. When he was finished, Tocmal asked a question.

'A-Bra-Ham, does this mean that in your culture, a person's first name is unique?'

Aaron saw where this was leading; inter-species communication could be the hardest part of building any relationship. 'No Tocmal, it does not. I can see where this will be an issue for you so may I make a suggestion? Use everybody's full name... my brother would be Jeffery Abraham. Does this help?'

'Yes a good solution,' Tocmal turned to Jeff and spoke, 'My greetings, Jeffery-Abraham.' This solution seemed to help both visitors understand human naming and how to ensure they were speaking to the right person. The conversation drifted around for a while until finally, Jason asked the question uppermost in everyone's mind.

'So where have you been for the last week Aaron?'

Aaron knew this question would be asked many times over in the coming days. 'For tonight, can we leave it until everyone is here? The answer is complex and we will be discussing both it, and the implications, next week at the palace.'

There was a reluctant agreement and the conversation drifted to the ecological situation on Earth, and how things deteriorated so badly. Tocmal was dismayed at some of the revelations: practices that had been deliberately or ignorantly done to damage the environment and that ultimately, served only to make a very few citizens extremely wealthy.

At 6.30 pm, Petra, Amanda, Sal and Sonia joined the group, far too many for Jeff's study so they adjourned to the dining room, with Jeff being enthusiastically encouraged to bring his scotch with him. They had an hour before dinner would be served, which gave Aaron an opportunity to satisfy their curiosity with an explanation of their sudden disappearance.

Phillip announced dinner and began serving while Mondrac continued telling part of the story. Another hour passed, desert was consumed and the table cleared as Tocmal added his final flourish.

Sonia sat, shaking her head, the information seeming to be too much for her. 'There's one thing I don't understand. You tell us that other races, from the inner realms, have visited us over the centuries, and that some have interacted with us. I can accept this, as historically, we have many examples of ancient depictions of aliens and space ships. But, when you say your people have been watching, but not interfering? This, I don't understand.'

Mondrac smiled. 'Sonia-Abraham, I can understand your confusion... indeed A-Bra-Ham had a similar reaction. Perhaps some sort of demonstration may help.' He paused and looked to Aaron. 'A-Bra-Ham, maybe you could demonstrate... show everyone the molecular control we taught you.'

'Are you sure, Mondrac?' Aaron was hesitant as he felt this could be a real issue for him and Petra. Mondrac nodded. 'Ok, but everyone please, it is imperative that no mention is to be made to anyone else outside this room.' He waited till everyone had agreed.

'Has anyone ever had the feeling that they weren't alone, even in a room that was empty with just you there?' The nervous smiles told him they had. 'Well, here is one possibility.' Aaron concentrated and altered his molecular vibration. To those in the room he seemed to become less distinct, less visible.

'Has anyone ever thought they saw someone who wasn't there?' Aaron disappeared completely and five seconds later his voice sounded again, this time from the other side of the room. 'Ever thought that you saw, or heard something or someone in two places at once?' Aaron suddenly reappeared back in his original position. He looked at the stunned faces before him. 'Looks like I've got a new party trick.'

Jason sprang to his feet, his face a mask of disbelief. 'You vanished?' How?

'Jason-Abraham, we Eldorans have the ability to control many physical things... the frequency of our molecular vibration is one. We have given A-Bra-Ham and Man-Nix these abilities... subconscious abilities they actually already possessed but did not know how to use.

'This quite simple manipulation is necessary for anyone dealing with some species in the inner realms whose entire existence is at a different vibration frequency. If we cannot match it, we simply cannot see them and, in some cases, they cannot see us, making any interaction impossible.'

Sonia was looking uncomfortable. 'So how long have your people been doing this?'

'Sonia-Abraham, we were an ancient culture before your species even existed... we were initially from this Galaxy. In fact, we left this realm before your primate ancestors began to walk upright but we were constantly drawn back, to see how you were progressing.

'Others, from the inner realms, began to accompany us. Unfortunately, many wanted to help your development, as they espoused. Some seeded their genetics... others took a more direct approach.' He turned to Aaron, as if asking for help.

Aaron came to his defence. 'Sonia, I have some images and data on the yacht that may assist you to understand more. How about we pause and I retrieve it. Then we can all sit down and work through this.' He turned to Mondrac. 'This is good... we need to be able to have a very succinct presentation for the President and the Council.'

'Mondrac, just one other thing,' Sonia asked, 'you seem to speak with a degree of knowledge and authority, almost as if you have witnessed our development. Just how old are you?'

'In your terms, I would be nearly 13,000 years old.' His words were greeted by stunned silence.

Jeff broke the silence. 'Then your people would have witnessed many things that we still argue over today: events that have caused wars; situations we have been trying to understand for centuries.'

'Jeffery-Abraham, I understand your thoughts but please

consider this. We Eldorans only observe. We have an overriding philosophy that negates any interaction. You are correct, we have witnessed many events but we cannot ever comment on them or, indeed, discuss them with you. Our philosophy of non-involvement is absolute, and for any of us to discuss our research would be a violation of that, and... what would it benefit your race?'

'There are issues we have fought over, some we still violently disagree on. Knowing the truth would stop all that,' Jeff insisted.

'Would it? How many times, in the past, has your species been given absolute proof of something, only to ignore it because it didn't suit the ideological mores of some? How many times have you destroyed the evidence because it didn't suit the "political narrative", as you call it?' Would the words from an old alien, who you do not know, carry any weight?'

Jeff looked Mondrac in the eyes, sensing nothing but honesty. 'You're probably correct Mondrac. It just seems that we could have answers to so many questions, but we do tend to shoot the messenger, if we don't like the message. Let's adjourn to the library. Aaron, could you get your data and join us?'

Aaron left and Jeff ushered the others out the door, pausing with Mondrac. 'You said you were committed to non-interaction... the current situation would seem to nullify that?'

Mondrac nodded. 'My new friend, you are correct. The current situation is new ground, so to speak. Never in our history has there been an incursion such as this. Yes, some races have coveted what others have, even between realms... just ask Tocmal about their interaction with Galdor.

But now we have a deliberate and co-ordinated plan to invade your realm, and we believe that someone here is part of it. So you are correct, our old ways may need to change, if the multiverse is to continue.'

His words were firm and Jeff began to realise just how much trouble may be coming their way. He nodded and walked with Mondrac in silence.

By the time everyone was settled, the data retrieved and activated, twenty minutes had gone by. The next hour was spent on the data stream that documented the events that happened on Junior, including being shot down, the subsequent battle and the return to the home realm. Mondrac and Tocmal filled in much of the information on the inter-realm council.

It all seemed so predictable until the images of Zarof and Nefaris were shown. A hush fell on the room, a hush of recognition and disbelief. Mondrac felt the anguish and confusion. 'Yes, as I said, some species from the inner realms interacted physically with your ancestors. Some built huge empires, based on them being gods, just for their own experimentation and enjoyment. This is what you now face, again. The same species want to resume their control.'

Strangely there was no discussion – the shock of what was displayed evidence enough. After a short silence, Jason announced he and Amanda were retiring. The others quickly followed suit, as if trying to avoid the awkward truth that had confronted them. Finally, only the two Ambassadors, Aaron, Petra and Grainger remained.

'Well, that went well. We have three days to fine tune this information for the Council... believe me that will be a much harder audience.' Aaron started to fill glasses with port; he handed them out and sat back down.

'I have known your people since the first encounter, Mondrac, but I never imagined any of this.' Grainger was at a loss, having no explanation that would refute the evidence before him. 'But Aaron is right, the Council will be much harder to convince.'

'I do not understand,' Tocmal clicked. 'Accurate and corroborated evidence is before you and *still* you find it hard to believe?'

'Welcome to the realm of human nature.' Aaron smiled as he raised his glass. 'Now you may start to understand why we allowed our planet to be so badly decimated.'

At 06:30 am, the house came alive.

As usual, Phillip was in the kitchen preparing breakfast, and soon very familiar and welcome aromas started to filter through to the dining area. Aaron remembered this from his childhood, the welcoming and comforting smell of a hearty breakfast being prepared. The meal was laid out in the dining room and everyone slowly shuffled in.

Jeff looked out of the window as he took a plate to the waiting buffet, feeling heartened at the sight of the dark, heavy clouds filling the sky. 'I hope the forecast for heavy showers is right,' he said to no-one in particular. 'It's odd, but it somehow feels right watching the sky and hoping for rain.' He turned to his brother. 'It's been a long time since we stopped trying to control weather... now that it's back under nature's control, things seem better.'

Aaron nodded his agreement adding, 'I must say, the sights of the desert areas now being farmed was impressive... a hell of a lot more has been reclaimed since I was last here.'

Jeff nodded. 'Yeah, all it ever needed was water... it seems so obvious now to re-cycle human waste, pity it wasn't considered centuries ago.'

In all there were twelve for breakfast. Sol had eaten

earlier and gone with the other flight crews to plan the days cover missions. Tocmal was engaged in a deep conversation with Salina, eagerly listening to her describe her work in rebuilding the devastated oceans. Mondrac and Grainger were discussing how to proceed with the reception in a couple of days' time, leaving the others to engage in family small talk.

The rest of Saturday was relaxed with no expectations. Petra decided to take Junior back to the dock and check on Condor. Aaron, Jeff and Mondrac spent the day touring the property with Mondrac showing strong interest in the cattle breeding program. He spoke of a growing movement back on Eldora where his people were beginning to return to an omnivorous way of life, citing a strong desire to begin a full breeding program for various meat producing animals.

Tocmal had taken another route. Fascinated with Salina's marine operation, he had accompanied her on an inspection of the facility she had shown Petra previously. He was regaling everyone with a description of his day when Jeff entered the room, a look of deep concern on his face. He called Aaron and JT over.

'Crompton just called... he's on his way here. Evidently there was some sort of incident at the Presidential Palace. I don't have any more details. JT, can you let security teams know? We really don't want anyone shooting him down... that'd really piss him off.'

JT smiled. 'Really, I never thought of that,' his reply filled with mock sarcasm.

An hour later Jeff's prediction came true as a very flustered Anthony Crompton, Director of Coalition Intelligence, met Jeff at the pod dock. 'Damn it Jeff, it seems every time I come here I'm targeted by someone. What gives with the fighters?'

'Malik's idea… he wants our guests protected at all costs. There's a company of troops as well.'

'Probably not a bad idea, considering what's going on… I hope you didn't have anything planned for the rest of the weekend?'

'Nothing special, just a quiet weekend, why?'

'Where to start… First: the two Raiders Aaron brought back are going to recover; second, our tech guys are having some difficulty with the data core he also retrieved and third; we have lost contact with Rhapsody.'

Jeff stopped in his tracks. 'What do you mean lost contact?'

'We can't raise her and there seems to be some delay in her arrival at Jacara. It could be nothing… you know, ship full of rich idiots suddenly decides to make an impromptu stop.'

'Bullshit, that's not what you believe, is it?'

Crompton looked worried. 'No it isn't. I came here to discuss what, if any, alternative ways of communication there may be with the ship. After all, Abracorp built it.'

'Crompton, I don't have all the details here but I'm certain that we built into that ship every comm system you know about. Hell, Albrect kept a very close eye on the costs and schedule. Believe me; nothing went onto that ship that he didn't want. I think you're clutching at straws. If that's all you came here for, I'm sorry, but you've wasted your time.'

As Jeff finished Aaron walked into the hall. 'Crompton, I didn't know you were coming for the weekend.'

'I'm not here for that… truth is I'm here to check on your guests. The President made it very clear that they are to be secure… I just need to check on things.'

'I don't think it will be an issue. We have a full company

of ground troops traipsing all over the place, plus JT has a flight of three fighters, with more on standby in Sydney. Security is well taken care of,' Jeff assured him.

'Well in that case I'll get back... if you're sure everything is ok?'

'Crompton, stop the bullshit! What's the real reason you're here? The Director of Intelligence doesn't make house calls.' Jeff was tired of playing twenty questions.

'You're right, to some degree. I really am here to check that the Ambassadors are ok, but the reason is different. Earlier this morning there was an attempt on the President's life. Don't worry, he's fine, but the security at the compound was breached, something that's supposed to be impossible. Malik called me and asked me to get here ASAP and check, so I'm here.'

'That's not all is it?' Aaron asked.

Crompton looked at Aaron before answering. 'You'd have made a good spook. No that's not all... in the sweep we made we have found several surveillance devices. Seems someone has been watching and listening to everything that has been happening in the Palace: private and confidential meetings; receptions and negotiations. It's possible everything has been compromised. We don't know how they were planted but there must have been someone on the inside, it's the only possible answer.'

'So the Political Protection Service is suspect? Where is the President going now? Surely he can't stay there?' Jeff regretted asking as soon as he spoke – the answer was going to be one he didn't like.

'That's another reason I'm here... I don't think any official building is safe. At the moment, a private estate would in all probability be much more secure.' Before Crompton could say more, Jeff spoke.

'And we have the bunker, what could be more secure... right?'

'Exactly what I was thinking; what do you say?' Crompton answered as Jason also joined the group.

'Crompton, what brings you here?' Jason asked.

Jeff turned to his father. 'Seems there was a breach at the Palace... someone took a shot at Malik... Crompton was wondering if we could step in and host the President for a while.'

He turned back to Crompton. 'You understand this isn't just a house, it is the headquarters of Abracorp and come Monday morning there will be several hundred employees back on the job. The bunker is still a work in progress... hell; we usually have up to three hundred down there.' Jeff stopped and shook his head. 'What do you think, Dad... you're still head of the clan.'

'No question. Tell Salim our house is his for as long as he needs it... just none of those useless PPS clowns... they couldn't protect a steak at a vegetarian congress.' Jason had made the decision.

'Thank you, I'll inform the President,' Crompton said as he entered the pod to return to his shuttle just as the sun was starting to set.

***

Thirteen thousand five hundred kilometres away, in Rio de Janeiro, Katie Albrecht's communicator buzzed for the fifth time, but there was no one to hear it. The call timed out and the caller was asked to leave a message. Katie and Simon had decided to take an early morning walk on the beach. Although the environmental disaster had caused sea levels to initially rise, the destruction of the North Atlantic Current and the subsequent freezing of most of the northern hemisphere had stopped the cycle, and sea levels had stabilised.

Rio had fared better than most other cities in South America and was still largely habitable. It was now mainly a research centre with an increasing number of vacationers making it a destination of choice. This had led to a resurgence of local traders and a small, but thriving economy had developed. This time of year it was balmy with the temperature sitting on twenty four degrees Celsius this morning. It was five forty five as Katie and Simon walked down the beach, the sun's rays just starting to break over the horizon. The Atlantic looked beautiful, calm and smooth, looking more like deep blue glass than an ocean. It was hard for either of them to believe that their holiday was almost over, but both happy their Captain had returned and extended their stay for a few days.

Centuries ago this beach had become famous for beautiful people, frolicking and playing in the sun. It was also famous for the thong bikini and Simon had been so enthusiastic for Katie to get one; even in the thirtieth century this was almost a rite of passage when coming to Rio.

So, without telling him, she had made the purchase the day before. This morning she had secretly put it on under her beach robe and was waiting for the right time to reveal almost all to the world. They stopped to watch as a large yacht cruised effortlessly by, beautifully framed by the rising sun. Katie decided that now was the time as Simon was concentrating on the yacht. Quietly she let the robe slip down her shoulders and drop onto the sand. Simon was so engrossed with the yacht he missed this completely.

It was when Katie took a few steps towards the ocean that his attention changed. This small amount of material, and the high price, was worth it to Katie, just to see his face as she turned around. Although they had seen each other naked countless times, she had never seen this reaction before.

'Well, if that is how you are affected by this little thing, I may never be naked in front of you again.' She giggled and started to run up the beach. Simon chased and they cavorted in the shallows for a while, till the sun was completely up and the beach started to receive more similarly clad women, taking the magic of their moment away. They walked back to where Katie had dropped her robe and then back to the hotel.

Katie looked at Simon. 'Well, I hope you enjoyed the show. By the way, when is it my turn? I'd love to see you in one of those, what are they called... yes mankini. But I warn you, they are not very comfortable when you get sand in the wrong place. I'm in the shower first!' she said, racing back to their villa.

Katie was already in the shower when Simon walked in to the sound of her communicator. 'Seems you have a message on your communicator,' he called as he picked the unit up.

'See what it is... it may be the ship.' Simon pressed the retrieve icon and a male voice, quite agitated, emanated from the unit.

'Katie, this is your father, call me urgently.' The message ended just as Katie came back into the room.

'That's strange... I thought your father was dead?' Simon queried.

Katie slumped into the nearest arm chair, looking very small and vulnerable. 'Well now you know, he's not. But he's a total arsehole and I will not have anything to do with him.' She held her hand up as Simon looked as if he was going to ask something. 'I don't want to talk about it, I just want to have a few more carefree days... maybe then I'll tell you about it, but not now.' Her voice was adamant and Simon knew better than to push the point.

She went back to the bedroom and quickly dressed with Simon following her keeping what he believed to be a safe and respectful distance. The rest of the morning was much the same. Katie was very quiet and withdrawn but just before midday she walked up to Simon and planted a huge kiss on his lips.

'I'm sorry for being such a bitch. I think you have a right to know just who you are with.' Simon started to protest but she would have none of it. 'Just shut up and listen.' She waited until he sat back and gave her the floor.

'My father is Damien Albrecht. He came to Argos and met my mother and I'm the result of their relationship. They never married but he would visit us whenever he was back on our planet... and then my mother died. He wanted me to come and live with him on Earth but, by then, I was at university. I had been accepted to the academy and my whole life was on Argos.

'Eventually, I made my mind up to come and see him but one of the guys at the academy had a brochure for one of his cruises... very explicit. It seems that my father is the biggest pimp in the known universe... you can imagine the effect that had on my social life.

'All of a sudden everyone wanted to be my friend. All the men wanted to see if I could get a discount for a cruise or if I was going to follow in the family business, if you get my drift.

'Anyhow, Damien turned up on a particularly bad day and we had an almighty row. I actually punched him, told him what a bastard I thought he was and that I never wanted to see him again. It seemed to rock him and he left. That was twenty five years ago and this is the first time I've heard from him since.'

She stopped as her eyes filled with tears. 'He was the only family I had and he turned out to be an arsehole.' She slumped back into a chair.

Simon stood and went over to her. 'Katie, while you may disagree with some of his business operations, he isn't doing anything illegal, he isn't hurting anyone, he isn't running contraband... he is just supplying a service. Don't keep hating until you know the full story... you're only causing yourself pain. Now he's reaching out and it sounds urgent. I think you should call him.'

Katie glared at Simon but said nothing; for the next ten minutes she just sat there. Finally she spoke.

'He was a great father when I was younger. My mother and I never had to worry about anything. 'Whenever he was in our sector he would spend time on Argos with us, or take us to some exotic place for a break... but he would always leave and I hated that. I was young and all I wanted was my dad, like all my friends. After our big fight I refused to take his calls... I returned any gifts and cut myself off.'

'You mean he did try to contact you?'

'Yes. I suppose if anyone was to blame for the end of our relationship, I think it is me.' She stood and started to pace.

'Then call him. All you need do is acknowledge the call,

see what he has to say and then make a decision... just don't let this chance go by.' Simon moved beside her and handed her the communicator. 'Just hit the recall icon, I'll be outside.' And he walked out the door giving her privacy to make the call.

Katie stood near the window looking at the communicator trying to decide what to do. Eventually she tapped the recall icon and the connection started. Immediately she tapped cancel; she did this several times, still undecided. Finally, she swore and tapped the recall icon again, this time allowing the connection to be made.

Albrecht here the voice at the other end announced.

'Damien; it's Katherine. You called?' she tried to sound matter of fact and distant.

Katherine, it's so good to hear your voice. He sounded relieved and genuinely happy. *How are you*? That was all it took for her emotions to overflow and she burst into tears. The voice on the other end was reassuring and he patiently waited till she regained her composure.

They talked for the next hour and a half; several times Damien had to tell others that had obviously come to his office to go away, the last time quite vehemently. As the conversation began to come to a conclusion he asked *Katherine, I want to see you. I know you're on Earth... please can I meet with you*?

This request caught her off guard; she took a couple of moments to register the request. Part of her, the old angry part, wanted to say no, to scream no in fact, but this conversation had been good, she felt as if a great weight had been lifted off her so she quickly replied. 'We are in Rio, at the new Plaza.'

Great, I can be there in an hour. He waited for a few seconds and, as there was no refusal simply said goodbye and cut the connection.

Katie was in a bit of a daze when she finally found Simon at the pool bar. 'We're going to have a visitor in an hour.' Simon simply nodded and ordered her a drink.

An hour later a sleek silver shuttle landed on the hotel pad. A well-dressed man, carrying a brief case alighted and headed to the lift area. As the door opened he was framed in the glow from the cubicle's light, he was tall and well built, his large frame moved effortlessly as he entered the lift.

He had deep blue eyes and well-groomed blonde hair, his face had been described as well chiselled, even handsome, but the overall look was one of confidence, a man used to getting his own way. It was the eyes that betrayed his true state of mind; furtive, they were constantly moving, constantly scanning and deciphering what he saw. His demeanour was one of readiness, readiness for anything.

He touched the icon for the lobby, the doors closed and the express dropped to the level in a few seconds. He left the lift and scanned the room, noting everything and missing nothing. Satisfied with what he saw, he went directly to the bar, obviously looking for someone.

It was just after 9.00 pm and the bar and restaurant was beginning to fill, everyone here looking for an enjoyable evening. He paused at the entrance to the restaurant, located who he was looking for and walked confidently toward them. His two targets were deep in conversation and didn't notice him until he was beside them.

'Hello Katie,' he said.

Katie and Simon both looked up at the man. 'Hello,

Damien,' she replied, waiting for a few seconds. 'Please sit.' She indicated the chair backing onto the large window. Instead of taking her offer he moved the chair to the other side of the table. Now backed up to a wall, he had a clear view of the entire restaurant.

'I prefer to be able to see who's here,' he simply stated.

Katie had agreed to see her father only after Simon had badgered her into it; she still harboured no good feelings toward him. 'Ok, I agreed to see you... now what do you want?' She almost spat the words.

Simon interjected before she could say more. 'Steady on. Let's have a civilised evening, ok?'

Katie relaxed a little. 'Ok,' she agreed.

Damien began. 'I know you don't want to see me but please listen. There are things happening that you need to be aware of, things that involve you being my daughter.'

Katie almost laughed. 'Stop being so dramatic; you would think this is some life and death issue.'

'It *is* life and death, and it could be your death, now shut up and listen!' Damien was in no mood to put up with his daughters sarcasm. 'As you already know, we launched Rhapsody last week.' He held up his hand to stop any protests.

'You have made your views on that vessel very clear, so no need to go into that. This morning we lost contact with her and I received this.' He produced a small communicator, touched the screen and handed it to Katie. She looked at the text that displayed and the images that accompanied it, the colour slowly draining from her face. The message was simple.

'*We have control of your ship. Do not inform anyone or*

your daughter will suffer.' The images showed Katie and Simon at the beach earlier that day.

'I don't know who sent this but I took it seriously and dispatched two of our best security guys here to watch you... they were both killed within an hour of arriving. That's when I knew I had to come here in person, to get you out.' As he spoke his communicator buzzed. 'Damn, they've found my shuttle. Do you have any weapons?'

Simon shook his head. 'Why would we? We're on leave, on a friendly planet.'

Damien opened his briefcase. 'I thought as much,' he said as he stealthily slipped a small blaster under the table to both of them. 'A blaster each and two spare energy packs, enough for sixty full power shots. Now we just sit tight.' He slid three other items into his coat pocket and closed the case.

'Not a good idea.' Katie looked around the room. 'Too many innocent bystanders... if this is as bad as you think, we need to get away from these people.' As she spoke, her communicator buzzed. She answered.

Petra's voice greeted her. *Hello, Katie. Sorry to do this but we may have a situation... we're issuing a recall.*

Katie replied. 'Sounds like we're both in a situation; I can't explain now, but can you have a shuttle sent for us... an armed shuttle?'

Wait one while I check. The comm went dead for a few moments until Petra finally spoke again. *Dave Carter has a shuttle fairly close to you, but the Captain will want to know... what is going on?*

'We may be the target of a kidnap attempt.' Petra could hear the fear in Kate's voice.

OK, David's on his way and the shuttle is armed... what's your sitrep?

'Not good. Damien Albrect is with us and we are armed. We are leaving the hotel to avoid any collateral damage... can you follow us?' Katie was concise as she could be.

Affirmative, the shuttle is locked onto your comms but he is still ten minutes away, head for the beach, Petra suggested.

The beach made sense as the shuttle could land easily. This caused other problems as it was completely exposed, but there was no available alternative. While Freebooters had no formal military, everyone did have the required training and both Katie and Simon had their fair share of interesting adventures so were able to adapt to this situation. Damien's abilities were unknown but, Katie thought, it was good planning to bring the weapons. She was now subconsciously re-evaluating her Father.

They left the restaurant via a side fire exit that led them through the parking area toward the beach, found reasonable cover in the garden and settled in to wait.

'When we move, keep low, using the vehicles as cover,' Damien commanded. Time seemed to slow, seconds seemed like minutes, it felt like an eternity waiting for the shuttle to arrive. Seven minutes later Damien called for them to move.

They moved from vehicle to vehicle, crouching to offer a low profile. Suddenly the vehicle opposite them exploded, showering them with debris. The ground beside Katie also spat upward as a number of small explosions erupted.

Simon drew a bead on the source and fired three quick shots, a window on the third floor of the hotel blew out and a body, cradling what looked like a long arm weapon, fell to the ground. 'One down,' Simon grunted.

Katie, what are you and Simon doing? It was David Carter's voice. *I'm bringing the shuttle in low over the ocean, need any help?* Before she could answer there were three more small ground eruptions, closer this time, showering her with asphalt.

Simon answered. 'Dave, we are taking fire from the roof of the hotel, can you do anything about that?'

Sure thing!

On board the shuttle, Dave Carter moved the control back towards himself, climbing the shuttle at an almost vertical angle. When he was slightly above the hotel roof he looked at the sensor screen; clearly visible were three shooters. He locked on to each of them and fired the shuttle's forward blaster array; instantly three shooters were no more.

Scratch three bad guys, head to the beach. Dave dropped the shuttle down to a couple of feet above the ground, remembering to engage the shields.

As the ship settled, the shield flared red as he took fire, this time from the ocean. He engaged more power and swung the ship one hundred and eighty degrees till he could see the large boat speeding toward the shore, long arm blasters firing continuously. These small weapons couldn't damage the shuttle, but no one could board with shields engaged.

Sorry guys, this is not your night, Dave chuckled as he locked the target and fired the forward blaster again.

The boat was heading toward shore at nearly 100 kilometres per hour, the energy blast that hit it being equivalent to several hundred kilograms of explosives. The result was spectacular – what wasn't vaporised flew up into the air in a bright display of pyrotechnics.

He didn't have time to admire his handiwork though as the view screen showed his shipmates running for their lives with four others in hot pursuit. He turned the ship through another ninety degrees and targeted the four pursuers. The angle wasn't good so all he could do was offer covering fire, enough to get the four to drop to the ground. But this was another problem, the four now were too low for his blaster to do any damage and they were starting to aim at his companions – only one thing to do. Dave lifted the ship ten metres into the air and pushed it forward over the heads of the others and then dropped it down to the deck again.

Now the shuttle was a physical barrier between the four attackers and his friends. He disengaged the port side shield generator and opened the outer airlock door just as his companions got to it. The three scrambled into the airlock and closed the door as Dave re-engaged the generator. He lifted the ship up to twenty metres and angled the nose so he had a clear shot at the attackers.

As if one man they threw down their weapons and put their hands on their heads, knowing that with just one shot from the ship they would all be dust. The scene behind the four kneeling attackers was changing. Flashing blue and red lights indicating the local authorities were moving in.

'Time to go,' Dave smiled as he turned the shuttle and accelerated out over the ocean, keeping very low just in case.

Simon jumped into the second pilot seat. 'Nice work Dave. Thanks for the help.'

'Help; I just saved your arses, but you're welcome. Boy, you two certainly know how to have a holiday... by the way who's the suit?' He laughed as he pulled the shuttle into a climb, pushing the throttle to full power just in case there was anyone following.

Katie replaced Simon in the second seat. 'This is my father, Damien Albrect.'

'Pleased to meet you, Sir,' Dave greeted Albrect.

Shuttle Tiberius from Condor... Dave have you got our people? Petra's voice sounded over the comm link.

'We're here, safe and sound,' Katie replied, 'but I need to talk to the Captain urgently... is he there?'

No, he's still at the house, wait one. A relieved Petra replied, cutting the comm. She returned a couple of minutes later. *He says to proceed to the following coordinates and he'll meet you there.* The nav console showed the coordinates. Dave entered them and the ship began to turn. *Keep your eyes open. We will monitor from here, Condor out.*

Even though he was, technically, outranked by both Simon and Katie, Dave was in command of the shuttle. 'Number two, can you take sensor control and keep our eyes open?' he asked.

'Consider our eyes open,' Katie replied and began to extend the scan range. The shuttle was now flying at twenty thousand metres and at four thousand kilometres per hour. 'Just over three hours to Australia,' she announced. 'It looks like we have company.' The sensor display showed an object following the shuttle over five hundred kilometres behind and at the same height. 'Simon, get on tactical.' Simon moved to the starboard side console and sat at the tactical post.

The shuttle may be small but Freebooter history had led to the development of very capable vessels. Dave, Katie and Simon were confident in the capabilities of the craft. Most Freebooter shuttles were much better armed when compared to shuttles used by the Coalition.

Many times Freebooters had found their expeditions to new worlds being greeted with overt hostility and small craft, like a shuttle, were easy prey. No longer was this an issue, and definitely none of Aaron Abraham's shuttles could be called easy prey.

They continued to monitor the following craft and noticed it was catching them, slowly and deliberately. 'At this rate he'll catch us somewhere near Hawaii,' Simon ventured.

As commander the call was David's. 'Condor from shuttle Tiberius,' he said into the comm unit.

Tiberius this is Condor, I'm aware of your situation and it is about to get worse. As if by command three more blips appeared on the sensor screen.

You seem very popular today.

These three were spaced out ahead and to each side of the shuttle and were closing at the same speed.

I estimate contact in twenty minutes... what do you want to do, Tiberius?

'I don't know, a couple of days R&R in Hawaii would be nice, Number One.' Dave could be very flippant, especially in times like this. 'Maybe we should do the unexpected?'

Your call, Dave... there's not much I can do except watch. Petra sounded concerned.

'Ok, power up weapons. Tactical, keep watching them... here we go.' With that, Dave opened the ship to full power and their speed increased to nine thousand kilometres per hour before he stabilized their acceleration. 'Call the vitals Number Two.'

'All in the green, deflector holding, hull temperature

normal,' Katie called out.

'Tailing ship is off the screen, we seem to have lost him, for now. Lead ships closing at thirteen thousand, ten minutes till we meet them. Target locked on front ship.' Simon read off his sensors.

'I hope you are all belted in, this is going to get a little rough.' With that comment Dave threw the shuttle into a steep dive. At their speed the G force would have crushed them but for the inertial dampening system. In the shuttle there was a mild sensation of an increase in the G force, but nothing like the twenty 'G''s they were actually pulling.

At five thousand metres he levelled the ship out and again applied maximum power. The speed shot to over eleven thousand kilometres per hour as Dave called for the Bubble.

Immediately in front of the pilot's seat a holographic bubble appeared with the shuttle in the centre and the three opposing ships arranged slightly ahead and well above them. The three chasing ships began to turn and descend towards the shuttle, increasing their speed. Dave kept the shuttle level at a constant speed of eleven thousand.

'Now we'll see if they really have the heart for a chase... vitals please?'

'Engines at three quarter power and smooth,' Katie answered. 'Speed eleven thousand; deflector holding; hull temperature two degrees above nominal, shields ready; and absorption battery at thirty percent capacity. 'Only problem is fuel; at this rate we'll expend all our drive plasma well before we reach New Zealand... what then?'

'Shit!' Dave exclaimed. 'Well, maybe we should slow down and ask these guys what they want... very politely of course.' The other two knew just what Dave was planning – time to fight. As he spoke, Dave threw the shuttle into a climbing turn to the right and again engaged full power.

The little shuttle seemed to leap into the sky, speed increasing to fifteen thousand by the time he had completed the turn and he pulled the throttles back to the mid-range position. This manoeuvre bled off speed, but also brought their turn much tighter, bringing the lead pursuit ship into range where he centred in his sights. Dave pressed the fire control stud on his control lever and the forward blaster spat a high intensity energy burst toward the oncoming ship.

The move took their adversaries by surprise and they were slow to react, too slow for the lead ship. It was engulfed in the energy blast and the front of it exploded. The other two broke and started a flanking manoeuvre, but Simon noticed this movement and called out a warning. 'Dave hard left and dive; full power!' Simon shouted.

Dave complied and the little shuttle again leapt ahead. The Bubble display now showed the two remaining pursuers facing each other, heading together at a combined nearly twenty thousand kilometres per hour.

They both took desperate avoidance action and barely missed, one climbing and the other diving away and directly in front of the shuttle. Dave manoeuvred the shuttle with skill and grace as he lined up the second ship.

Again the blaster did its work, this time almost completely vaporising the opposing vessel. Dave throttled back as Simon searched for the third ship, but it was heading away at over ten thousand kilometres per hour.

'Seems they don't really want a fight,' Dave said as he turned the ship back on their original course and brought their speed down to cruise. 'You've got to give it to the

Captain though; he certainly knows how to build a shuttle. How's our fuel?'

Katie again consulted the screen. 'If we don't have any more adventures we should be fine, just go easy... no more high speed runs.'

'I hate to spoil things,' Simon interjected, 'but three more bogies are heading our way... thirty thousand metres and moving at sixteen thousand.'

Shuttle Tiberius, this is Coalition Space Corps flight above you. Would you like an escort to Sydney? The comms system announced.

'Coalition flight, this is Lieutenant David Carter commanding Condor Shuttle Tiberius, your company would be much appreciated. Who is leading the flight?'

Captain JT Abraham, the reply was from the lead ship as it settled in front of the shuttle. *You certainly gave a good account of yourself back there. Seems Freebooter shuttles aren't all they appear.*

'Well, Captain, we do like to entertain. Hope you enjoyed the show.'

The rest of the trip was uneventful. Dave handed control to Katie, reclined his seat and was soon asleep. Three hours later Simon roused him as they were within a couple of minutes of Sydney. Dave again took control and Katie gave him their vitals, completing it moments before the communicator again sounded.

Lieutenant Carter, do you have enough fuel for another ten minutes? JT asked.

'Yes we have enough reserve.'

Good, follow me. It seems your Captain would like to have

a word with you, hope you didn't bend his shuttle.

The other two fighters peeled off and Dave pulled behind JT's ship. They headed over the mountains and on to Orange; ten minutes later they were on the ground at the Abraham compound.

Aaron, Jeff and Crompton were waiting for them inside the hangar; Dave opened the side airlock and exited the shuttle. Dave and Katie did a quick walk around to make sure there was no damage.

As they finished their inspection, JT walked up to them. 'Lieutenant, I want to shake your hand. That was very impressive flying back there. If you ever want to join the Space Corps, I'm sure we would welcome someone who flies like you.'

'No thanks Captain,' Dave replied as he shook the offered hand. 'I think I might find all that marching and saluting just too tiring.' They both laughed and joined the others.

Introductions and pleasantries over, they took the pod to the house, where they were all soon sitting in Jeff's study. Once settled, Aaron addressed his crew members. 'Ok, so just what happened in Rio?'

It was Damien who replied. 'I think I should explain this,' he said, proceeding to inform all of the day's events. He finished with, 'in truth, I have no idea who sent the message but I was sure it was genuine when I saw the photos of Katie and Simon and found out the two security guys were killed.' The story was met with a stony silence.

This silence was interrupted by the sound of approaching shuttles. 'Looks like our guests have arrived,' Jeff said as he and Jason stood. 'I'll leave Crompton to explain... we've got people to greet.' They left the room as Crompton began to speak.

The first shuttle to land was one from Abracorp Robotics, with a number of additional androids for the household staff. Aaron and Crompton had decided that artificials would be much less of a security threat than temporary human staff.

The second vessel held President Malik and his wife, Hiba. They were met by the security officer and escorted to the pod, which conveyed them to the house. Sonia had joined the growing group and began directing staff to take luggage to various rooms and apartments. Once again, the Abraham house was fully occupied but never in its history had it seen such extensive security.

As the group began to disperse to their respective accommodations, President Malik pulled Jeff aside. 'I want to thank you again for this and apologise in advance for the disruption we will cause. But I have one more request, could we meet soon? I want to get things moving and I believe time may be short.' His tone and demeanour told Jeff that Malik was both rattled and resolved to set things right.

Jeff nodded. 'Mister President, I suggest we meet in an hour, in the bunker, if that's acceptable.' Arrangements now agreed, Malik took his leave and followed his wife to the elevator.

An hour later, the elevator door opened and the President led them into the meeting room. The recognition of who was in the room brought home the seriousness of the situation to the Rio escapees.

Now gathered were Mondrac, Tocmal, Salim Malik-President of the Coalition of Earth Planets; Madam Collard-senior member of the Coalition Council; Fleet Admiral-Skye Wilson; Admiral Sam Grogan-Space Corps Commander; General Ivan Klastok-Commander Coalition Ground Forces; Anthony Crompton-Director CID and Allen Grainger-Freebooter Prime.

The newcomers were given translators and introduced to Ambassadors Mondrac and Tocmal.

Crompton pulled a data stick out of his coat pocket as he scanned the room, his eyes finally resting on Damien Albrect. 'Albrect,' he simply acknowledged and was rewarded with a similarly surly 'Crompton' in reply. 'It is probably time I brought all of you up to date.'

Crompton held his hand out to Katie. 'So I finally get to meet Damien's daughter... you are every bit as attractive as your mother.' He looked back at Jeff. 'How secure is the room?'

'Better than your office... the whole structure is completely shielded. Nothing gets in or out if we don't want it to,' was Jeff's answer.

Crompton seemed to relax and he sat down. 'First I need to clear up something about Albrect. For the past thirty odd years he has been an independent contractor for CID. His unique business model was, shall we say, very attractive to us.

'It has enabled us to gain Intel on many situations and keep an eye on people we would, otherwise, have no chance of getting near. As his ships operate in free space, no law enforcement can touch those on board; they sometimes let their guard down and, well, things are said... or just happen.

'Until today, he has been one of our best assets in maintaining the status quo, but after this thing in Rio,' and here he stared at Damien, 'we may need to clarify your allegiance and loyalty.'

Damien glared back at Crompton. 'I always told you my daughter would come first and you agreed to keep her safe. Seems to me you failed that, so don't question my actions.' The threat was bare for all to see, and it caused a few nervous smiles around the room.

'Ok, I get your point, but you must admit, two unmarked shuttles destroyed and seven, no nine... if we include the two operatives we sent... dead seems a bit excessive. The favours I have had to call in to shut this cluster fuck down are unbelievable. Still, we now know that the threat was real,' Crompton replied.

'Yes,' Damien replied while maintaining his defiant look, 'and I'll do it again if I have to, so what now?'

'I think we should go back a bit and explain to those

present. Damien, you tell it.'

'Six months ago, I started to get weird communications alluding to Katie's safety. I couldn't do much myself as she wouldn't even take my calls so we started to try and trace the callers. Then, about two weeks before the launch, we had a breakthrough when CID received information about a possible rebel uprising.

'The interesting thing was, it was going to be on a number of planets and involve very disparate groups, but the information was corroborated. Much appeared to revolve around Rhapsody and a possible hijacking; with all the dignitaries who had booked we had to take it seriously. If they took the ship, the rebels could hold these dignitaries for ransom so, with CID help, we had a number of operatives inserted into the guest list.

'The problem is that a last minute booking change left nearly all of these operatives stranded and we only found out after the departure. Obviously, someone very well placed in my own company, or CID, was involved, so an investigation started. We found the culprits easily... unfortunately they were in no condition to talk... all dead. Then, this morning I received the communication stating that they had the ship and threatened to harm Katie if we informed anyone.'

Crompton interjected. 'We copied the communication and despatched two operatives to Rio immediately, to watch and secure, if necessary. Within an hour of landing they were both dead, that's when Damien went rogue.'

Damien's reply was to close his right fist and extend his middle finger and all got the message. 'And now, Crompton, we have lost the ship and your great secret security plan is in tatters.'

Crompton smiled. 'Well, you agreed to it so we were all fooled, anyway it's not a total loss. Janice Barker is still active... at least she was before the ship went dark. Hopefully they don't know about her or they don't believe one operative is a threat, so we do have a glimmer of hope.'

'I know about Janice but she's not alone... I contracted someone independently of the Directorate.'

'What! Who is it, and bloody why?' Crompton blustered.

'First, you heard what I said, I have an independent contractor. Why? Well your spymaster act hasn't been that good lately, has it?' Damien answered forcefully.

Crompton slumped back into his chair. 'Unfortunately, I have to agree. There have been too many leaks, but you didn't answer who?'

Damien studied Crompton for a moment. 'Sorry, confidential,' he said at length. 'I had a few suites and some cabins held back for special consideration, you might say... all in all ten rooms. The deal was I booked all available rooms: to different people; different companies... hell, two were even family suites; so he could be any of them, or none. Damien teased, 'if he's as good as his price suggests, he may already have been on the guest list, or he just slipped aboard. All I can say is he is referred to, in certain circles, as the Doctor.'

Crompton sucked in his breath. 'You're kidding! Didn't he end the siege on Galagos a few years back, and the Andarian coup... reportedly his work... we may have an edge after all.'

'What I don't get is why hi-jack Rhapsody in the first place? Even though the ransom angle seems to fit, I don't swallow it... no, there must be another reason,' Crompton mused.

'What is so significant about this ship?' Mondrac entered

the conversation.

'Nothing, it's just a big cruise ship,' Albrect answered. 'The only thing I can think of is that there are many very wealthy and influential people, all in the one place. If this is indeed a kidnap for ransom ploy, they certainly have a huge number of options.'

'Maybe it is not about ransom, as you call it,' Mondrac addressed the group. 'What is the size of the vessel?'

Jeff answered, 'Rhapsody's 7,000 metres long and slightly less than 2,000 in diameter.'

'And how many can board it.'

'Including all crew, security, entertainment and guests, just over one hundred and fifty thousand,' Albrect answered.

'And its drive... what displacement can it achieve?'

'A maximum cruise of 15, a little more for short duration, why?' Jeff asked.

'I think it is time to explain what we discovered in the Tenth Realm.' Mondrac said, and for the next hour, he, Tocmal and Aaron recounted their experience in the tenth and eleventh realm, culminating in their capture of the two Tragarian Raiders.

'So you are saying that these other aliens intend to use our old Exodus Gates to invade?' Crompton sounded amused by what he just heard. 'How many are still left?'

Wilson answered that question, her voice flat and firm. 'Twenty are still operational: most are in care and maintenance; but some are used for freight operations; mainly mining... getting the ore to processing plants quickly and cost effectively. So they would have plenty of options.'

'Admiral, do you have locations for all of them?' Mondrac asked.

'No Ambassador. When they were sold off, we lost control and any movement reporting was left to the operators. Part of their licence to operate a Gate is to keep its location up to date with the authorities in the system it's located. Space Corps has no interest, to date.'

Malik spoke, concern visibly playing across his face. 'Well Admiral, it would seem that Space Corps now has a vested interest in locating all of these units, would you agree?'

'Yes Mr President, I do.'

'Then I suggest you make it a priority to locate them all. Now, what progress has been made with the data core Captain Abraham retrieved?'

'We have been having difficulty powering it up, it would have been better if we received it with its power coupling intact.' Crompton gave Aaron a disapproving glare.

'Sorry, Crompton, we were in a bit of a hurry,' Aaron fired back. 'With the destruction of the ship imminent, the power coupling was the least of my concerns.'

Tocmal interrupted the conversation. 'Maybe if I could examine the unit... I do have some understanding of engineering.'

'Not a chance,' said Crompton, on his feet now. 'We're not giving that unit to any alien... we'll sort it out ourselves!'

Tocmal's eyes started to change, the redness now becoming evident. 'If it wasn't for *this alien*,' he said, 'you wouldn't have the unit, so I don't understand your problem with me inspecting it.'

Jeff intervened. 'Crompton, is there anyone in any universe you don't piss off?'

Malik settled everyone. 'Ambassador, I apologise for this

insult, we will be very appreciative of your input.' He turned to Crompton. 'Have the unit despatched here immediately.'

Mondrac had been thinking while the others bickered; now he spoke. 'If the rebels, or whoever took the ship, are going to use it for any purpose, they will need to remove the people on board and they will need to find somewhere they can secretly transfer them to. Somewhere isolated and not regularly visited. Do any of you have any idea where that may be?'

This brought everyone back to the present. Crompton called his people and arranged for the data core to be transferred while the others attempted to locate where Rhapsody could dock.

'There is another issue we must ponder, Gro-Gan. We found significant Trisidic radiation at the site in the tenth realm. There is no appreciable source of the ore and definitely no facility to refine it there. Any fuel for these reactors must come from this realm... that may be another reason to take such a large ship.'

'Ambassador Mondrac, it would do them no good to use Rhapsody. As soon as any processed Trisidium was placed in the ship, the ship would be useless to transport any beings. The radiation would contaminate the whole vessel,' Grogan replied.

'What about the Coultrane, we haven't heard anything of her since she was taken?' Grainger suggested. 'What if they intended to use one for the Trisidium and the other to bring their forces here?' The room fell silent as the vision of what they were facing was coalescing and it wasn't something anyone wanted to see. 'It's time to stop pussy footing around,' he said firmly.

'We all know what this scenario is, so let's stop ignoring the problem. Somehow Sarclan has survived... probably he has joined forces with Tragarian and his pirates... and now he has allies from other dimensions who are intent on invading this realm. In all probability he is behind the attack on the President.

'Sarclan must be the key so, we need to find him. To do that we need a command centre that can communicate with all our forces, and I include Freebooters in this.' He looked to Aaron. 'I'm sorry Aaron but I'm sure you see what we are facing.'

'Unfortunately I do, and I agree with your assessment. This is one fight we can't sit out.'

Grainger nodded his acceptance of Aaron's commitment. 'Mr President, I will discuss this with our council of seniors, but I am sure they will agree to join forces. Let's not forget the Krell... where will they stand in this? Aaron... can you investigate this? You do have the strongest relationship with the Empire.'

'Yes Sir,' Aaron agreed.

Malik stood and walked around the table. 'In this room we have the leader of the Freebooters, the Coalition and representatives from the inner realms. Between us, we must devise a plan to finish this threat once and for all time... Crompton, how long before that core arrives?'

'It should be here within half an hour, it's at our Sydney base.'

'Good, when that arrives I want you and Ambassador Tocmal to start working on it, the information on it may be our key. Admiral Grogan, do we have any word on the Coultrane?'

'No, Mr President, but I believe Admiral Morris will be here soon, he may have more details.'

'Well, it seems we are waiting on quite a lot,' Malik stopped behind Jeff. 'Jeff, it seems we have half an hour to kill... any chance of that quick look around we discussed last time I was here?' Jeff nodded and the two men left the room.

While they waited, the others started to take stock of their new operations centre. The old bunker, the Second's Folly – as the Abraham family referred to it – was now the centre for the defence of the human race, but the technology that it held was several hundred years out of date. Assessments were made and calls placed to various supply depots. Within hours, the old halls would be ringing to the tunes of 30th century technology.

4

Daily life aboard the luxury liner went on as usual. There had been a slight change in itinerary, and they had dropped out of sub space for a few moments but all passengers had been assured *this was just a routine test for the new ship's drive system*. There were rumours of another ship docking with the liner, but generally everything was proceeding as normal.

It was early morning and Anton Alvaris was hungry, quietly relishing the thought that baked Spanish eggs would soon quell the growling of his stomach. He walked with purpose, heading for the diner he knew in this section served what he desired.

Physically, Anton was an average person, or so he looked; average height and an unexceptional face that could be forgotten as soon as it had been seen. His black hair was kept in a common non-descript cut, but his eyes were unforgettable. They were deep blue and had the ability to seemingly cut though steel; many had felt the effect of his stare and none ever forgot it.

He was extremely fit with a well-muscled frame that wasn't over toned and he worked hard at maintaining this condition. Though he never considered himself rich, he was comfortable, with a growing and successful business.

Doctor Anton Alvaris headed up Omnicron, a Geotechnical company that was started by his great-great grandfather. Omnicron was a medium sized operation but probably the only corporation that boasted its own planet as headquarters.

Anton's grandfather had been convinced that, given an ever expanding human population and the scarcity of available habitable planets, the process of terraforming should go to the next level.

To prove his idea, he had sunk almost all of the company's funds and income into terraforming a medium sized planetoid approximately two thirds the size of Earth that held all the precursors of being able to develop an atmosphere. Everything was on track for it to become a life sustaining planet; however, this would take millions of years. Indeed Bellangra, as it was known, was described as a *planet in the making* by many scientists.

The terraforming of this planetoid took almost a century and nearly bankrupted the company, but in the end the Omicron process succeeded and became the standard for planetary engineering.

Unfortunately, after the continuous stress of one hundred years of fighting for the survival of his dream, Anton's grandfather's health deteriorated to such an extent that he could no longer run the operation so the reins were handed to Anton's father, Jose.

Jose proved to be an excellent administrator and the company thrived. Over the next two hundred years, it grew into the preeminent terraforming operation in the galaxy. Fifty years ago a young Anton Alvaris graduated from Altor Major Institute of Technology with a PHD in Geophysics and joined his family's company, but his passion was not in terraforming.

He worked in several divisions till he discovered his true calling. While working on a remote terraforming operation he found himself involved in a rebellion where his true skills came to the fore. He found he had a natural gift for espionage and other services.

Finally he had a purpose and, on his return to Bellangra, started a small private security operation, the sort of operation that specialised in tasks that no one wanted to know about but still wanted done. This side of his business flourished and expanded into an organisation that took on more visible security tasks, but Anton and a few special operatives continued the covert side of the business in complete secrecy.

When his father decided to retire, the mantle of CEO fell to Anton as eldest child, but as he wasn't interested in company administration, the appointment fell to his sister, Alethea, to act as CEO. Anton remained as Chairman of the Board and a special consultant on Geophysics, giving him both time and cover for his many absences. For nearly thirty years he had been living this double life and it was still his driving force.

What he did was a very closely guarded secret and his cover worked very well. It had been several long years since Anton had taken any real leave and the opportunity to indulge was irresistible, but he left his decision too late. The marketing hype surrounding the imminent launch of Rhapsody meant all available rooms were taken, but on a whim he left his name on a reserve list. When he had been notified of a sudden cancellation, he had wasted no time and had booked the platinum package which entitled him to unlimited access to all of the ships distractions.

The diner came into view and he quickened his pace;

hunger and the thought of this simple yet exquisite breakfast utmost in his mind. He entered the diner and was quickly seated at the table he had reserved the night before. He ordered his meal with extra chilli and smoky bacon and as his first coffee arrived, he relaxed to savour the deep rich brew.

He closed his eyes and took his first sip and allowed it to swirl around his mouth. Coffee was another of his passions and this was some of the best he had ever tasted. He made a mental note to try and get the blend recipe; it would make a great addition to his pantry at home.

'Doctor Alvaris?' his indulgence was interrupted by a voice. Anton opened his eyes to see one of the Bellhops standing before him.

'Yes?' He replied curtly, not welcoming the interruption to his morning.

'Sir, I am sorry to interrupt but this was left for you at our main reception before we left Earth with instructions to deliver it to you now.' The Bellhop seemed somewhat intrigued and handed the envelope to Anton.

'Thank you,' Anton said as he casually took the item and glanced at the attendants name tag, 'Ellery', he added. He placed the envelope in the inner pocket of his jacket and nodded his dismissal of the Bellhop.

His meal arrived and he decided that nothing was going to spoil his enjoyment. He ate slowly, savouring every mouthful; the Chorizo and Tomato base complimented the eggs beautifully. He finally finished and ordered another coffee; time to see what was in the envelope.

He opened it with little movement, years of covert living shaping his every move. Into his hand he dropped a coded key card and a piece of paper that read:

Security Storage level 5; row 8; bin 23

Interesting, I didn't put anything in security storage, he thought. Anton took the last sip of his coffee then rose and went to the desk, handing his room key to the attendant. The attendant tapped his key against the console and recorded his morning meal; his package included all meals and beverages.

He moved slowly towards the concierge board and located the security storage area, three floors above him. To enter the security area he needed the key card so he retrieved it from his pocket and ran it through the scanner. Next, the scanner asked for his right index finger for a print identification.

'Very interesting,' he said to himself as he offered the required digit. 'I don't remember giving my finger prints for the ticket?'

Welcome Doctor Alvaris, the digitised voice welcomed him. *Please proceed down this corridor to room four... your security box will be delivered to you.*

Anton nodded and walked to the room, opened the door and sat at the small table; a few moments later the security box was deposited onto the table. It was common practice on these up market cruise ships for passengers to use these security boxes to transport their valuables: jewellery; money; in fact anything, as the contents of each box was known only to the person assigned to it.

Anton hadn't arranged for any of this and was starting to have a bad feeling about what was happening. The box itself was standard security issue, made of a very special amalgam of metals and composite materials; they were almost indestructible and without the correct access, impenetrable.

Anton inserted his card into the reader slot and a small ocular reader popped up. *Please place your left eye to the scanner,* the box asked.

Anton smiled to himself; *someone has gone to a lot of trouble*.

Most ocular scanners used the right eye – in fact this model security box always did – but Anton's right eye had been severely damaged on a job. Its replacement was a very special, and highly secret, biomechanical implant. To the casual observer it looked like an ordinary eye, even the colour was a perfect match for his real eye, but it would never pass one of these scanners.

He complied and was rewarded. *Thank you, Doctor Alvaris,* the box said. *The room is now sealed and fully filtered. Just insert your card in the door reader when you wish to leave. Enjoy your day.* The box latch disengaged and the lid slowly opened.

Anton's blood ran cold as he saw what was inside. He reached in, removed the object and pushed the box to the rear of the table, placing the object in front of him. A briefcase, or so it seemed; but this was a very special briefcase that only a few people even knew about; even less had access to it.

How the fuck did this get here? His mind screamed.

He placed his hands on the spots indicated and spoke quietly. 'Alvaris, Anton,' he softly commanded, 'open.' At the same time, a red beam interacted with his ocular implant and the case opened.

A combination of biological cues was needed to open

the case: his finger prints; voice analysis; and electronic communication. The case opened to reveal a normal briefcase interior. Inside was an assortment of papers, pens, a micro console and a few personal items all seemingly benign, though this was far from the truth.

Anton placed his thumbs inside the top corners of the case and tripped a catch, dropping the top of the case down to reveal six perfectly balanced throwing knives and one large antique combat knife. Satisfied, he replaced the secret compartment. Then his attention moved to the bottom of the case, where he again pressed two hidden release tabs. He removed the false base to reveal two blasters and six spare energy packs.

These weapons were very special as they were designed to be undetectable to any security scan, as were the energy packs. Where a standard pack gave approximately fifty full power shots, these were designed to triple that. In this case, he had enough firepower to start a small war if necessary.

Carefully, he replaced the base and closed the case; his mind was racing. He only ever used this case on the most extreme operations and then only if things were known to be going south. How had someone got hold of it and how did it get here with all his secrets laid bare?

He knew he needed to be calm so he commenced his calming breath exercises. Within a few moments his heart rate settled and his mind was clear. Now he noticed something else in the box; a data stick. Curious, he reopened his case and removed the console and inserted the stick into the connection point.

The screen came to life with an image of this vessel on it, before a disguised voice began to talk.

Doctor Alvaris, you are no doubt intrigued by all this but I need you to listen very carefully. There are things happening that have the ability to severely compromise our society and I fear that this ship will be part of it. I need you to be sharp. I don't know what or when anything will happen but I do know something will.

There is one person on board that I urge you to meet and trust, as I do. She will be in the main arboretum at two each afternoon, she will be wearing a blue security uniform with the rank of Commander and her name is Janice Barker. If you assist in this matter, we will deposit ten times your normal fee into your company account. Thank you and good luck.

The screen died and the data stick automatically erased. Anton looked at his watch. Just after eleven hundred hours, he noted, time to get back to his room, change and plan his next move. Although not being in control irked him, his interest had been piqued; the only way to satisfy his curiosity was to meet her. In any case, he really didn't have any way of refusing the commission.

He replaced the console in the briefcase, picked it up and left the room. As he left the security area the digitised voice followed him.

Goodbye Doctor Alvaris, enjoy your day.

Back in his suite, Anton quickly removed his clothes and placed them into the sanitiser. He showered and opened the wardrobe. All his clothes were specially designed to conceal a great deal of weaponry when required. He chose a pair of light weight cotton trousers that had a special pocket each side for two energy packs. The shirt was made of a plant fibre, a derivative of Hemp grown only on Altarus. It had four concealed sheaths for his throwing knives.

From the briefcase he removed a holster and shoulder harness which he donned before finally putting on the same jacket he had worn that morning. Then he picked up one of the blasters and quickly stripped it to run function tests. Satisfied, he placed the weapon into the holster and stood in front of the mirror, making sure that there was no evidence of what he was carrying.

Next, he moved to a belt rack where he selected a wide leather belt with numerous studs and trimmings. He decided it was a bit of overkill and he selected another that was less artful but still with a few glittering adornments.

It was just before 2.00 pm when Anton entered the arboretum, not realising how close he had cut his arrival. He didn't need to worry. As he entered, he immediately caught sight of the security uniform over near a large Elm tree. He casually made his way towards the tree, noting the Commander insignia on the left sleeve.

He moved with caution, not knowing what to expect. Quickly he scanned the area. No other uniforms but that didn't really reassure him – just because there were no uniforms didn't mean he was clear. So, what to do?

To hell with it, he thought and walked briskly over to the officer. 'Janice, I didn't expect to see you here,' he said in a friendly tone.

'Doctor Alvaris, so good to see you again,' she replied as she turned to him. She was taller than Anton and slightly built, some might say skinny, but they would be wrong. Under her clothes she was well muscled and wiry; her long, red hair was pulled up under the beret worn by the security team. Her light brown eyes darted back and forth as she constantly scanned the area, an obvious professional.

'Perhaps we could have that drink you suggested the other night?' she asked. Anton agreed and they left the arboretum and headed across the foyer to a quiet bar. They selected a private table that afforded a good view of the bar and the foyer and ordered their drinks. When the drinks arrived Janice began.

'So tell me, Doctor,' she said, 'what brings a Geophysicist to this ship? Shouldn't you be digging up rocks somewhere?' Her eyes sparkled with mischief but instinctively Anton knew this banter should be light as they were likely under surveillance.

'Seems to me you need some education,' he replied cheekily. 'Geophysics is more about how things work... the physical properties of a planet, or other heavenly body... how it is made up and held together... gravity, magnetism, even the weather. Geology looks at what the rocks are made of; we look at how they are held together and how everything interacts,' Anton continued.

After two more drinks and what looked like a catch up between old acquaintances, they parted company, agreeing to meet later for dinner. Anton decided to make the reservations, so he went up to the main restaurant precinct, four levels above and selected a BBQ restaurant; it had been quite a while since he had had a really good smoky BBQ steak.

He decided to wander down the wide boulevard that formed the central part of the precinct to check things out. About half way down the boulevard, he noticed something that looked out of place; two hundred metres ahead, access had been cut off and three heavily armed security types were stopping everyone from going any further.

Surreptitiously, he ambled closer to see what was going

on. What he saw was a couple in a heated discussion with one of the guards, demanding why they were being stopped as they were meeting friends for drinks and were already late.

To his credit, the guard was very politely and calmly explaining that there was a maintenance issue being attended to and could they please return once the task had been completed. This didn't initially impress the couple who were obviously agitated. Finally, with the guard persuading them their delay would be minimal, the couple retired to a nearby cafe to wait.

What had Anton intrigued was the show of force. Three security guards, each with a side arm and carrying a long arm blaster, seemed pretty gross overkill for a simple maintenance issue. It seemed smart to find out more so he walked up to the guard and started a conversation.

Looking past the guard, he saw an open maintenance access hatch where he could make out two workers doing something just out of sight. He looked round and checked out the cafe the couple had retired to, noting that from there he would have a much better field of view. He casually walked over, ordered a coffee and sat at one of the outside tables.

When he had been injured and told he would lose his right eye, Anton was devastated but, thanks to some good investigation by one of his employees, he was able to find an excellent surgeon who could fit him with a very special prosthesis. His new biomechanical eye was state of the art and was upgraded regularly. Two of its most used features were magnification and zoom, allowing him to see much further than before.

Now as he sat at the table, seemingly lost in his coffee,

his right eye zoomed in on the maintenance access. He watched the two operatives as they worked on the water supply. They were clearly attaching something to it.

It could have just been a problem with the purification system, he supposed, but his gut said otherwise. He moved to his right, slightly, to get a better view. He could now see the canister that they were attaching which appeared to be a simple replacement purification canister.

It was possible the main purification system had a glitch. Even so, something about the canister raised an alarm – it just didn't look right. *Mental note*, he thought. *Only drink bottled water for a few days, just in case.*

Without being able to find any real problem, Anton decided to cut his losses and move on. Just as he rose from his table, the guards and the maintenance people moved away after resealing the access door. Anton casually walked past the access door and took notice of the seal that had been placed on the lock – not standard issue – this one had a small power supply and transmitter; any interference and security would know in seconds. This only added to his suspicions so a quick tour of some other levels seemed wise.

In the next two hours, he covered six levels and found three similar maintenance issues, all with the same seals on the access hatches. His mysterious employer may have some basis for his suspicions after all. He decided to return to his suite to contemplate his next move.

As a matter of habit, Anton always used many unobtrusive ways of securing his property and rooms; nothing overt, but indicators that told him if anything had been interfered with.

At once it was obvious that housekeeping had been –

the bed was made and fresh towels and robes were in the bathroom. The other areas that he was concerned about though were his wardrobe, the fittings and fixtures. If any surveillance equipment was in place, there were many places to hide them.

Quickly, he opened his briefcase and activated the console. To the screen, he called up part of a lecture he had given to students at his old school but it was his implant that was doing the work. While to any observer he appeared to be just editing his lecture, his right eye was simultaneously doing a number of scans of the room. Within seconds it located three devices in this main part of the suite; he found another in the bedroom and even one in the bathroom.

Degenerate bastards! Anton thought, continuing his casual walk around his suite. Finally, his tour complete, he returned to the console and continued with his editing. In reality, this editing was a cover for transposing code over his lecture; he took almost fifteen minutes to finish the work. When he was satisfied with the result, he activated the communicator and called Janice Barker.

Barker, can I help you?

'Janice, Anton Alvaris here. I have taken the liberty of transcribing a lecture I gave to my old school a few months back. I was wondering if you would like to read it? You showed an interest in my field this afternoon and I thought it might be a good idea to better inform you of what a Geophysicist does before we meet tonight.' He deliberately tried to sound condescending, to any eavesdropper he wanted to seem like a slightly arrogant nerd trying to impress.

Janice caught his message. *Thank you, Doctor... I would be only too glad to read it.*

'Good. I'll have a bellboy bring it to you... what is your room location?'

Just tell him room three in the security quarters. I look forward to more discussion tonight... goodbye. She severed the connection.

Anton rang for a bellboy and shortly was rewarded by a knock at the door. He gave the Bellboy a data stick and the instructions of where to take it. Any action was a risk but if Janice Barker was who he thought she was, she would be able to define the code in the lecture and get his message.

The door annunciator chimed.

'Come in,' Steve Harris, Captain and majority owner of Albatross called. The door opened and Greg Lewis, one of Steve's business partners and second in command, entered.

'Morning Steve, how's everything looking?' He asked as he sat opposite his Captain. Greg was a large, jovial person, always ready to lend a hand and always ready with a joke. This morning though, he seemed a bit subdued, his brown eyes looking bloodshot and he seemed much slower than normal. This was to be expected however – they had just loaded 8 dart fighters, spares, equipment and crew into a hold that wasn't designed to hold fighters.

'You look like shit,' Steve commented.

'Yeah, 18 hours straight to load those Darts is enough for me. I thought we were here to pick up spares for the mines on Delangra... why the change?'

Steve looked up from his console, his blonde hair falling across his face. He was taller and slimmer than Greg, and his hair was always long. He had been described as temperamental, except those close to him knew he actually had a long fuse and when he did lose it, there was usually a good reason.

'Evidently the mine has closed for a while… something to do with these rebel activities we keep hearing about. Thankfully, the Coalition needs these Darts at Star Base 462 urgently and the fee is very good. This deal will make the trip pay off.' He turned the screen so Greg could see it.

'Shit, they must be desperate to pay that much!'

'Simply right place, right time… but that's not what I wanted to discuss.' He changed the screen. 'What do you make of this?' On the screen was the text of a message from Condor, advising all Freebooters to be extra vigilant due to increased pirate activity.

'What's up with Aaron?' Greg shook his head. 'The only pirates are the Raiders and they've never been a real threat.'

'Normally I'd agree, but he's been doing some weird things lately. He disappeared for nearly a week and now he and Grainger are both on Earth… I think something's up.' Steve stopped, stood, and walked round his desk.

He paced across his ready room a couple of times. Then mid stride – he stopped.

'Ok, you get some sleep. I'm on watch but I want this ship kept at yellow alert till we find out what's going on.'

'Yellow… that's costly,' Greg replied. Running a ship at a constant elevated alert status used energy – more energy used meant more energy needed to be generated. This, in turn, created maintenance issues and that increased costs.

'I know, but it's cheaper than battle repairs.'

'Good point, I'll get it started before I head to my cabin.' Both men now had vested interests in not damaging their ship, as insurance didn't cover everything – especially battle damage.

On the bridge, Greg found Zab'ata Gollti at the command station. He approached her and, after a brief conversation, she opened the ship's internal comm system.

'This is the Second Officer. We will be running at an elevated alert status till further notice. All hands, all stations yellow alert... I repeat, yellow alert.' She cut the comm and turned to Greg. 'What are we looking for Sir?'

'I don't know,' Greg chuckled. 'We had a communication from Condor about increased pirate activity. We're just trying to be sure, Zab.' He smiled. It was common knowledge that Greg Lewis was more than a little interested in Zab'ata Gollti. How she felt, nobody knew.

Zab'ata was a Zatarian and very hard to read. Though humanoid, Zatarians were very different to Earth Humans. Their skin was a light blue and they were totally hairless. Zab's eyes were large and a deep indigo, something that fascinated most who met her. The intensity of her gaze meant not many could look her in the eye. Zatarians were a very tall race; Zab was no exception and her body was elegantly thin.

As she turned back to her console she spoke softly so no one else could hear. 'I'm off duty in six hours... perhaps we could meet in the wardroom... to discuss any strategy?' Her words were all work but her tone was inviting.

'Excellent idea,' Greg looked at the time, 10.45 am. 'I've been on duty for eighteen hours, how about we make it eighteen thirty hours? I'll be ready for dinner around then.'

'Good, eighteen thirty in the ward room,' Zab replied.

Greg Lewis left the bridge with a new spring in his step – this was the first time he had been able to get Zab to commit to meeting off duty and she instigated it. He went straight to his quarters, showered and went to bed, setting his alarm to make sure he was on time.

The alarm sounded at exactly 17:45hrs, just as Greg had programmed it. Slowly he left the bed, stretched and headed to the bathroom. He showered again, dried himself and started to decide on what to wear – technically he wasn't on duty for a few hours so a uniform wasn't required. Finally he chose casual, giving himself the once over before he left his quarters. He reached the ward room a few minutes early, selecting a table where they could have some privacy without looking like they had something to hide.

At 18:30hrs, Zab'ata entered the room and its patrons fell into an immediate silence. Everywhere she went she seemed to make a statement. She was dressed in a long silver dress that was mostly translucent. It had dark blue embellishments strategically placed and looked more like something that would be worn at a formal engagement, not just to the ward room.

Greg greeted her. 'You look stunning,' he said in awe. 'I feel totally underdressed.'

Zab laughed. 'No, this is normal casual attire for my race.'

'Then I apologise, I must admit I know very little about Zataria... hopefully after tonight I'll be better informed.' They ordered drinks and their meal. As usual the ward room had a limited choice but the food was always well prepared. Zab told Greg all about her home world.

Zatarians, she explained, were basically humanoid, mammals who gave birth to live young. They reproduced the same as humans and lived mostly in similar community groups. They had one major difference though; being amphibian, they could breathe under water by utilising a gill like structure in their respiratory system. In fact, they needed to do this even when in space.

'Fortunately, when I was offered the position on this ship, Captain Abraham arranged to have my cabin refitted. He had a special bath tub installed. It is large enough so I can submerge; that way I can make sure I stay in good health.' She hesitated and then continued.

'Greg, I know you have tried to strike a friendship, even asking me out a couple of times. I apologise for not responding. It is difficult for me, being the only Zatarian on board. We tend to be quite insular, some say we are aloof, but that isn't the reason. We look similar, but sometimes the differences cause unease for others. I didn't want to go through that again.'

'Then why suggest tonight?'

'You have never treated me differently... you have always treated me like anyone else on the ship.' She seemed to blush as she said this, which in a Zatarian that meant a deeper blue hue to her face, 'and I like you, not just as a fellow shipmate, but... ... .' Her voice trailed off and Greg reached for her hand.

'That's why I kept asking. I wanted to get to know you better from the first day you came aboard. You are an extremely competent officer, you have made this ship a much better place since you joined, but that isn't all.' Greg stopped and took a long drink from his wine glass. 'I find you very attractive, as a woman... ' He stopped. This wasn't how he wanted to say it but suddenly words failed him.

Zab squeezed his hand. 'I understand, I feel similarly, but I don't want to cause any problems.'

'What problems?'

'Some people think we are too different, we breathe water, we need to live part of the time in water and our physiology is different.' She held up her hands and spread her fingers. She had five, as did every human but between each was a thin blue membrane, and the fingers could spread much further than any human's. 'Our feet are similar, we have these membranes between each toe and we can extend fins each side. Some people... humans... find this confronting.'

Greg looked at her and smiled. 'I must confess to something too... I have a large dark birthmark on my backside, shaped like a pair of horns.' Zab shook her head, and smiled back. 'Don't worry; I did know about that... I've seen your employment records.'

Greg leaned across the table and almost whispered. 'I believe those membranes can be very sensitive... at the right time.'

Zab looked at him very intently 'You have no idea!'

'I'm willing to find out' he responded mischievously. The evening continued very well until just after the desert course when Greg's communicator buzzed. He left the table and answered, just as Zab's did the same.

'I'm wanted on the bridge,' Greg said. 'Sorry.'

'So am I,' Zab answered, both wondering what could be so important as they left together.

The bridge was almost silent as they entered. 'What's up?' Greg asked as he went to his station beside the captain.

'462... it's not there,' Steve answered.

'What do you mean not there?'

'Just what I said... we dropped out of the worm hole, half a million kilometres from the station as normal, but the station just isn't there.' Steve pointed to the view screen; all that was evident was a large glowing debris field.

'What do the sensors tell us?' Greg asked. As First Officer, his main duty was at the operations console.

'Not much. The debris field has some very large pieces of wreckage. I can't pick up much more, there's too much interference from all the bits floating round. I could launch a sensor probe… that might help.'

'Good, do it!' Steve answered. 'Comms, get Captain Markwell up here… looks like he and his flight are homeless… and contact the nearest Coalition base, advise them of what we have found.' He looked at the screen. 'What's the function of this station?'

Greg was already working on this. 'It's a science station, set up to study some sort of quantum anomaly that appears here from time to time, there's not much info about it. Maybe they had an accident… a failed experiment.'

'Possibly, but why would they request a flight of Darts for a research station; and why pay the huge premium for us to get them here so bloody quick? No, this doesn't add up.' Steve paused as if looking for something. 'Number One, bring us to full battle readiness, I have a bad feeling about this.'

After all the years he had spent working with Aaron Abraham, Steve had developed a good sixth sense and it was now itching like never before. Greg Lewis had much the same feeling and wasted no time sounding the red alert alarm.

'What's the flap?' Brian Markwell, commander of the Dart group asked as he stepped out of the bridge pod door.

'Captain Markwell, that's what's left of your new post,'

Steve replied as he pointed to the debris field in the view screen. 'Star base 462 is no more. It appears you got here a bit late. Now, care to share what you know?'

Markwell looked at the cloud and spoke. 'Can we use your ready room?'

'Number One, you have the con,' Steve said as he led Markwell off the bridge.

Steve closed the door behind them and turned to Markwell. 'Well, what have we gotten into?'

'I really don't know. Several weeks ago we noticed an increase in Raider vessel sightings... we didn't think much of it. We're so close to the Badlands we do see them from time to time, but lately they seem to have become much bolder. Then two weeks ago, the station was buzzed by a couple of them, so Command decided it would be prudent to have some back up. The station had only basic defences so they thought a bit of a show might deter any further incursions,' Markwell explained.

'What was going on here? Why would Raiders want this station?'

'Seriously, I have no idea. The station was set up to monitor a quantum anomaly that occurs every seven months... it's not even classified. The only people who are even interested are a few quantum physicists. We were to be here for the next couple of months until the next appearance of the anomaly.'

'Then what happened? What could cause this damage?

Markwell shook his head, 'Again, no idea! Even if the main reactor went critical, it had an ejection fail safe. And in any case, when was the last time you ever heard of a MAM system failing... never, right?'

'Agreed, but something caused this. They weren't involved with any secret weapons development?' Steve was baffled by what he saw. If there was no possible internal source of this destruction, then it had to be external and that only meant an attack, but by who?

As if reading Steve's mind, Markwell spoke. 'If nothing on the station caused this, the only other explanation is an attack.'

Steve turned and called the bridge. 'Number One, check for any ion or heat signature trails.' He was already on his way back onto the bridge. Every ship leaves some evidence of its passing in space: a latent heat signature; or a trail of charged ions generated either by the ship's drive system or by causing the minute particles in space to change their static charge. Now Albatross had something to look for.

As they entered the bridge, Markwell pulled Steve aside. 'Captain Harris, as part of our standard deployment kit we have 100 sensor probes if they are of any use.'

Steve turned to Zab. 'Number Two, can we use the Coalition sensor probes?'

'Yes Sir, they're the same as ours. The systems match perfectly.'

'How many do you need?' Steve asked.

'Twenty, if you can spare them.'

Markwell smiled, feeling better at least now he could contribute to the operation. 'I'll have my guys bring them to your forward torpedo bay.'

'Ensign,' Greg called to a young officer at the rear of the bridge. 'Go with Captain Markwell and help.'

'Yes Sir,' she called as she took position following Markwell.

Steve sat back in the command chair, watching the screen. 'Ahead slow, let's get a bit closer.' The helm responded and Albatross slowly began closing in on the debris field. At 200,000 kilometres, Captain Harris again called all stop. At the same time, eight sensor probes were launched from the forward torpedo tubes. These units were similar in appearance to a standard torpedo but, instead of the usual warhead, they held a variety of sensor suites. It only took a couple of seconds for them to reach the debris field where they began a series of slow sweeps.

The Comm operator called for the Captain's attention. 'Sir, message from the Coalition... the Colombia is on route to our position and should arrive in less than an hour. They ask that we wait and observe only. They ask that we do not interact with the debris in any way as it may interfere with their investigations.'

Steve turned towards Markwell. 'The Colombia... Space Corps is sending one of its newest and most powerful warships to investigate this incident?'

Markwell looked just as perplexed as Steve was. He was about to speak when the Comms again called the Captain. 'Sir, you have a priority one message from Prime Grainger... I'll send it to your ready room.'

'This just keeps getting better,' Steve said as he stood. 'Number One, you have the con.' He entered the ready room, locking the door as it closed. A priority one message from the Prime was never about how trade was going. He felt a cold shiver run down his spine. The console activated and Steve watched as the face of Allen Grainger, Freebooter Prime, appeared on the screen.

Captain Harris, I wish I was sending better news but things have transpired that we need to be part of. I can't go into too much detail but I must ask you to be very diligent in what you are now doing. If you agree, we will ratify a new contract for Albatross.

This contract will place you in the employ of the Coalition Space Corps. They will be picking up all costs associated with your current operations. Captain Satria, commander of the Colombia, has been informed and asks that you only observe the debris field. Under no circumstances are you, or any members of the crew to enter the field.

Use any and all sensor activity you have, but no incursions into it. I am sending some confidential sensor settings to you in this message. Have your sensors scan for these readings and report to me or Captain Abraham only, on what you find. If necessary, we will pass the information forward... Grainger out.

Grainger's face faded and was replaced by a copy of the contract with the Coalition. Steve scanned it, clearly happy with the terms, but one clause made him pause. A few words caused the uneasy feeling he had to grow exponentially.

Any and all Freebooter vessels and personnel as requested and agreed, from time to time. The three words 'any and all' were the key – something really big must be coming. This type of commitment could only be done with a majority agreement from the Council of Seniors.

He sighed, this was way out of his understanding, but the terms were still very enticing. If the Coalition was happy to pay, then he was very happy to accept. He called Zab. 'Number Two, can you come to my ready room?'

A few moments later the door annunciator rang; Steve unlocked it and Zab entered. 'You wanted to see me?' she asked.

'Yes. Can you set up a sensor scan like this?'

She looked closely at the specifications, 'yes, easily.'

'But can you do it without anyone knowing?'

She thought for a while. 'I take it you don't want the results displayed?' Steve shook his head. 'Then I'll need to set up a sub-routine that will scan and record the findings... where do you want them sent?'

'This console, the secure data core, and tell everyone you're leaving the bridge to change... perfect cover.'

Zab looked embarrassed. 'Sorry Sir, I came straight from dinner.'

'I'm not reprimanding you, it's a good thing. Gives you the perfect cover for being off the bridge for the time you need.'

Steve entered the bridge and took his seat. The ship was stationary and the feed from all the sensor probes were being analysed and fed into the Bubble. The 3D image was astounding. The station had suffered some sort of cataclysmic event, where pieces of it had been flung out over 100,000 kilometres from its prime location.

Markwell was staring at the image in the Bubble as if trying to will the pieces back together. 'It must have been the reactor... what else could do this amount of damage?'

Steve was also at a loss to explain what he saw in the Bubble. Star Base 462 was a standard design, looking like a huge barbell. There should have been two domed sections, one at each end. These held accommodation, administration, and commercial areas at one end. The other was for engineering, dock facilities, life support, and power generation. Between these was a long tube that had many functions. It could house scientific and astronomical operations, or a myriad of other functions depending on the purpose of the base. Also, 462 had a large ring round this centre tube used for collecting data on the anomaly it was studying. But none of this was now here, except in varying sized pieces in the debris field.

'What was her complement?' Steve asked Markwell, quietly.

'About four hundred I believe,' Markwell replied, his voice sombre.

The bridge was quiet while everyone took in the scene before them. Zab returned in uniform and went back to her station. One of the probe icons in the Bubble began to flash; it was on the far edge of the field about to return.

'Ion trail,' Zab announced, 'something passed here.' She kept working on the data trying to find a drive signature. Minutes passed slowly with Zab at her console working every angle. She brought two more probes to the location and started them in an ever widening global search; then she brought another two into the pattern.

No-one made a sound; every mind was willing her success. 'Got it,' she called, 'definite drive signature, three actually.' She went silent again as she fed the data into the recognition program, everyone on the bridge waiting for the results.

Finally Zab stood back from her console and announced, 'Three distinct drive trails... signature appears to be Tellurian. The course is indicated in the Bubble now.'

Three definite drive signatures could be seen heading away from the scene. Zab sent one of the probes off along the trail, mapping the path of the ships. It ended 875,000 kilometres away, where there were indications they had activated their displacement drives.

'Navigator, can you hypothesise from this information

where they could be heading?' Steve asked.

'Yes, but nobody's going to like the answer,' the navigator said as he brought his findings up on the main view screen. 'Best guess is the Badlands. Looking at their course, entry angle and what I can make of the intensity of the worm hole, that's the most logical destination.'

Markwell stood, his head shaking slightly in disbelief. 'That fits with the reports of Raiders in the area, but this makes no sense! There's no gain for them to do anything like this, and in any case, three old Tellurian ships just don't have the fire power. There must be something else, something we missed.' He looked at Zab. 'Can you do another sweep?'

Zab looked to her Captain who simply nodded in response. She re-tasked all the probes setting them on a slow, grid search to cover every part of the debris field. As she finished, she announced that the Colombia had arrived and fed the data into the Bubble.

'Colombia is hailing us Sir,' the Comms Officer called.

'Steve sat back at his command chair and activated the link. 'ECS Colombia, this is Captain Harris of FTS Albatross. Welcome.'

Captain Harris, I'm Captain Satria, have you found anything yet?

'In a manner of speaking, yes we have. I would prefer to discuss this in person however, if you agree.'

Satria looked young to be in command of the ship, which told Steve she must be very good at her job. His personal console flashed. Greg had brought up the information they had on Captain Satria and Steve's suspicions were correct. At only 120, she was indeed young to be Captain of one of Space Corps newest and largest star ships.

I agree, Captain, she replied. *Let me get my ship parked. I look forward to meeting you in person... say ten minutes?*

'Agreed, ten minutes suits me fine. I have Captain Markwell on board; shall I bring him with me?'

No need, he'll be staying with you, for the time being, but transmit your sensor logs, we can discuss the results when you're here... Colombia out. The comm link terminated.

Steve turned to his comm officer. 'Can you get me a sub space link to Grainger?'

'No need Sir, I have a call coming through from him now.' The comm officer looked stunned – coincidence was something no-one on this ship had any faith in. Steve left the bridge and went into his ready room. The delay between Earth and the ship was now only seven seconds but was still enough to make conversation difficult. He accessed his console and Grainger's face filled the screen.

Captain, I'll make this short. I take it Captain Satria on Colombia has arrived? Grainger waited for an answer then continued. *Good, work with her... give her whatever she needs, especially the data I asked you to collect... it may be critical.*

'Yes Sir, but may I ask what I'm supposed to do now?'

When Captain Satria is up to speed, if she doesn't need your assistance, you are to come straight to Earth. Captain Abraham and I will be here... understood?

'Understood Sir, I'm about to go and meet with Satria now. I'll call you when we've finished... Albatross out.' Steve cut the link, connected his data pad to the console and copied the secret sensor logs to it. He walked back into the bridge, handed command over to Greg and left for the shuttle bay. Although there was a larger shuttle in the Captain's

Yacht hangar, Steve decided to take a standard unit. It was prepped and ready for flight when he arrived. A quick check of the operating systems and he left Albatross.

The trip to Colombia was short and the sight of the massive cruiser was impressive. It was at least three times the size of Albatross and ovoid in shape. There were no obvious protrusions, except for a communications array that had been raised.

The flight controller from Colombia called and gave Steve the data to enter the ship. He fed this into the nav system and Colombia took control of his shuttle, automatically sliding him into the shuttle bay near the centre of the ship.

The shuttle door opened and Steve saw a young ensign waiting at the end of the gangway.

'Welcome, Captain Harris. If you would follow me, Captain Satria is waiting in the conference room.' Steve nodded and fell into step behind her, very aware of the two armed marines only a few paces behind him.

The dock was huge, capable of holding up to 100 fighting vessels. At this time, it held 25. The walkway they were using was clearly marked and the centre was divided into two lanes for transport vehicles. They quickly covered the 75 metres to the closest pod where the Ensign and Steve entered; the two marines taking position either side of the entry.

'Sorry for the muscle, but we are at red alert status making life aboard quite tense.' She explained as the pod sped them toward their destination, first horizontally then transitioning to vertical. Finally it stopped and the door opened, the Ensign again leading the way. Stopping at a door, she activated the annunciator.

Come in, a voice sounded from the panel and the door opened. The woman sitting at a table looked up. 'That will be all, thank you Ensign.' The door closed behind Steve as the woman rose to greet him. 'Ellen Satria... pleased to meet you.'

Steve was taken back by the lack of formality; every other Space Corps Officer he had met had always insisted on using rank formalities. He took a good look at this Ellen Satria: medium length brown hair; eyes a light green; and her face round and attractive. In all, she appeared to infuse a feeling of confidence.

'Steve Harris and the pleasure is mine Captain.' 'Please, can we ditch the rank?'

'Of course, if that's what you prefer.'

'Believe me, all day, all I get called is Captain. I'm starting to think I don't have a name and we are, after all, equal. We both command ships,' she said pointedly.

Steve chuckled. 'Comparing my old girl to this is somewhat of a stretch.' They returned to the table where Steve handed the data pad to her. 'This is the data that Prime Grainger had us compile from the sensor probes.'

Satria took the pad and connected it to a console behind her seat. It took a few moments for the systems to normalise and the data to begin to download. At the same time, she initialised a comm link to Earth; Admiral Grogan and Prime Grainger's faces appeared on the screen.

Satria and Steve made the normal greetings before Satria announced she was starting the analysis they wanted. There was silence from the comm link and in the room as they waited for this to complete; finally the results came up on the screen.

'Admiral, as you suspected… a high concentration of Trisidic radiation now out to one hundred and fifty thousand K from the original position,' she turned to Steve. 'I think we should get our ships back a bit, say… half a million?' She activated another comm link, this time to the bridge as Steve did the same.

'Number One, please move Albatross back to the 500,000 kilometre mark.

'But Captain, we think we have some life signs. We should send a team in to check,' Greg Lewis pleaded with his Captain.

'Greg, move back now, that's an order! I'll explain later but at this point, no-one is to enter that debris field, understood?'

'Aye Sir, understood.' Within moments, Albatross started to move back. Steve stood at the view port and watched as Colombia also started to retreat.

'Ok, I've just ordered my ship out of harms' way… how in hell did a Coalition research station, become irradiated by Trisidium?'

Grogan answered. *Captain Harris we believe that this was a test of a new weapon that the Tragarian Raiders have gotten hold of. There is nothing to gain for them in this, except to prove the weapon. Captain Satria, proceed with your patrol of all the border outposts, although I don't think we'll see any more incidents.'*

Steve couldn't help but protest. 'Admiral, what about the life signs Albatross detected? We can't just ignore them!'

It was Grainger who replied. *Captain Harris, Steve, please understand, we don't like this any more than you do but your ship and crew would not survive. And even if you did, there is nothing you can do for people irradiated by Trisidium... all you could do is euthanize them and you'd be condemning both yourself and your crew to the same fate if you try to intervene.*

'He's right, Steve, there's nothing we can do for them,' Satria spoke softly. 'The best we can do is finding where this weapon is coming from and destroy it.' Deep down he knew they were right but Steve Harris riled against just leaving someone to die in space – it went against everything Freebooters believed in – but there was no alternative.

Grainger's voice boomed from the comm system. *Steve, come to Earth, bring the Dart flight with you and we'll explain everything then. How long do you estimate the trip will take?*

'About three days.'

Good, we'll see you in three days. And the link to Earth was cut.

Satria closed the console and handed Steve his data pad. 'I know how you feel,' she said. 'It rips me up to leave anyone stranded, but killing ourselves isn't the answer. Come on, I'll take you back to your shuttle.' They travelled back in silence, both locked in their battle between their conscience and their orders. It seemed like no time till they were standing beside Steve's shuttle.

'Well Ellen, I suppose this is goodbye. I wish we could have met under better circumstances,' Steve said with an empty feeling in his stomach.

Ellen Satria held out her hand which Steve took. 'I agree Steve. Maybe next time we'll have a chance to actually get to know each other... I'd like that.'

'Yes, so would I... until next time then.' He smiled, let

her hand slip from his grasp, turned and walked down the gangway into his shuttle.

Ten minutes later, Steve Harris entered his own bridge. 'Navigator, set a course for Earth... I want to be there in 3 days.'

Greg Lewis moved to Steve's side. 'Can I have a word in the ready room?'

They both left the bridge as Zab took the con. The door closed behind them and Greg started.

'Are you fucking for real? There may be people still alive in that debris field, and we're just running off to Earth?' He was angry, angrier than Steve had seen him in a long time – probably the whole bridge crew was feeling the same. 'Why are we leaving them?'

Steve dropped into a chair, indicating for Greg to do the same. 'One simple problem Trisidium... the debris field is full of Trisidic radiation... we'd all be dead if we went in there, that's why we're leaving.'

Greg was about to protest but Steve held his hand up to silence him. 'Grainger and the Coalition suspected something. They sent us some special sensor settings and Zab programmed it secretly... remember she left the bridge to change? Well, that's not all she did. I took the results over to the Colombia as instructed and they analysed the data. This whole area will be quarantined, probably out to 1,000,000k or more. We just need to get away.' Greg's face looked stunned at the revelation.

'I don't believe it, Tellurians wouldn't be so stupid! It kills them as fast as it does us.'

'We don't think Telluria has anything to do with this. Apart from the drive signatures, there is nothing to point to them.

But Raiders may be another issue and they use a lot of Tellurian ships and drives.

'Bullshit! Raiders wouldn't attack an outpost like this. Where's the gain for them?'

'Fucked if I know, but then I don't have a clue about any of this! Why is Grainger on Earth and why is he so cosy with the coalition all of a sudden? The only way to get answers is to get to Earth and ask the questions,' Steve vented at Greg.

'Yeah, good point but we better bring the rest of the crew up to speed. There are some very unhappy people out there.' Greg pointed to the bridge door. Together they went back to the bridge. Steve handed Zab the data pad and asked her to input the data and analysis, she compiled the data as requested and displayed on the main screen.

Together, Steve and Zab went through the data and analysis, bringing the whole bridge up to speed and nobody said a word. The evidence was plain and all agreed that entering the debris field was a death sentence and not an option. They realised that also bringing any survivors out remotely was just as bad.

'If they were to come aboard Albatross, the entire ship would be compromised,' Steve said rubbing his hands over his face as he started to gain an understanding of the reason a group like Tragarian Raiders would use a weapon like this. 'A miss is almost as good as a direct hit,' he muttered. 'If the initial blast doesn't kill, the radiation released will finish the job.'

Finally, the analysis was complete and the navigator broke the silence. 'Sir, course for Earth laid in. Displacement factor of eighteen will get us there in just under three days.'

Steve looked round his bridge crew. 'I know this is a hard

thing to do, but we have no choice. We get to Earth and find out what's going on, and hopefully find a way to stop this ever happening again.' He paused letting that sink in.

'On a lighter note, technically we are still working for the Coalition so this trip will be profitable for all of us.' While not what he wanted to say, he desperately tried to end the conversation in a positive vein. The nods and smiles showed him it worked, albeit weakly.

'Helm... engage course to Earth... how long to insertion?'

The helmsman consulted his console. 'Twenty minutes, Sir.'

Exactly twenty minutes later, the displacement drive initiated and Albatross slipped quietly into the relative safety of its worm hole.

Sunday morning dawned and dark brooding clouds held the expectation of rain. Although the last few days had been similar, little rain had fallen, but today held more promise.

Captain JT Abraham had just returned from a patrol flight that had taken him over much of the adjoining regions. Since the discovery of the security breach, things had become complicated, with his family home and headquarters for Abracorp fast turning into the seat of government for the Coalition. The Palace and Parliament buildings had been compromised – even Space Corps headquarters in Perth had been penetrated.

A full security sweep of the entire compound including the house, all the offices and also the resurrected bunker, had been requested, before being approved for the President. Then, before anyone had arrived, Admiral Grogan and Mondrac had left for Perth to attend a highly covert meeting.

The entire Earth defence system had been brought to high alert, all the satellite weapon systems were initialised, and even ground forces had been dispersed. The decision to secure the President and his party at the house was causing a large degree of upheaval. Ground troops had been deployed to protect from any land based incursions and JT had been given command of the air cover. He and Sol had flipped for duty – JT lost and got the night shift – with twenty fighters constantly covering the region.

All the activity was starting to affect company operations and this had Jeff Abraham fuming. Staff arriving Monday morning would have to be cleared by security before starting work. All the activity in the bunker would cause major disruptions to the renovation schedule and blow a huge hole in David's budgets. This caused JT to smile; everyone wanted him to leave the Corps and join the company. Now he was relieved that this option was off the table for the foreseeable future.

How did this all come about so fast?' The question kept roaming in and out of his thoughts. *Friday had been a normal day and then Saturday; all hell broke loose... the attempt on the President, then the discovery of surveillance equipment at the Palace.*

As a precaution, every Coalition facility had been checked and more were found to be compromised. Every department, every building, was under intense scrutiny – so *much for PPS security protocols.* He shook those thoughts away as he walked towards the house.

He consulted his watch, 05:25am. Phillip should be in the kitchen and there was a good chance of a quick bite before he went to his room. Having been on duty for 12 hours, he felt the need for sleep but he was hungry. He walked into the kitchen to find Phillip already on breakfast duty. With all the extra mouths to feed, he now had four other androids working on food preparation.

'Good morning Mister Abraham,' greeted Phillip, pausing his chopping.

'Morning Phillip, any chance of something to eat,' JT

smiled as he spoke, remembering sneaking in here often as a child and grabbing a quick snack.

'Would bacon and eggs suffice?'

'Perfect,' JT answered in fascination. Perfectly chopped carrots flew from Phillip's knife, each piece exactly the same dimension as the previous one. Phillip looked over to one of the cooks and issued the necessary instructions.

Twenty minutes later, JT pushed the now empty plate away, sat back and sipped at his cup of tea. He was amazed at the amount of food being prepared.

JT had watched the preparation as he ate, wondering how many it was for, 'Phillip, why so much food?'

'Evidently, we have more guests arriving today; your mother has asked that we prepare a dinner for forty people. That's all I know.'

Great, thank heavens I've got the night shift JT thought. He thanked Phillip for breakfast and headed to his room to get some sleep.

***

The buzzing of the communicator woke JT instantly. He recognised the caller and answered, 'Abraham here.'

Captain, can you please join us in the conference room in ten minutes?

'Yes Admiral.' JT broke the connection and headed straight to the bathroom. Ten minutes later the elevator doors opened and he entered the assigned room.

'Sorry to disturb you, but there are some new developments,' Sam Grogan announced as he greeted John in the ante room. 'Star Base 462 has been destroyed... the President is considering putting the Coalition on a war footing.'

The Admiral's words were blunt. They crossed into the conference room where the President and the other leaders were gathered. JT saw a vacant chair beside Sol and quickly sat without the usual banter. The situation was far too serious and the grim looks on the gathered faces demonstrated that.

'Last night, Ambassador Mondrac and I examined the surveillance devices we found in a number of our buildings. The results are not good. First, they are a blend of both Human and Alien technology. Second, we now believe that the issue of Eugene Sarclan's involvement has been proven.'

There was a distinct murmur around the table as Grogan spoke. 'I know nobody here wants to think that Sarclan is still a threat but, if what Ambassador Mondrac has to tell you is even half accurate, the threat is real and much worse than we could imagine. Ambassador, perhaps it would be better if you explained.'

Mondrac stood and began. 'The equipment we examined is a clever melding of technologies from your realm and from one of the inner realms from a planet called Galdor. Before I go any further, let me explain.'

Mondrac described the true nature of the multiverse and the different realms. To some it was a revelation – almost a confirmation of long held ideas – but for others, too much to grasp. There was a period of disbelief and argument until Aaron spoke up.

'Ladies and Gentlemen, we,' and he indicated Petra, 'have been there. We have seen it with our own eyes. Everything the Ambassador has told you is true. Now either you accept that we live in a universe much bigger and more diverse than you ever thought, or you stick your heads in the sand and wait for it to roll over you.

'Believe me, I have fought these people and they are formidable. If they have teamed up with Sarclan, we have a serious threat to counter.' Like a hammer blow, his words stunned all back to reality.

'Excuse me Captain Abraham, but where do Freebooters stand in this? Aren't you non-aligned?' Madam Collard, the senior Council member asked.

It was Allen Grainger who replied. 'Madam Collard, this is true, but I have asked the members of our Council of Seniors to join us on Earth. They should be here later in the week and we will discuss this situation. As it stands, I do have the authority to offer some Freebooter support, but only our council can make that support unilateral.'

'I understand Prime Grainger. But Freebooters are traders... what can you offer in this situation?' Collard was fishing for something.

'Madam Collard,' Grainger interjected, 'without Freebooter help you don't have the capacity to defeat this new enemy. The rebellions have stretched your resources past their breaking point. You have no reserves left and the Krell Empire seems to be involved in some diabolical internal political drama so their assistance may be limited. You need Freebooters much more than we need you.'

'*Enough!*' Mondrac was on his feet, his fist smashing on to the table. 'Enough of this petty bickering... your very survival is in the balance and all you do is start a... ... ' he seemed to search for words, '... yes, a pissing competition! I think that is what you call it.

'Make no mistake... if Galdor and Nileros have joined with this Sarclan you all seem to fear, then the very existence of your species is at risk. Tocmal and I have come here to try and assist but if all you are going to do is bicker and play at your foolish politics, we will leave you to your fate.'

Aaron had never seen any form of anger from an Eldoran before, and he decided that he didn't want to again.

'Mondrac is right, we all need each other,' Aaron replied. 'As I said, we have fought Galdorans and they can match anything in this realm, plus they have numbers. The only way we can win is by working together and being smarter than they are.' As he finished, the door opened and in strode Admirals Wilson and Morris.

'Mister President, my apologies for being late… may I?' Wilson pointed to the console. President Malik nodded and pushed it toward her. 'Thank you Sir,' she said as she inserted a data drive. 'We have found the Coultrane. She is in the Dacarian system, heading for the Badlands. Fortunately, we have several monitoring stations in the system so tracking her won't be an issue.' Wilson sounded pleased with the discovery, even bordering on smugness.

Crompton couldn't help himself. 'So, we can now watch while one of your biggest battleships gracefully flies off into the waiting arms of our adversary?'

Wilson smiled. 'Sorry Crompton, we're not doing that. We're going to destroy her. Mister President, I hope everyone in here is cleared for top secret.'

'I don't think that really matters, now, do you?' Malik answered.

Wilson stopped and looked as if she had an answer, but thought better of it, 'Probably not.' She continued working at the console. A few minutes later she looked up. 'All our larger ships have been set up with a remote kill switch, a program that, once initiated, will cause a cascade failure of the MAM system. The result is the total destruction of the ship.'

'And you have control of this?' Crompton asked, quietly.

Wilson shook her head. 'Not exactly… for the system to be activated, it needs three separate codes to be sent simultaneously, plus it must be originated by the commander of the ship. Thankfully, Captain O'Neil was able to initiate the system before the rebels took control. There are only five senior officers who have codes and we have three in this room. Gentlemen, please enter your codes.'

She stood back as Admiral Morris moved in, completed the Bioscan and entered his code. Sam Grogan followed suit. 'And now I will enter mine.' Wilson did this and looked to the President. Sir, once I activate this it cannot be rescinded… will you authorise it?' She paused until Malik nodded his agreement.

'Now, all I need to do is this.' She pressed an icon on the screen and sent the message. 'Now every sensor buoy, every comms relay and every security picket will be a potential weapon to destroy Coultrane.'

'What about the communication delay?' Collard asked.

'It's only about 10 seconds, it's already been received.'

'Now you know where it is, why not retrieve the ship? Surely those rebels aren't familiar with the ship, at least not enough to be a problem.'

'Madam Collard, we simply don't have anything close enough to her to intercept before she reaches the Badlands. I'm sorry, but unless you wish to give our enemy one of our best warships, this is the only way.' The room fell back to silence, the truth of the situation starting to hit home. Everyone waited.

Time dragged painfully by, and nothing seemed to happen for ages. Then suddenly, the console chimed. One of the sensor probes had detected the ship. The console flashed a message.

CODE DELIVERED

Everyone waited again. The main screen started to flicker and all eyes were now on it. A shape began to appear and very slowly, the shape coalesced into the Coultrane, now stopped in space.

One could only imagine the activity that would be happening on the bridge at this point in time. There would be panic, of course, and noise – commands being barked as the crew frantically tried to bring the critically wounded ship back to life.

Just as suddenly, the screen flared a brilliant white and went black. Wilson's fingers worked the console and slowly the screen came back. The image was different now. Where the Coultrane had been was now a slowly receding glow; debris was very limited. A MAM cascade leaves very little behind; even something as large as Coultrane was vaporised.

No-one spoke, the enormity of what had just happened hanging like a huge weight on the heads of everyone in the room. 10,000 rebels had just died, one of the Coalitions best ships vaporised and all done from a single data console.

Wilson quietly shut the console down and looked to her President, her voice quiet as she spoke. 'Sir, I know they were all your people on that ship, but there was no other alternative.'

'I understand Admiral. After all, it was I who authorised the action. They made their choice and suffered the consequences, now please all of you go about your allotted tasks.' He moved to Wilson's side. 'Admiral I need to contact Ummah... I shall inform the Government of the situation.'

The room began to empty as people moved away to their allotted work spaces in the bunker. Soon, only a few were left and Crompton now spoke to Admiral Wilson. 'That took some balls, Skye, I'm impressed. Now all we need to do is find Rhapsody before she becomes more of a problem.'

Wilson looked hard into Crompton's eyes, 'any word from either of the operatives?'

Crompton shook his head. 'Nothing... and we don't have any trace of the ship. It's like it vanished.'

Albrect entered the conversation. 'Not surprising... she had left Dalroth 4, heading for the Stygian Nebula. There's no surveillance in that sector and the transponder has gone dark I'm afraid. But what else is out there? Something they need? We need to find it, and fast!'

'We have a team working on that, looking for options, but there's not much in that region... a couple of old mining operations and that's all,' Wilson replied.

'Mining... what mining?' Crompton asked.

'Don't really know. They are old operations, mostly abandoned, but some are in care and maintenance. Why?'

'One of the things that many of the mining operations needed was somewhere to house their workers and maintain their equipment. If memory serves me, many of the operations in that region are mainly asteroid based, with no atmosphere and limited space.

'Didn't Cordoba set up some large stations? You know accommodation, processing and maintenance plants?' Crompton's voice was animated as he called up some files on the console. Finding what he was looking for, he continued.

'Yes, here it is. In order to exploit the ore, they set up a number of huge stations. The ore was transported to these, processed, and then sent on to the eventual destination.'

Again he stopped and looked round the room; he saw his target about to leave. 'Grainger,' Crompton called, 'can you spare a minute?'

Allen Grainger turned and acknowledged the call. He excused himself from the group he was with and joined Crompton.

'What is it?'

'Prime, what do you know about the Cordoba Corporation mining operations in this sector?' Crompton brought the star map up on the main screen, highlighting the area in question.

Grainger studied it for a while before answering. 'Not much, it's mainly played out. There are some rumours that they have found some more viable ore bodies, but nothing has happened as yet. Why?'

'If I recall correctly, Freebooters had the transport contract with Cordoba; if so, you would have the locations of their processing stations.'

'Not me personally... I believe Aaron has some contracts now, but this area was closed down before he came on the scene. I think Colin McKenzie, or maybe his father, had the contract for that region. Colin's on his way here for the Council meeting... I'll send him a message, see if he has the information. But why is all this so important?'

Crompton smiled. 'Remember what Ambassador Mondrac said? He believes they need these large ships to move troops. The passengers may still be of value, as hostages, but they'll need somewhere to off load them, accommodate them, and keep them secured. One of the processing and accommodation plants would fit the bill.'

Wilson spoke up. 'But nearly all of these stations have been shut down. Some have been converted into hotels and moved and, because we don't have total authority, only some local systems would know what is in their region. It's like the old needle in a haystack.'

'Yes, but it's all we have at this point in time. Don't you think it's worth looking for those needles?'

Wilson looked at Crompton, and saw he was serious. 'Ok, I'll see what resources we have. Maybe we could use the Astrophysics department at the Academy?' She suddenly seemed to accept the idea. 'They have the equipment and staff to do the job. I'll get it moving,' she said as she left the group.

It was 19:30hrs and the door annunciator buzzed.

Anton activated the door viewer and saw Janice Barker waiting. She entered and handed him the data stick.

'Thank you, I found your lecture very informative,' she commented. She was dressed casually in grey jeans, a light blue shirt with a loose grey jacket to match her jeans. On her feet was a pair of sturdy, but flexible boots. 'I thought as we are going to a BBQ tonight, I should dress casual.'

Anton had decided similar attire would be best. 'Seems our thoughts were similar,' he quipped. The one thing neither commented on was the weaponry they both carried. 'Shall we go?' he asked. As they left the room, he tapped an icon on the console and his makeshift security system was activated.

They took the transport pod to the main restaurant precinct and slowly ambled down the wide boulevard, looking like most other couples out for an enjoyable evening. As they approached their destination, Anton pressed a small round case into Janice's hand; it looked like an amulet which she immediately placed into a small space cleverly designed into her shirt.

The device was a scrambler designed to cover their

conversation. It did this by emitting a sub audible sound that scrambled any vibrations in the air surrounding the wearer. To anyone close, their conversation would sound like gibberish and, as Anton wore a matching unit, they could talk normally. Another feature was the unit's ability to scramble the air movement close to them, confusing any listening devices that may be nearby. To any eavesdropper, their words would be lost to a breeze.

Janice looked at her companion. 'Why doctor, you seem full of surprises,' her voice was clear only to Anton. 'Have you tried to contact anyone outside of this ship?'

Anton shook his head.

'Won't do you any good, there appears to be some sort of dampening field disrupting all communications. I asked the Captain about it and he only gave some vague explanation of some cosmic interference, but I know some of our passengers are getting a bit angry.'

'Do you have any idea what's going on?' Anton asked, moving his head slightly every few seconds so any visual surveillance could not get a clear read on his lips; lip reading was a basic skill for any would-be spook.

Janice was just as skilled and did the same as she answered. 'No, but I'm pretty sure the crew are no longer in control. If this is a simple hijacking, they have gone to great lengths to keep everything as normal as possible.'

They arrived at the restaurant and were seated by a waiter. Anton ordered a couple of beers as they consulted the menu. They ordered their meal and the waiter left them. 'If this dampening field is being generated on board, there must be a way to breach it... it can't reach every part of the ship,' he mused.

'Correct,' Janice replied. 'I worked through the ship's schematics this afternoon and I believe that there is one place where it can't reach and at least one place that we can. Why?'

'If we can get there, we may be able to get a signal out or at least receive one. I was contacted by someone by way of a note left for me before we left, probably even before I boarded the ship. Whoever left it arranged for it to be delivered to me at a precise location and time… no-one knows me that well. The one thing I still don't know is why? I have no instructions, no mission parameters, just you as my contact, so what gives?' Anton was visibly concerned by this revelation. 'I know you must be CID or something, and you now know more about me than anyone still alive, so please give me some reason not to walk away from this.'

Janice's stare bored into Anton's very soul. 'Ok, I report directly to Director Crompton, head of CID.'

'Interesting… I know who Crompton is.'

'We became aware of a plot to hijack this ship a few months ago; with all the dignitaries on board it is a prime target for any number of dickheads. From political coups to simple ransom, you must admit this trip is rich pickings. We tried to get things changed, to stop people from joining the trip and we succeeded with some, but in the main, we had no real evidence only rumour and whispers. Crompton decided to insert me into the crew but he never said anything about help. I assume that you are the infamous doctor I hear so much about?'

'What the hell? Yes, I am the Doctor, but just drop the infamous, ok?'

'So, someone, who you don't know, has contracted you to

do something you also don't know. Shit, you could be one of the hijackers for all I know,' Janice responded.

Anton smiled at her. 'No, not in my repertoire… still, I can see why you might be suspicious. But I have just admitted who I am… do you think I would do that if I was a bad guy?'

Janice didn't have time to answer as the waiter appeared with their steaks. Anton switched off the security field so their conversation became more normal. They discussed Anton's work in terraforming at length and he was pleasantly surprised that she had actually read his lecture, not just the coded message he had placed in it.

While they were eating, Anton had scanned the area with his implant, looking for any anomalies that may suggest they had been compromised. They finished their meal when Anton's gut alarm sounded; something wasn't right. He rescanned the area again, this time noting four security officers standing a small distance down the boulevard.

Re-establishing the security field he said quietly, 'I think we are going to have company any minute. Four security types, just over your left shoulder looking at our table… whatever happens, follow my lead.' As Anton finished, he turned the field off again and dropped back into talking about terraforming.

They didn't have to wait long, with the four men moving over towards the restaurant a moment later. Two took up flanking positions about ten metres either side of the entrance whilst the leader and a fourth were moving inside. The leader stopped and had a quick discussion with the Maître De before he walked to their table.

'Doctor Alvaris, may I introduce myself?' He didn't wait for an answer before continuing. 'I am Major Korder, head of security. How is your evening?'

Janice saw a flicker of recognition in Anton's eyes as Korder introduced himself, she filed it for later. Taller than Anton, Korder had facial features that had plagued him all his life, earning some very uncomplimentary nick names such as rat face. As a child, Korder had been bullied and made the butt of many jokes until he joined the Coalition Expeditionary Forces. Here he had found his calling – brutality.

Once enlisted in the CEF, he had quickly climbed through the ranks until his interrogation methods had come to the attention of his superiors. It seemed at the time, that his methods were unacceptable, even if his results were singularly impressive. He was summarily removed from the force and became a contractor, working for some of the worst scum in human history. So why was he here on Rhapsody?

'Ah yes, Major Korder... a pleasure I'm sure. Would you care to join us?' Anton gave his best disarming smile as he stood and offered a chair to the Major.

'Thank you, but no,' the rat smiled cunningly. 'I was wondering if you would care to join me in a tour of the ship.'

'Very kind,' Anton said, 'I was just trying to work up the courage to ask Commander Barker for exactly that... and now you are here offering the same! He turned to Janice. 'Care to accompany us, my dear?' Janice nodded and stood up. 'Again, thank you Major, please lead on.'

They all left the restaurant with the Major in the lead, the guard who accompanied him to the right of Anton and the other two about five metres behind. Anton kept up meaningless small talk with the Major until they turned right into a security access way. He turned the security field on and said, 'Get ready, the two behind are yours,' and turned the field off again.

He raised his left hand and rested his thumb on his belt, surreptitiously removing one of the studs. He lazily moved his left hand upward and, using his middle finger and thumb, flicked the small item onto the back of Korder's neck. Two second later the Major stumbled and fell against the wall. 'Major, are you alright?' Anton enquired as rat face slumped to the ground. As the guard beside Anton reached down for Korder, Anton's hand snaked out, striking the guard's throat like a piece of steel. The guard crumpled immediately, his larynx crushed. The other two guards leapt forward only to be dropped in their tracks by Janice's fists and feet. In all, the altercation took no more than a few seconds but in that time their escort was reduced to zero.

'What just happened?' Janice asked.

'Just a little drop of Togarilium Bloat Fish venom... he'll be ok in a few minutes. Meantime, we need somewhere to put these three.'

'Well, at least one won't be a problem anymore.' Janice rose from the guard with the crushed larynx. 'Your reputation is well deserved.' She moved off to the left and found a small maintenance space. 'In here should do.' They picked up the two unconscious guards, stripped them of their ID and administered a sedative prior to dumping them. The dead one they hid behind an air supply duct and returned to rat face.

'We need somewhere to have a quiet discussion with this asshole,' Anton mused.

'I know just the place. Do you need any help with him?'
'No, he'll walk on his own.' Anton brought out a small tube

and shunt from his belt. He inserted the shunt into a vein on Korder's left arm and squeezed the tube. Within a few seconds Korder was aware of his surroundings.

Anton spoke to him softly and menacingly. 'Now listen, Rat Face, you have been poisoned with bloat fish venom. I have just given you a small dose of antidote, not enough to counteract the poison, but enough to keep you alive... for a while. Now, if you want the rest,' Anton held up another tube of liquid, 'I suggest you do what we ask.'

Korder nodded his answer, his eyes showing both fear and anger at the same time. 'Oh, and don't get any clever ideas. If anything happens that I don't like, you'll be dead before you can blink... understand?' This time fear was the only emotion showing in his eyes. 'Ok, let's move.' Janice led them off down a narrow tunnel to their left. They had gone about two hundred metres when Janice called a halt.

'There is a security field just ahead. I could get through with my ID but we can't risk using his yet, so what now?'

Anton reached behind and pulled a small, wafer thin piece of material off his belt. He held it in front of him and focussed his ocular implant on it. The implant sent a low energy light beam to the material and it started to change. Multiple colours ran across its surface and it started to emit a soft hum. 'We're ready now, just walk ahead.' He pushed Korder in front of him. 'Now be a good boy and play nice, I don't want to have to punish you.'

Korder got the message and walked in step with the other two. They passed the security station without incident, walked along the corridor and then finally into a small room. Janice locked the door and the lights in the room came on. The room was sparsely furnished with just two consoles and four chairs. The wall in front was a large view screen, which

Janice activated.

'I'll do a quick scan to see if any of our handiwork has raised any concerns.'

Anton pushed Korder to one of the chairs before he pulled about three metres of cord out of this belt and tied the captive. Janice had finished her scan and was shaking her head. 'What's the problem?' Anton asked.

'That belt... what don't you have in it? Where did you get the idea for it anyhow?'

'I take it you aren't a fan of 20th century superhero vids?' Janice shook her head and he continued. 'I always liked Batman,' Anton explained. 'He always had whatever trick he needed in his utility belt, so I decided to have one made... well actually I have several and they work very well.' He seemed very proud of this piece of kit. 'This one has many tricks and it will pass any security inspection. The guy who makes them for me is an absolute genius. Now Mr Rat Face,' he said, addressing their captive, 'I think we need to have a little talk.'

The talk lasted for nearly an hour. Korder required some encouragement from time to time, but eventually they had the information they required.

'Eugene Sarclan,' Anton mused. 'He was supposed to be dead years ago but now he's running this little operation? So we know they are going to offload all the passengers onto some artificial station, then take this ship elsewhere to transport men and material. Where and when, who knows?' Anton turned to Korder. 'For such a bad arse, you really don't know much, do you?'

'So what do we do with this piece of work now?' Janice glared at Korder. 'He doesn't look well.' She moved closer to Korder, his eyes were glazing over and his breathing was becoming laboured. He was sweating and he had an obvious fever. She gave Anton a questioning look.

'Well, I wasn't totally truthful,' admitted Anton. 'The blocker I gave him is wearing off and the poison is taking over... from here he'll lose all bodily control. It could get very messy, he'll be paralysed and slowly his body will shut down. It may take a while but he'll die, slowly, painfully and silently, an apt end for him.'

Then he walked over to Korder. 'I know what you did to the colonists on Sofria when they rebelled against the government. You liked to skin children alive in front of their parents, even if you knew they had nothing to do with the uprising! You see Korder, we are both professionals, both contractors, but unlike you I have some scruples. I think you're getting off far too lightly for what you've done.'

Anton reached into his belt again and pulled out a small, thin device which he attached to Korder's wrist. 'Don't think that there will be any rescue. Even if your friends do find you, this will finish the job.' Anton smiled and patted Korder on the hand. 'Goodbye, Major.' Then they left and locked the room, leaving Korder to die alone.

They turned left on leaving the room, the disruptor field masking their presence from any of the security scans they passed. They hadn't gone very far when Janice looked at her companion, 'a mercenary with a conscience... now that's a new one.'

'Not really,' Anton replied. 'I don't accept every job I am offered and I try to work with clients whose moral code I can live with. I was very young when the Sofria uprising went down, doing my required term in the Coalition military. Our unit was sent to mop up the mess... that's when we found what that bastard did. I have spent most of my working life hoping to catch up with him... now it's over.'

'Is it?' questioned Janice. He isn't dead yet.'

'No but he soon will be. That device I attached to him monitors his vitals. When they cease, or change too much, it ignites and will vaporise both the body and anyone else in the room, so I don't think he'll be a problem much longer.'

They passed through three more security checks successfully using the ID tags they took from the three guards until they reached the final one where Anton was forced to produce Korder's tag. This immediately allowed them access but flagged a message on the door console. It seemed that someone wanted to know where Korder and his guests were.

Anton knew that not to answer would flag a problem and very soon they would have more guards to contend with, but the wrong answer could have the same, or worse, repercussions. He studied the message, still looking for a clue as to how to answer when Janice pushed in front of him and typed a short answer.

Just showing our guests around, we should be there in about 10 minutes.

'Great, now we only have ten minutes until all hell breaks loose,' Anton growled.

'Ten minutes is more than enough. We need to get to the centre of the ship... from there we can use the central conduit to move to the forward deflector array. There we'll be able to get a signal both in and out, so just follow me.'

Janice moved off to her right and found a small access tube that disappeared into the centre of the ship. 'No security scans here, we should be clear right down to the main conduit.' She carefully locked the sensor switch in the closed position before opening the access door; once inside she closed the door and locked it. 'No way out now. It's all the way or we die in this tube.' And she started to descend the ladder. It took almost half an hour before they reached the access hatch, their muscles aching and tired from the exertion.

'There's no gravity in this conduit... it runs through the exact centreline of the ship, so it should be easy going once we're inside. There are security scanners in here though. What's the range of your little toy?'

Anton checked the battery of his field disruption generator by accessing the data with his implant. 'Power is about fifty percent so if we wish to prolong its usefulness, we need to stay within five metres of each other.'

Janice nodded and opened the junction box on the side of the hatch tube. She located the hatch cover sensor and ran a bypass so the hatch would indicate it was closed then nodded to Anton who turned the locking wheel anticlockwise and the hatch opened. They entered and quickly reclosed the hatch.

Although Anton's training program included weightlessness, it had been a long time since he had experienced it on a job and it took a few seconds for him to accustom himself to the sensation. Janice waited as he acclimatised and finally they moved off. Even though the conduit was large – over twenty metres in diameter – there was not much room and they were forced to proceed in single file. Hand over hand they pulled themselves along a cable tray; cables as thick as Anton's arm carried the energy needed to run the ship's deflector system.

By Anton's reckoning, they had travelled almost two

kilometres before they got a glimpse of their destination – the central forward deflector housing. Thankfully, zero gravity meant that the effort to move was minimal and both were feeling good. They passed another scanner and it suddenly changed colour from green to amber.

'Janice, slow down,' Anton commanded as he consulted the battery condition again. 'We need to close up... battery power is going down faster than I estimated.'

Janice moved back closer to Anton and the scanner indicated green again. Hopefully the change could be put down to a glitch.

They moved more purposefully now, maintaining very close proximity to each other. Ahead was the entry access port to the housing; again Janice opened the junction box and bypassed the security system. They opened the port and slid through, closing it behind them. Inside there was good atmosphere and some gravity – about fifty percent of normal – so maintenance workers could operate more efficiently. It was a welcome relief to Anton.

The array housing contained: the power supply; control system; a small workshop; and a small room where maintenance workers could eat and rest during their shifts. Thankfully there was no need to have a crew here most of the time and Janice scanned the maintenance schedule which revealed that the next scheduled inspection was not due for another sixty hours. Finally it appeared they had some breathing space.

It was Janice's turn to show her ingenuity as she pulled several small objects from her clothing; she assembled these and seemed happy with her handiwork. 'You're not the only one who has a utility belt, she said with a grin. 'Now we have our transceiver.'

She moved towards a console, ducked down below the bench it sat on and pulled open another junction box. She took time examining the various cables before making four new connections to her transceiver. Satisfied, she replaced the cover and stuck the transceiver to the underside of the bench. 'Now let's see if anyone is listening.' She switched the unit on and, using the console, typed a short message and pressed the transmit button. 'Now we wait… any idea how we can pass the time?'

'Just a moment,' Anton called. He was busy with a console on the wall. He pulled yet another small, thin device from his belt and attached it to three of the cables in the back of the console housing. The device was easily secreted inside the console housing; to all intents it appeared that the console had never been tampered with. His fingers flew over the icon pad and finally, he stood back. 'That's better… now this room's security shows everything's normal and we don't need the disrupter field, thankfully. Power is now down to ten percent… I need somewhere to recharge it.' He looked round the room and saw a power outlet on the far wall. He removed the disrupter pack and pulled an energy cord from the rear of it, plugged it into the socket and turned back to Janice smiling. 'Now… you were asking what we can do for a couple of hours.'

***

Sunday passed quickly on Earth.

With a number of different groups desperately trying to bring some sense of order to the last few days, the old Bunker had become a hive of activity. Mondrac, Aaron, Petra and Tocmal worked with a group of Astrogators from the Academy trying to define possible locations for the Twelfth Realm Exodus Gates. Once they had this information, they used the inter realm data from Junior to come up with several plausible alternatives. This took all day and part of the night.

The next task was to correlate this data with the findings from Wilson and another team from the Academy who had been investigating possible locations for stations large enough to take all the passengers and crew from Rhapsody. The hardest part was the use of computing time. No-one could be sure that any official systems were clean, so the Abracorp system was all they could rely on. Though a state of the art unit, it wasn't designed for the huge amount of additional traffic so a system of time sharing was arranged. The next day would be worse, as Monday would see all of the Earth staff back at work – then problems would be compounded.

Mondrac stood and looked at Aaron. 'A-Bra-Ham, this is ridiculous. We need more capacity, and you have it. It may be time to release information to everyone.'

Aaron nodded. He had been thinking the same for the last 3 hours. 'Ok... Petra, prep the yacht... I'll get some of the others.' He switched his link to the ship back on. *George, prepare Condor to receive some guests.*

Yes Sir. I take it you're finally going to use our abilities?

There really was nothing worse than a smart arse computer, but George was right, this time. Aaron didn't answer, just headed up two floors to meet with the others. He spent ten minutes explaining to Wilson and the others before asking them to prepare all their data for transmission. The senior members of the group accompanied him to Junior, the others – necessary to the operation – followed in four shuttles.

Setting everyone up on Condor would take time so, to keep any delay to a minimum, all data so far gained was fed directly into the computer. Now it was time for the reveal.

Aaron stood and asked for everyone's attention. 'As you all know, we have a special working relationship with Eldora. We trade with them and we obtain much technology in return. One thing we do is to ascertain if the technology transfer is beneficial to our species and we trial most of it ourselves. This ship is equipped with a great deal of Eldoran technology, one system being the computer.' He paused, unsure of what to say next.

Mondrac came to the rescue. 'What A-Bra-Ham has here is a fully functional synthetic human brain. It is fully integrated into the ships operating system and computer... it is also fully integrated into A-Bra-Ham's brain. The difference between this computer and a natural human brain is it has full use of all its capacity. More than enough for what we need now. A-Bra-Ham, can you introduce the computer?'

Aaron smiled. 'George,' he spoke aloud, 'please introduce yourself.'

My pleasure, welcome to Condor. George's voice emanated from the comm system. *As you heard, the Captain has given me a name though not what I may have chosen for myself. What Mondrac said is correct... I can access every part of my cerebral cortex to work on a problem. So... how may I help you?*

Aaron answered. 'Thanks George, please start analysing the data we have transmitted.'

There was no indication that anything was happening, no lights flashing and no sound of circuits working, just normal ambient sounds of a space ship in dock.

Aaron noticed the quizzical looks. 'That's one of the strange things I have needed to get used to, there is no indication of what George is actually doing, he just does it. Now, our chief Engineer, Dianna Holland,' he pointed to the woman standing at the rear of the room, 'will show you to your stations. Most of the crew is still on the surface but will be returning very soon so things may get a little crowded.'

Everyone turned to Dianna who started working out where everyone would fit. Normally Condor only had a complement of 150, already there were 100 on board and the crew was still absent.

Petra beckoned Aaron. 'Why don't we put the senior people in the upper observation lounge? It's big enough and it'll give the rest some distance, let them do their work without others staring over their shoulder.'

Aaron agreed and she started moving the senior people. Soon the room was almost back to normal when Dianna returned.

'Skipper, the crew is returning, any instructions?' she asked.

'I think we should prepare for a quick departure,' Aaron replied.

Dianna looked perplexed, 'nothing else?'

'Not now. I have a lot to explain but for now we don't have enough information. One thing though, most of the senior traders will be arriving in the next couple of days and we have a full meeting of the council to attend. Till then, I want the ship ready to leave at a moment's notice.'

'Yes Sir.'

As she left, Mondrac's voice entered Aaron's mind *A-Bra-Ham, can you meet me in your cabin. We have much to discuss.*

I'm on my way,' Aaron replied.

Aaron walked into his cabin. Mondrac, Tocmal and Petra were already there looking very serious.

'What's the problem?' Aaron asked.

'No real problem, just a possibility. I know the computer will give us a few possible scenarios but I already believe we have found a main contender.' Mondrac turned the console toward Aaron. 'Here in Sector 215... something called Cordoba Green... do you know it?'

'Not really, I've never been to it. It's one of the ore processing plants we are looking for. Why is it important?'

Mondrac continued. 'Two reasons: First, it occupies a region of space that intersects with a sub space convergence, where we discussed the possibility of using a pair of your gates to form a stable sub space breach; the second is more complex. We believe they are using Trisidium as a power source for their gates and there is a significant body of ore in the region. We need to have a look at this facility; if it is being used to process the ore, we must assume it is because of the proximity of the convergence. If this is the case, we should find one of the gates very close by. This scenario needs to be confirmed, but we must send a ship to investigate and Condor is the only one that can achieve this.'

Mondrac was referring to the Jump Drive. 'This may be one time when we need to make an assumption. We can take it from your work with the drive that it is not harmful to human physiology. It might be time to start manufacturing it in this realm; you have our permission and any trade details can be sorted on our usual terms.'

The fact that Mondrac said this demonstrated to Aaron

just how serious he believed the situation to be. The entire human race only had two ships *jump* capable, and Aaron Abraham owned both. While he didn't know the detailed workings of the drive, Dianna did. He considered what Mondrac had said, came to a decision and called Dianna to his quarters.

'You may be right, Mondrac.'

'There is one thing more, A-Bra-Ham,' Tocmal spoke for the first time. 'The resin formula, I give you permission to manufacture it here... how do you say it?

Aaron helped him out, 'under licence.'

'Yes, that is acceptable. We can work out the trade arrangements later; for now we feel it is imperative your people have our assistance.'

Aaron nodded. 'Thank you my friends. We will post date any royalties we agree on. I will have my Proctor draw up some documents, to protect both parties.'

Tocmal stood. He appeared hurt. 'You do not trust me?'

Aaron shook his head. 'No, I trust you with my life... it's some humans I don't trust. The documents are how we guarantee trust, mainly for your benefit in this case.'

Tocmal accepted the explanation and resumed his seat as Dianna entered the room. 'You wanted to see me Sir?'

'Yes Dianna, could you build a jump drive?' Aaron asked.

'Yes, I believe I could. Some of the components are different from what we use but they don't present an insurmountable problem. Given the resources, I think we could have one ready in a few months.'

'What would it take to get it done in a week?' Aaron asked.

'Shit! I don't know... a full manufacturing facility, a crew of top flight engineers and no distractions... not to mention a few million credits.'

'Point taken... let me see what I can arrange. For now, assume we can get whatever we need and start collating your requirements.' Aaron looked at the faces in front of him, all showing signs of weariness. 'George, how's your analysis coming?'

Even with the capacity we have it will still take time... several hours I believe.

'Right, everyone here is tired, I think sleep is in order. What time is it anyhow?'

Petra looked at the console, 'twenty one thirty, it's been a very long day.'

'I agree, time to call it a night,' Aaron said. 'I'll talk to the group in the lounge; they really don't need to stay.' He left the room accompanied by Tocmal and Mondrac. Mondrac went to rest in the room across the hall from Aaron's while Tocmal declined, saying he would sleep better in the cabin on the yacht.

The group in the lounge comprised the Admirals, Jeff Abraham, Allen Grainger and Crompton. He explained the situation and suggested everyone needed some sleep. Jeff agreed and offered accommodation in the hotel section of the dock complex. Once this was organised, they all left the ship.

As Aaron returned to his cabin, he heard the sound of the shower; he quickly stripped, dropped his clothes into the sanitiser and opened the shower door. There he found Petra waiting, wet and glistening. He placed his arm round her waist and pulled her to him, her firm buttocks pushing against him.

'Finally alone... I thought we would never get rid of them.' He whispered into her ear as he gently nibbled it.

'Steady my love.' She reached down and took hold of his growing erection. 'We're both tired. First some sleep and then... well, we'll see.' Petra turned and kissed him. Aaron quickly had his shower, dried himself and went to the bedroom. Petra was already in bed and from her steady breathing, knew she was asleep. He smiled, lay down beside her and within minutes fell into a deep sleep himself.

***

The buzzing of a communicator roused Aaron. He looked at the console across the room – 05:01. *Who the fuck is calling at this time?* He thought. 'Abraham,' Aaron said groggily as he answered.

'Crompton here, we just had a comm from Rhapsody. How's the analysis coming?'

'I'll check and call you back.' Then subliminally, *George got an answer yet?'*

I wouldn't call it an answer, more a set of probable solutions. Sometimes Aaron thought the bloody brain was so arrogant.

'Well, would you care to share?'

I have downloaded my analysis into the main system... anyone can access it there, but here is the short version. The most probable place to offload the passengers and crew is Cordoba Blue. From the data I have, the ship should reach it in five hours, probably take the same to offload everyone and then the data suggests that it will head for Cordoba Green in Sector 215 as that appears to be the most logical area for the gate.

Aaron reached for his communicator and Crompton

answered immediately. 'Cordoba Blue in Sector 085 is probably where they will offload everyone.'

'Now we can get our operatives working... how long till it gets to the station?'

'Around five hours.'

'Thanks.' Crompton ended the call, already compiling the message to Barker.

The two hour dwell time until they could receive a message was busy for Janice.

First she hacked into the ship's security system via a back door only known to her and two others who were not aboard. Into this hack she spliced two independent transfer circuits; the first was to their audio communication system and the second linked Anton's ocular implant directly to the ship's video security. With this done they could relax a little, convinced they should get ample warning of any pursuit. They sat at the small table in the maintenance crew room.

'I could do with something to eat,' Anton griped.

Janice walked over to the row of storage cupboards and began to look through them. 'There's plenty in here if you want to get something.'

She returned to the table with a ration box.

Inside was a complete meal designed for the maintenance crews to easily and quickly feed themselves during their shifts in this section of the ship; Anton returned with one and they commenced to eat. The contents were surprisingly tasty and easy to eat and packed with the nutrition and essentials needed for the strength to work deep within the bowels of the vessel.

They had almost finished their meal when Janice's communicator buzzed. 'Finally, a response,' Janice said in a relieved voice as she listened to the message. It was short, with three important statements: first confirming their suspicions; second the estimated point to offload the passengers; and finally their instructions.

'Well, what did they say?' Anton asked, his impatience growing.

'They confirmed what we surmised about the hijack, but it's a lot more, including confirmation that the Sarclan Sedition is back and they are the ones behind the hijacking. It's part of something much larger, no explanation as to their final intentions, but something pretty big. Seems that Damien Albrect is who contracted you and he and Crompton are working together on this. Our instructions are to lay low until the passengers are off the ship, then do whatever we can to disrupt the endeavour, including destroying this ship if necessary.' Janice paused for a moment to allow this to sink in. 'Seems we're collateral damage... there's nothing about how we get away, just do anything and everything to stop this ship.'

'So where are we going, or didn't they know that?' Anton asked.

'Nothing concrete, but the consensus is Cordoba Blue to unload passengers in about three hours. Then on to Cordoba Green where they will load something on board and then somewhere else... don't know what or where after that.'

'Not much to go on, but we really don't need to know everything. Time for a recce I think.' Anton used his implant to access the ship's main computer and do a systematic sweep of all the main systems. He checked all critical engineering areas, command and control centres and life support and was not happy with what he found.

After twenty minutes he spoke. 'Not good. This ship is locked down tighter than the Sultan of Ummah's Harem. The two of us will never get close to any critical system to do any damage worth talking about. There are guards everywhere, seems that passengers are now being ordered to their quarters and locked in.'

'Sounds like things are moving,' Anton said, his voice having an edge of excitement to it. 'We better come up with a way to knobble this vessel, and quick.' He never felt quite alive until the chips were down and life was looking very short.

'I already have,' Janice interjected. 'Right here, the deflector; no ship can travel without deflector screens. If we *knobble*, as you call it, the deflectors, the ship will be torn apart.' Her logic was sound; unfortunately her engineering knowledge of the ship wasn't.

'Slight issue with that,' Anton pointed out. 'This ship runs five forward, four lateral and three rear deflector arrays. To cause any severe damage we need to take out at least three of the forward arrays and, as they are separately operated and have their own control stations, not an easy task so... we need to disable them all at the same time. Now, that may not seem too much to ask but the other control rooms we need to access are a couple of hundred metres in different directions. Also, the power supply for the disruption device we used before won't last long enough to get us anywhere near the first control room, let alone both.' He paused to think. 'But there might be another way,' he said as a solution came to him.

Moving over to the view screen, Anton now faced the emitter array. Basically it was a lattice work of antennae that projected a force field that deflected any solid objects away from the ship. The Acrilan composite cover that made up the outer surface of the ship could withstand considerable impact events but, at the speeds that ships travelled, it wouldn't last more than a few seconds without the deflector. Most star ships had emergency override systems that stopped all motion in the event of any failure of the deflection systems, and Rhapsody was no different. As Anton now kept saying, *knobble the deflector* and the ship would automatically stop, or be destroyed.

He was deep in thought when his implant sent a warning to his brain. 'Looks like we may have some trouble,' he announced. 'The first guard we despatched has just been found and it seems that Major Korder is unable to be contacted... we need to move fast. Did they give any indication of how long before the passengers are to be dropped off?'

Janice checked the message again. 'Not sure... looks like about two or three hours. Why?'

'We don't want to do anything until they are clear and the ship is back to full speed. Maximum disruption to the bad guys' plans will come if they have to drop out of displacement prematurely. Then we need to give them a bit of time for repairs before they can get going again so,' Anton paused again, 'we need a multifaceted failure... one that will cause multiple delays.'

The small convenience room had three view ports and Anton moved between each of them as if looking for something. Finally, he stopped at the one facing the central core. 'Those main conduits, is there a way into them that won't set off any alarms? I don't think using our stolen security keys would be a good idea.'

Again, Janice moved to the console and called up the ship's schematics. It took her almost five minutes before she stood up, triumphantly. 'Yes! There's a small port just above here... no monitoring and it doesn't have a secure entry system. Problem is, we have to access it **through** the antenna array itself. Not something I would normally contemplate given the electromagnetic radiation out there... but it is our only unsecured point of entry.'

She moved back to the view port facing the array and pointed to the small hatch just thirty metres away. 'Normally nobody goes anywhere near the array while it's powered, for safety reasons, but there should be some emergency suits in here that will allow us a few minutes out there.' Janice began rummaging through various cupboards and drawers.

Finally she found what she was looking for. 'Here! Janice said triumphantly, holding up what looked like a head to toe coverall made of a very finely woven metallic mesh. Trailing from the centre of the garment were two cables, each two metres long, ending with a contact clip. The clip was obviously designed to be placed over something else and slid along it. 'We simply put these on and connect the sliders to the grounding bar,' she said, pointing to a metallic bar running from the cubicle to the end of the array structure. 'There are supports every ten metres so we will need to unclip and reconnect the trailing cables one at a time. That will at least give some protection from the array. But remember, this is designed for emergency use only and, as far as I know, not when the array is at full power, so we need to be very quick.'

Anton reached out to take the mesh garment she offered to him. 'Ok, I agree,' he replied, 'it's the only option we've got. I suggest we use the bathroom before we leave, don't know when we will have the chance again.'

Janice nodded and moved off towards the small bathroom at the rear of the room. While she was there Anton consulted the schematics again and found what he was after, a smile crossing his lips as he closed the console.

After taking care of bodily needs, they donned their mesh suits. They both now looked like some of the more radical inhabitants of Ummah; nothing was visible, even the eye slits were covered with a fine mesh. Janice went to the door. She paused momentarily as if undecided on the course they planned. Then just as quickly she purposefully operated the mechanism that unsealed it before they stepped into the array. Even with the protective suits, the power of the deflection field could be felt – almost like a physical blow – as they exited the room. Thankfully, it was focussed forward or else their flimsy mesh cages wouldn't survive more than a few seconds.

Moving became a little easier when the trailing cables were attached to the ground rail, effectively shunting the residual field through the suits. While the mesh coverall was designed to fully cover anyone inside and protect them from the magnetic field it still hampered their efforts. Designed to be in constant contact with a ground plane, the suit had more than a metre of mesh constantly on the floor and, coupled with the twin trailing cables, made walking slow and difficult.

A full seven minutes later they reached the hatch. Carefully, Anton reached his encased arm into the hatch release and, with some difficulty, operated the release mechanism. The hatch lifted easily and Janice entered the small space; Anton followed but it was a difficult fit. When they were inside, he quickly closed the hatch before they could remove the coveralls. He ran through a test of his implant and was satisfied that it was undamaged.

'Are we likely to need these again?' He asked as he held up the coverall.

'Not unless you want to do a return trip.'

'Not likely, but I think we should bring them, you never know.' They folded their suits and placed them into the tool packs they had taken from the control room.

'Ok, we are here… now what do you have in mind?' Janice asked.

Anton thought for a moment then began. 'We have about two hours to reach Blue, three, maybe four hours to disembark, another hour to get back to full speed, then, at a rough guess, about twenty to Green. So, we have thirty hours to cause as much mayhem as we can!

'I was thinking of several separate failures, timed to happen in sequence so that we totally disrupt their time frame. I had a look at the schematic you had on the console; about two hundred metres down this conduit we will come to a branch point. That's the main weak point in the system and the last possible failure point.' He held his hand up as Janice opened her mouth to object.

'The right branch will take us to the forward array power node; that will be our first target… we need to find a way of making it fail in around ten hours. If we can set it up correctly, it should cause at least two to three hours delay for repairs, then we do something similar to the lateral arrays about five hours later, another three hours for repairs and the grand finale… sabotage the inertial stabilizers! The best we could do is to delay them for about ten hours… I hope it's enough.'

Janice considered his ideas before answering. 'Let me get this straight... we sabotage the forward deflector array... the main defence against the ship being torn apart... somehow... then we do something similar to the lateral array. Finally, we damage the inertial stabilisers... just one question... how do we do all this?'

'I didn't say I had all the answers; just call it a work in progress,' Anton replied, 'unless you have a better idea?'

Janice shook her head and started toward the branch point, two hundred metres away. 'We had better get going on this work in progress of yours.'

Anton smiled and gave a satisfied chuckle as he followed her lead.

They reached the conduit branch and turned right toward the forward deflector array power node, Anton still mentally working on his plan at the same time. It had taken longer than he estimated to reach this point and, if his end game was to work, they would need to move faster.

The problem they faced was the number of security scanners they encountered, which forced them to use the cloaking device, further depleting its battery. If the unit failed, they wouldn't be able to carry out his final piece of sabotage. Glancing down, Anton saw the power reading in his implant, twenty two percent – not enough. *Looks like the work in progress just hit the wall*, he thought to himself grimly.

They entered the power node and scanned for any security devices; thankfully there were none so he turned the cloak off. The power node was the main distribution point for the forward deflector array supplying the energy needed to keep the ship safe. They stood at the entrance and studied the layout. Filled with conduits, cables and bus bars, the room connected the various power systems to the array itself. Unfortunately, there seemed to be no accessible weak point.

Slowly and cautiously, they moved through the various marked walkways, constantly searching for any exploitable weakness. Suddenly they felt spatial compression, followed by a sense of vertigo.

'Shit! We're dropping out of displacement,' said Anton alarmed. We need to hurry! I don't think we can be subtle now. The only sure way to disrupt the array is to remove power to the main and secondary bus system.' He knew how dangerous it was to go anywhere near the high voltage bus systems that fed the array, but they didn't have any other option.

They back tracked and moved down another corridor that led to the two bus systems. These systems were large copper bars suspended and separated by a special support and insulation structure, made of a composite insulation material. What they needed was some way of bridging both groups of three bars.

Janice tapped Anton on the shoulder. 'What about the coveralls we used to move through the array? If we could rig them to drop across the bars, would that do what we need?'

Anton pulled his coveralls out and began examining their structure. Made of a copper and carbon impregnated composite fibre, the fine weave was the secret to protecting them from the electromagnetic radiation in the array chamber. If the composite was strong enough and held the other materials in its matrix, it may be able to last long enough to cause some serious damage. At worst, it would trip some breakers and cause the ship to drop out of displacement. At this stage, any delay was worth the risk. In any case, the energy taken to vaporise the fabric would cause some serious concerns on the bridge.

They studied the layout. A small overhead service trolley ran the length of the chamber; if they could position this directly over the bus way they might have a chance. They set about the task, constantly watching for any unwelcome intruders. The trolley proved to be easy to move now that the ship was stationary, but they would need to secure it above the target and reprogram its cradle so the system would record it as secure for displacement.

Working as fast as they could, it still took almost three hours to rig their trap – Anton's utility belt proving its worth again. He removed two of the four remaining studs and attached them to the cords supporting the coveralls; each stud held a small but extremely powerful explosive charge, enough to sever the cords and the support they were attached to.

Janice shook her head again. 'I'll bet you're great fun at parties... what else does that belt hide?'

'Not much now. We've used most of my party tricks, just a few more explosive studs and some other, less lethal things.' He replied sadly, 'First time I have ever used so much hardware... think I need a new design.' They walked back to the entrance. 'Can you get another message through from here?'

Janice opened her communicator and touched the screen. 'I think so.'

'Good, I've set the timer for four hours, can't make it

any longer. Tell them we have done all we can and we are leaving the ship.'

Janice looked puzzled; their orders were to stay with the ship.

'There's nothing else we can do. With all the passengers and unnecessary crew offloaded, I guarantee they will shut down most of the ship, no life support, gravity or anything else not needed. We wouldn't last ten minutes so we leave and see what else we can do.' His logic was sound; Janice agreed, coded and sent the message.

'Now, how do we get off?' She asked.

'Simple, Commander Barker. You found a stray passenger in an off limits area and are escorting him off the ship!' Anton beamed.

'And if they get suspicious?'

'They won't,' Anton said dismissively. 'Has there been any mention of us or our friend, Korder?'

Janice consulted the ships comm system, shaking her head as it showed nothing.

'I thought not, they are on a tight schedule, we won't be an issue because we are getting off. One problem though... you are somewhat out of uniform.'

'And very pissed that my dinner with the handsome Major Korder was interrupted because of one very naughty absent minded scientist who wandered into the wrong area and we were forced to leave our evening to find him.' She smiled, now getting into the act. 'Ok that's settled. Now, how do we get back?'

'I think I have a way... the service elevator. We ride it up from the maintenance tube, stopping at a number of levels as though searching, finally arriving at the main dock area.' Anton consulted the power level left in the cloak. 'Not much charge left, probably no more than ten minutes.'

Janice looked toward the elevator. 'About three minutes to the elevator, two more waiting if it is not there, two more to level eight, we get out and straight back in, one more minute, then one minute to level ten; there is a blind spot in the security grid on ten, just ten metres from the elevator. We get there, turn the cloak off and I start admonishing you and ordering you to disembark… not much room to move but it could work.'

'Good,' Anton replied as he headed out the door.

They made the elevator quicker than expected but it was on another level and took what seemed forever to reach them. At level eight they opened the doors, but didn't exit; the doors closed and they went to ten. Here they exited the elevator, turned right and walked swiftly toward the blind spot Janice mentioned. They followed the corridor as it curved around the hull and there in front of them were two guards lounging against the wall. Anton's implant showed a flashing red light, the battery was dying and they only had seconds of power left. 'We've got no power,' he said. 'We have to take these two out!'

As he got the words out the battery failed and they started to lose the cloak. It didn't fail immediately; there were a couple of seconds where they would have seemed to solidify. To the guards they looked like an apparition taking solid form, just what was needed.

The conflict was quick and deadly. Janice leapt toward the guard closest to her, her feet and hands slashing at her target. Before the guard could utter a sound she was dead. Anton neutralised the other one with his knife, silently slicing through the base of his palate, through the soft tissue of his oesophagus and finally severing his brain stem; silent and effective with very little blood loss.

'Nicely done, Doctor,' Janice admired his effectiveness. 'But what are they doing here? This section should be empty.'

'Don't know, don't care. We need to get rid of the bodies and get moving.' Anton paused, studying the two bodies. 'Is she about your size?'

'I think so, why?'

Anton had opened a door to his right which led into one of the cheaper cabins. 'In here,' he called and began to drag his victim inside. Janice followed and closed the door behind her. He began stripping the guard; Janice got his idea and did the same. Anton quickly removed his own clothes and redressed in the guard's uniform. Janice was a bit slower and it gave Anton plenty of time to gaze appreciatively at her lithe form.

'Having fun?' she said as she saw where his eyes lingered.

'Most definitely, you really are a surprise package.'

Janice was facing him buttoning up the guard's shirt and covering her firm but ample breasts. 'Sorry, we don't have time for the full show; we have a more pressing problem, now what about these two?'

'Remove all her clothes,' he bent to the male body and started removing the last of his clothes. 'These two were in here for a bit of fun, and it all went wrong. They fought and both died.' He stood back looking at the two, now naked bodies on the floor. To a casual observer it could look like a lovers-fight gone wrong. Anton shook his head. 'It's weak, but it's all we've got.'

Janice moved to the female, placing Anton's knife in her right hand and stood back. 'There, that looks a bit better. Now, let's get out of here!' She went to the door and activated the view port. 'All clear, come on.'

Anton took his second last explosive device and placed it against the external porthole, setting it for four hours as well. They had just left the room when a security captain appeared from the direction of the elevator.

'You two, did anyone come this way from the elevator?' He barked.

Janice stood at attention and answered. 'No Sir, we've seen no one till you arrived.'

'So this level is clear?'

'Yes Sir. We have completed our sweep, no one's left here, and all doors are locked.'

'Good. Ok, now get to the main exit on level fifteen, time for you to leave as well.' He turned and continued down the corridor.

Janice and Anton saluted the officer and went back to the elevator, entered and selected level fifteen. When the doors opened the scene that greeted them was one of organised precision. Most of the passengers were already off the ship, now only personnel essential to its operation would be kept aboard. Merging with a group of security officers they quietly walked down the gangway to the airlock. Before exiting the Rhapsody's airlock Anton placed his last little stud just inside the seal. Though uncertain what damage it would do, he decided to use it anyhow. Something was better than nothing.

Twenty minutes later, they watched as the huge liner eased away from Cordoba Blue and quickly moved to the outer marker. Once there, it engaged the displacement drive and vanished. Anton consulted his watch. 'Fifty two minutes and things will start to get interesting on that ship.' He smiled. 'Now we need to find some less conspicuous clothes and see what mischief we can create here.'

Back on Earth, Crompton and Mondrac continued to interrogate the captured Raiders.

A brief encounter with Mondrac's telepathic persuasion was all they needed to convince them to talk – after that, information was freely given. Neither knew very much; they had been sent to a set of coordinates to test a new weapon. They were given the order to fire, and did so knowing nothing of the terrible consequences of their actions. As soon as they launched the Hyper Torpedo – as their commander called the device – they had initiated a displacement insertion and were long gone before the missile detonated.

Later, they met up with a larger ship, one they didn't recognise. All they could say was it was huge and the design nothing they had ever seen before. At the rendezvous location, these two had become suspicious and had secreted themselves in the small emergency area where they were found. What happened after that they had no idea, believing that they were subjected to some sort of sedative; the next thing they remembered was waking up on Earth.

Crompton closed the door on the interrogation room, 'Mondrac, your thoughts?'

'Crom-Ton, I believe them, there is no indication that they

are concealing anything. I think they are as mystified as we are about what happened. They mentioned *Mechanista*… to what are they referring?'

Crompton smiled. 'Many centuries ago, our culture began playing with something they called virtual reality, a computer generated world. Some even started to travel this way, not in person, but in their virtual world. It spawned a whole new industry – gaming. Everything from simple card games to full war scenarios became commonplace, becoming even a form of sport. Some ended up trapped in this world… unable to face the real universe… they chose to stay in their programed reality.' He paused, noting a look of disbelief on Mondrac's face.

'You are saying that some Humans traded the real world for an artificial construct?' Mondrac asked.

'I can see how that must seem strange to you, but it was their choice. When we started to de-populate Earth, this group wanted to continue existing in their virtual universe. They chose a planet and set up a colony, deep underground where they continued to develop their particular technology. Their world and lives were served by this technology and the machines they devised… their reliance on their machine world is symbiotic. The Mechanista cannot live without their machines and the machines have no existence without Mechanista.

While most Human colonies use some automation and technology, we have deliberately limited its use. Centuries ago we saw the results of becoming too reliant on it and the social problems it caused, that's when we decided to severely limit the use of robots or androids. The Mechanista are the opposite, but that's our clue.' He stopped talking, his eyes sparkled and he suddenly became very animated as the inspiration hit him.

'Of course,' he continued, 'that's why they're involved! Trisidium! I'll bet the Mechanista have developed machines that can function in Trisidic radiation. Come on, let's ask them.' Crompton opened the door and he and Mondrac started questioning the captives again.

***

It was 07:30 and already many Abracorp staff members were arriving. The added burden of security checks slowed operations down markedly. The day before had demonstrated the seriousness of the current situation. Most staff arrived at varying times – depending on their duties – but yesterday the security checks had meant that it was almost midday before the company really began to function. Today however, was different; starting times had been staggered even further and the checking process streamlined, but it still caused delays and frayed tempers.

President Malik stood looking out of the window wondering what the day would bring, as if the huge black clouds were a portent of things to come. *At least the interior of Australia will be appreciative,* he thought, *even if perhaps city dwellers are less enthusiastic.* To rural residents, rain meant life but to city cousins, it could be an inconvenience. Malik moved away from the window, his mind still wrestling with the conversation he had with General Al'Hadi late last night.

Two weeks ago, the rebellion on Ummah had begun with fundamentalist rebels swamping the capital and taking the government captive. General Al'Hadi, on orders from the then President, had not intervened. But in the days following, he had witnessed so many atrocities by the rebels that he had no option but to institute martial law. The hard core of the rebel group had managed to seize the Coalition battleship Coultrane and had left the planet. With a form of peace now in force, Al'Hadi had called Malik to discuss the situation.

All parties on Ummah believed there was only one person who could rescue their usually harmonious society from the mire of religious violence that now plagued it. That person was Salim Malik. For several hours last night, the General and many of the Imams had discussed the situation with Malik, some begging him to return to unite the people again. The weight of responsibility was firmly planted on Malik's shoulders as he watched the procession moving through the security check point.

Malik's wife saw the pain in her husband's face. 'Salim, what troubles you so?'

'Oh, my dear... look what we have brought to this beautiful place. Armed soldiers, fighters constantly overhead and this... ' He gestured to the security gate, '... this imposition on the lives of all these people.' He shook his head as he watched the scene below. 'It is raining but still they are forced to go through this imposition and for what... our safety? It is too high a price.'

Hiba smiled. She knew how Salim's mind worked. While he was angry at what he saw, that wasn't the real reason. 'I think you have more pressing problems than that,' she said gently. 'The Abrahams have willingly allowed us to use their facilities. I heard no one complaining about that yesterday, except you. So what is really bothering you?'

The rain had eased to a very fine drizzle. Salim Malik – President of the Coalition of Earth Planets – turned to his wife. 'No matter how important I think I am, you always seem to know me better than I know myself. I spent most of the night talking to General Al'Hadi and the head of the Imam Council. They want me to return to Ummah and form a new government... it appears that I am the only person they all agree on.'

'But your Presidency still has twenty six years to run. Can you do both?'

'No, the constitution is clear... a President cannot hold any other office. To return home, I must resign. But to leave now would destabilise the Coalition, and probably terminally. Whoever is behind all this is masterful... they knew I would want to help our people. No, this adversary is far too clever, they have far too much information about us and we have almost nothing about them. But there *is* something else I can do. I'll talk with Graham Argort about it.' Salim moved away from the window. 'But for now, it is time we joined the others for breakfast.'

***

By the time breakfast was over, the stream of employees had diminished and Jeff had a relieved smile on his face. While he was the main protagonist for the enhanced security, he regretted exposing his employees to the ignominy of distrust.

The sound of a shuttle overhead interrupted his thoughts. He glanced at his watch, 08:20, time to get back to business. He was hoping that he could return to Abracorp and away from the politics that had hijacked both his time and now, his home. Jeff stood and excused himself from the table, noting that his father and Malik were deep in conversation by the coffee pot. As he approached them, he heard the tail of what his father was saying.

'A good idea, Argort's the only person to talk to.' He

stopped just as Jeff moved closer.

'Excuse me Mr President, I was hoping I could have a few moments with my father, we have some business to discuss,' Jeff asked.

'Jeffery please... as long as I am in your house I would prefer to be a friend, rather than the President. Please call me Salim, and yes, you can most definitely have some time with your father.' Malik smiled as he returned to the table.

'I thought I heard Graham Argort mentioned?' Jeff said as he poured himself a coffee.

'Yes, Salim has an issue of constitutional procedure he's unsure of and Argort's the best man to ask for advice,' Jason replied.

'You spent twenty years on the council and probably know the constitution as well as anyone, how come you need Argort?'

'I am not going to advise the President on any constitutional issues, I'll leave that can of worms to the experts,' Jason chuckled in reply.

For the next ten minutes, father and son discussed business issues and the new Manta program. As they finished, Jeff noticed the room was nearly empty. Malik and Madam Collard had gone to the meeting room on level 5 of the bunker, with Aaron and Grainger being pressed into joining them, leaving just Petra and the wives at the table. Jeff and Jason quietly slipped out of the dining room door and went their separate ways. Jeff was about to enter the pod when he heard Petra call for him to wait.

'Can I hitch a ride to the dock, there's a few things I need to do on Condor?'

Jeff smiled. 'Of course, but be warned... I may be a little

late tonight.'

'Suits me,' Petra replied as they entered the pod, 'with all that's happened in the past week or so, I could do with a day of ship life.'

Jason took the elevator down to his office, thinking about what Malik had discussed with him and, while he was certain that Argort was the ultimate authority on all constitutional issues, he was confident he already knew the answer. He left the elevator and walked the short distance to his office, happy to be back working again.

Aaron and Grainger had stopped on the fourth level of the bunker; this level was vacant and made for a good location for their discussion.

'Why do I have to be involved, I'm not a fucking politician?' Aaron's voice filled with frustration.

'Aaron, we're all involved… you of all people should see that. You're the only one of us to have actually gone through and experienced the sub space barrier and you're the only one to have actually seen and fought the enemy. So, you're the only human who has any real idea of what we face. You know the stakes, so tell me why you shouldn't be involved?' Allen Grainger asked.

Aaron paced, trying to find a hole in Grainger's argument, knowing all the time there was none. Finally he stopped, with his shoulders drooped for a moment before he straightened up and turned back to the leader of all Freebooters. 'You're right… but I still don't like it.'

'Neither do I,' Grainger replied, 'and from what I hear none of the council like it either but there is one simple fact we need to face: we are all dependant on one another. If the rebellion succeeds, our way of life will be drastically altered, possibly irrevocably. If that's not worth fighting for, I don't know what is.' He paused, giving Aaron time to digest what he just said. 'Now, I think we should get to this meeting.' Turning, he led the way back to the elevator.

Aaron and Grainger were the last ones to enter the meeting room. Mondrac had returned from interrogating the Raider captives with Crompton and Tocmal; Madam Collard had left to address the Coalition Council, leaving Malik and Admiral Grogan filling the other two spots at the table.

'Now these two have arrived, I can start my briefing,' Crompton began. 'First, we have had fruitful discussions with the two captives who have confirmed much of what we have already learned. Sarclan is indeed alive and orchestrating this uprising with his goal: the total destabilisation of the Coalition. How he intends to use the Galdorans and others, however, is still unclear. But Sarclan never does anything without a back-up, so I believe he will use all the help he can get. But his end game has always been Sarclan first, last and always.' He stopped and took a sip from the glass of water in front of him.

'Now for some good news,' he continued. 'Our operators on Rhapsody are taking steps to delay that ship. With any luck it will need to return to Cordoba Blue for repairs. What we need to do now is to get some firepower to the station and finish the job.'

'How much time do we have?' Sam Grogan asked.

'From our discussions with them – and remember they have been very cryptic – about ten hours.' Crompton smiled, believing he had just given them a minor miracle.

'Ten hours, is that all? We don't have anything close

enough to reach the station in anything less than twenty!'
Grogan shook his head. 'Nothing... do you get that?

'Yes we do!" said Aaron. 'Condor can be there in plenty
of time, although what good my one trader will be, I don't
know.'

'Bullshit, no ship can travel from Earth to Cordoba Blue
in less than eighteen hours. It's not possible!' Grogan
interjected.

Grainger spoke. 'Believe me, Condor can do it. But I
agree with Captain Abraham, what good is one trader? Yes,
Condor is very well weaponised but she is still only one
ship. Rhapsody is many times larger, plus we don't know
the defences that Blue has.'

Grogan stood and took the floor. 'Rhapsody has minimal
weaponry, one of the reasons we were so concerned with
the design. As for Blue, it has some disruptor and blaster
banks. We should also assume these have been reinforced
with torpedo bays and possibly some drones. What if we
could fit some fighters, or better still, the Manta and drones
in Condor's holds? That may even the fight a bit.'

Aaron called a halt to the discussion. 'Look, we can talk
about this for hours and get nowhere. I think the only way
is to get to the ship and work with my people to see what
will fit.' His point made, Aaron stood. 'I'll head back to the
dock and start things rolling. Admiral, if you could have
your people meet me there it'll make things go smoother.'
Grogan agreed and Aaron left for the elevator, glad to be
free of the meeting.

As he entered the pod he contacted the ship via his
subliminal link. *George, what's the status of the crew?*

George answered instantly. *As we speak, the First Officer*

is recalling all those still away. Shuttles will be sent to collect them.

Excellent, Aaron replied. *Have all senior officers meet me in the ward room, I should be there in about fifteen minutes and there will be a few Coalition officers joining us.*

Aaron exited the pod and saw Junior, still in the hangar. He ran up the access ramp and into the bridge. The start-up and initialisation took longer than he remembered, *maybe I'm getting a bit rusty,* he thought as the main reactor came online. While everything was settling down, he called the controller and requested permission to leave. Aaron had forgotten about the military red tape now affecting all vessel movements in and out of the compound. Fifteen minutes later, final clearance was granted and Junior soared free from the shackles of Earth.

Aaron parked Junior in a vacant dock opposite Condor; he had a feeling space would be at a premium this trip. As he entered the airlock he saw Petra waiting.

She smiled and greeted him. 'Welcome back, Captain. Everyone is assembled in the ward room... the Coalition crew is also here.' She stood aside to allow him to take the lead.

The ward room was full, all Condor senior officers and a number of Coalition people were already there. JT and Sol were at the front of the group as Aaron and Petra entered.

'Ok, if you can find a seat, I'll try and be brief.' Aaron began. 'This ship is equipped with a new drive technology which will allow us to intercept Rhapsody at Cordoba Blue. The issue we have is being only one ship, and a trade ship to boot. Our firepower is limited, so we need to work out how we can improve the odds. One way is to take a number of fighters, but I would prefer to take Valiant if she will fit. Dianna,' he said, turning to his chief Engineer, 'can you work with JT's engineers and see if we can fit Valiant in the main hold? Also, let's see how many drones or fighters we can fit in the auxiliary holds and shuttle bays.'

'On it Sir,' Dianna replied.

'Now, before we go any further,' Aaron called for everyone's attention, 'please listen up. Prime Grainger and the majority of the Council of Seniors' have agreed to join the Coalition in this fight. We are now on a war footing and all trade will cease, so the possibility for profit is off the board. As we are a free society, I can make no commitment for you. Any Freebooter who feels they are unable to continue with us, speak now. There will be no adverse action against you and you will be looked after here until we return but, understand this, we may well be in the fight for the survival of our species and I give no guarantees as to our chances. Please decide quickly as we need to get moving.'

JT moved to Aaron's side. 'What are you doing?' he asked quietly.

'JT, we aren't like the Corps,' Aaron whispered back. 'Every person on this ship is contracted to me... to the company. We have no right to demand they risk their lives... each must make their own decision.'

'But we're wasting time, we need to get moving!'

'Listen, nephew,' Aaron replied sternly, 'Freebooters will decide what they'll do and when they'll do it... no one will simply order them. Do you understand?'

JT nodded his understanding and reluctantly, stepped back.

Dianna Holland spoke up. 'Sir, do we understand that this

is war? And if so, are the normal terms for warfare invoked?'

'Dianna, as far as I am concerned that is the case but I will discuss it with Prime Grainger.'

'Then Sir, I can speak for the engineering staff... we're in,' she replied. Within a few minutes, all Condor crew members had agreed to the venture.

'Ok everyone, thank you; I sincerely appreciate your decision. Now, we need to be away in five hours tops.' Aaron summoned his navigator. 'Simon, meet me in the ready room in five.' Simon acknowledged the request and left the room. Simon was sitting in one of the lounges when Aaron and the others arrived. With him were Petra, Katie Albrect and Dave Cross.

'Right now we have our work cut out for us. Simon, I need you to calculate the jumps to get us from here to... ' Aaron paused and brought up the display of Cordoba Blue, 'here. I would prefer if we could arrive in some manner that concealed our arrival from the station.'

'I can do it but I'll need all the correct mass figures,' Simon replied.

'In that case, work with Dianna. Once the engineers figure out what will fit, we'll have the numbers you need. Dave, as we are heading up this little expedition, I want you to take the lead on all tactical issues. Now, before you say anything, I'll have a word to JT. We need one tactical commander if we are to succeed.'

'You're the boss!' Dave answered.

'No Dave, in this case you are actually the boss, I'll merely be another pilot. Now Kate, how are our supplies?'

Kate looked up from her data pad; she had been expecting the question. 'I'll have a list of resupply items needed over to the stores in about ten. Oh, nearly forgot, the Proctor is in your observation lounge.'

'Henry's here?'

'Yes Sir, he arrived only minutes before you.'

'Fine, you all have your assignments. Number One, you're with me.' Aaron rose and everyone filed out, headed to their tasks.

Aaron and Petra took the pod to the private deck, stopping outside his quarters. 'How do you feel about moving your things in here?'

'Only my things or do I come with them?' Petra teased, lightening the mood.

Aaron laughed. 'You should come too... I don't think much of your stuff would fit me.' He moved past the door and into the forward observation lounge.

'Henry, what's brought you here?' Aaron said as he entered the room.

'Oh, I don't know. A message that you had taken off in the Yacht and didn't return... some thought you were lost. I decided to come and see if I could find you, seems you were just off on a bit of a jaunt... I should've known,' Henry chided. 'By the way, I have the contract for Harper if you're interested.'

'Shit, I forgot! Petra, can you find Harper and bring him up here?' Aaron asked, Petra left to collect the cadet. 'Henry, how much have you been told?'

'Not much, except that you nearly got yourself killed.'

'Yeah, I suppose I deserved that. Look, things are crazy now so here's what we need to do. Grainger has invoked the war provisions, the entire council is coming here but I won't be available. I won't explain... it'd take too fucking long. I want you to take my place on the council. Just draw up any documents you need.'

'There's nothing to draw up, just a company minute giving me your proxy, but what is this all about?' For the first time since Henry had met Aaron, he thought he detected fear in his friend's voice.

'There's too much to explain, I'll have Grainger brief you, he should have more time.' The doors opened and Petra ushered cadet Harper into the room. 'Mr Harper, you know our Proctor?' Aaron asked.

'Yes Sir, how are you Mr N'Gabo?' Harper stammered.

'I'm fine, Mr Harper. Aaron tells me you are doing great things on this ship.'

'Thank you.'

'That's what we want to discuss. The company wants to work with you to develop your ideas... we'd like to negotiate a rights agreement for the sensor program.' Aaron looked at Harper. 'What I mean is, we want to market it for you and we have an offer, if you're interested?'

Evidently Harper had been expecting this – he had discussed the possibility with Professor Fraslok and had a proposition in mind. Negotiations of this nature usually took many days but the offer Aaron made was generous – even if it did mean that he would be one of the main contributors to Fraslok's future research.

An agreement was reached and Harper authorised the deal, which stipulated that a separate company be formed to handle this and any future advances made by Fraslok and Harper. Henry could action the necessary documentation from Earth so things were finalised on the spot. The first distribution of the program was to be on Valiant; Junior had already been upgraded as part of Condor. Henry would action the various documents and transfer funds as required when he reached the surface.

Petra escorted Harper back to the pod and back to duty. Henry watched him leave. 'That's one smart kid. He had it all worked out… whatever you do, don't lose him.'

'I don't intend to. Now, what to do with you, did Jacinta come with you?'

'No, it's just me.'

'Ok, I'll call Jeff. I'm sure he'd be happy for you to stay at the station, especially as we now have a few things that we can trade with Abracorp and Greenbach.' Aaron reached for his communicator, called his brother and arranged to take Henry to his office. They left the ship and took a ground car to the administration centre. Jeff had arranged for an office for Henry by the time they arrived.

'So where are you off to?' Jeff asked.

'Cordoba Blue, if we can fit Valiant in our hold. After that, I have no idea but I do know that things will never be the same after this,' Aaron replied.

'Look, I know this isn't the right time but I have to say this. I was wrong, all those years ago… so very wrong and I apologise,' Jeff said with conviction.

'Thank you, but as I remember it there were two hot heads there at the time, and I should have behaved better, so I owe you an apology for that. But let's leave it there… when all this shit is over, we'll sit down and sort it out, Ok?'

Jeff looked at his brother. 'Deal, just don't do anything stupid.'

Aaron smiled and nodded. 'I better get back. I think I'm still the Captain.' Aaron left the office, feeling better than he had for years. Finally the brothers were starting to sort out the feud that had almost destroyed the family.

He left his ground car at the charge station and went back aboard Condor. Tocmal, Mondrac and Grogan were there and the look on their faces told Aaron something was up, something he wasn't going to like.

'Morning,' Aaron said as he walked up to them.

'Yes, good morning. How's the conversion coming?' Grogan asked.

'Don't know as yet. Come with me, we'll see where they're up to.'

Aaron led the trio towards the main hold area, all the while waiting for them to reveal why they were really here. The airlocks to the main hold were open and, as they entered, they ran into a heated debate between Dianna, Amy Rodregas and JT.

'Look, I'm not going to make that call, only the Captain can,' Dianna said as Aaron walked to her side.

'What call can only the Captain make?'

'Sir, we can fit the Valiant in here, no problem. But Captain Abraham and Dave want to take forty drone Darts. The only way we can fit them in is if we use the auxiliary hold for their control systems. The drones themselves will need to go into Junior's hangar and the shuttle bay but, to fit twenty into the shuttle bay, we need to leave most of our shuttles here.'

'So, we won't have enough shuttles in the event we need to evacuate the ship... is that what you're saying?' Aaron asked.

Dianna breathed a sigh of relief. 'Exactly, we would only have five of the larger shuttles, not enough to get everyone off the ship.'

Aaron caught sight of Dave Cross and called him over. 'Dave, regale me with the reason as to why we need to leave most of our shuttles behind.'

Before he could answer, Sam Grogan spoke. 'My idea, Captain... these drones are quite special and you'll need all the firepower you can get. I know your shuttles are well armed but they are only shuttles. Forty remotes will give you much more firepower plus, we know that Sarclan has more KL10N cruisers. It appears that some on the Krell Council made a few backroom deals and they disposed of the ships, complete. So we believe he has at least another six, possibly more. If our scenario is correct and the ship returns to Blue, you can bet Sarclan will call for back up and we don't know where these are... they could turn up at any time... but what if they're cloaked?'

Aaron interrupted. 'We can see them even if they're cloaked. I'll install the sensor program on Valiant so they can as well... but what about support from the Coalition?'

Grogan shook his head, 'Nothing for a while I'm afraid. That's why I came here to brief you.' Sensing that the information would be confidential, Aaron decided not to push further.

'Ok Dianna, as much as I don't like the solution, it is the best option we have... leave the shuttles.'

'And the Yacht?' she queried.

'Yes, that too,' Aaron turned back to Grogan. 'Follow me,' he said as he led the way out of the hold. As they walked, Petra joined them. Once they reached the ready room

Aaron asked Grogan, 'So we won't have support from any Coalition ships? Just what is going on Sam?'

Sam Grogan slumped into a chair 'We really don't know. Somehow the Fleet has been dispersed, sent to places that have no relevance. The orders for this seem to have originated from either Morris or Wilson, but that's not all. They've gone missing.'

'Who?'

'Morris and Wilson... they seem to have vanished, and one of our latest ships, the Otamah, is also missing.'

'Great, not only are we facing who knows what at Blue, we could also be facing one, or more Coalition ships... seems like Space Corps is falling apart,' Aaron added. 'What about Dokad? I haven't seen him around.'

'He went back to Gaddok Prime, summoned by the High Council... haven't heard from him since.'

'What a fucking mess,' Aaron exclaimed, 'what else can go wrong?'

Mondrac spoke. 'A-Bra-Ham there is more. Grogan has located only sixteen of the twenty gates known to still exist. I fear that we may have another three in the tenth realm. We need to go back there to start searching for them and, we need Man-Nix to pilot Junior.'

That stopped Aaron mid stride. 'What! You expect me to take this ship into an almost one sided battle without my first officer?'

Petra stood. 'Gentlemen, can you excuse us for a couple of minutes?' Her tone told everyone not to argue; they filed out leaving Aaron and Petra alone.

As the door closed she spoke again. 'Aaron, you know I

have to do this... I'm the only one who can. Neither Tocmal nor Mondrac know Junior like I do. You need to be here; I need to go back. Maybe between us we can stop this invasion... we have to, and you know that.'

'Doesn't mean I like it. I'd rather we fought together.'

'We will, just not in the same dimension,' she smiled.

Aaron nodded, knowing it was the only alternative they had. 'Ok, you have permission to take the Yacht, but bring it back in one piece, and yourself too.'

Petra shook her head as she threw her arms around him. 'I fully intend to and remember, I still haven't had my wicked way with you yet.' They melted into each other and their lips locked in a desperate kiss. They finally broke apart and Aaron opened the door to ask the others back.

'Petra has agreed to this plan and reluctantly, so have I,' he announced. 'Now, is there anything else we need to know before we get going?'

Sam Grogan nodded, 'Yes. I think you should check this out before going to Blue.' Moving to Aaron's desk, he inserted a data drive into the console. 'We believe this is where they are processing the Trisidium... we also believe this is the first mission for Rhapsody... to pick up the Trisidium and take it to the tenth realm.'

'But that'd make Rhapsody unusable... seems a waste of a ship,' Aaron interjected.

'Normally I'd agree, but it seems that the Mechanista have developed an effective containment system so transporting the enriched ore is safe. Also, if they have done this, then it could be a viable power source for the gates.'

Again Aaron interrupted. 'Why bother? MAM technology is more efficient. Why risk using Trisidium?'

Mondrac replied, 'Trisidium is Sarclan's baby. I believe he wants to use it just to show us he was right. Remember what your Father said about his ego? Sarclan may be a genius, but he's also an egotistical madman.'

'So we need to take this processing plant out... where is it?'

'Cordoba Green,' Grogan answered, 'Sector 215, also close to where we believe another gate is located.' He worked the console and another image filled the screen. 'Here, just three parsecs from Green, we tracked down another operational gate and, from what Mondrac has told us, this is another good location for a bridge to operate.'

'And, A-Bra-Ham, we also believe this will give us the location of another operational gate in the tenth realm. The only thing they will need is the Trisidium to power it. We believe there is enough already there for some operations but they will need large shipments to continue. That is where both of the Cordoba sites are critical.'

Grogan interjected. 'First: we need to stop Rhapsody... without that ship they will not have the capacity to fully utilise the gates... second; we must destroy the processing plant... to stop their production... and third; we need to destroy the gates. Then we will have stopped them once and for all.' He made it all sound so simple.

Aaron looked at the images on his screen. 'Yes, I can see what we need to do, but we are very short on ships and this is a lot of work.'

'I'm working on getting our ships back ASAP. I just need you to stop Rhapsody!' Grogan looked to Aaron, waiting for an answer.

'Then consider it stopped.'

It took a full two hours to prepare Junior for the trip back to the Tenth Realm.

During this time, Condor was a hive of activity with the Dart drones – or ROV's as the military preferred to call them – arriving and being installed.

Aaron caught up with his engineer as he was about to leave Condor to farewell Junior. 'Damn good job Dianna. I didn't think we could get this done so quickly.'

Dianna smiled. 'Thank you, I'll pass it on to the troops; they've pulled out every stop on this. Now about those remotes... we can fit Valiant in the main hold; twenty remotes in here; and another twenty in the yacht's hangar. But... if we can put the controller hub in the secondary hold, that will allow at least another ten or more.' Dianna's thinking was sound.

'Then I'll leave you two to finalise the details... how long?' Aaron asked.

'We need a few mods to the holds... maybe two or three hours for full load out. Then, Simon and I will need time for mass calculations and drive programing so I think four hours at the most.'

'Ok get cracking, we're on the clock,' Aaron commanded

as he turned for the door.

It took Aaron ten minutes to reach the yacht's dock bay as other issues needed his attention on the way. Petra, Mondrac and Tocmal were already on board waiting to leave. He bid farewell to Mondrac and Tocmal and Petra escorted him to the airlock. They embraced silently – there were no words as they both knew what had to be done.

'Time to save the universe,' Petra finally said as she unlocked her arms from around Aaron. They shared a farewell kiss and then Aaron knew he had to leave. He stood by the view port and watched as the yacht slid effortlessly out of its bay; it sliced through the dock's force field, and was gone.

Aaron tried to refocus, but he had a feeling of dread, something in the back of his mind was nagging, something he couldn't quite grasp. He stood for a few minutes, looking vacantly into the dock entry portal, trying to understand what this feeling may mean. Finally he gave up and headed back to Condor.

Already there were a number of ROV racks – each containing four of the sleek weapons – waiting to be loaded into Junior's now vacant hangar. Aaron decided to have a closer look and called JT to meet him. He was already studying them when JT arrived. While they were the same design as their manned counterparts, the size difference was obvious.

Only two thirds the size of the manned units, these ROVs carried the same weaponry: disruptors, blasters and a type of torpedo fitted with the new antimatter warhead Valiant's crew had developed. They were a formidable vessel; speed and manoeuvrability were very impressive and the lack of any life support made them a singular fighting machine.

The fuselage was long and thin with winglets protruding from each side about half way back from the sharp nose. The leading edge of these – and the front section of the fuselage – also formed the deflector array, while emitter ports for the energy weapons were located top and bottom of the winglets. The four forward torpedo launchers were grouped around the nose with a further two aft of the wings. Each ROV was powered by three small MAM reactors located inside the hull behind heavily shielded bulkheads. Control was by way of a highly classified system developed by Greenbach Technologies that allowed both human and independent operation. Not only was this a very impressive weapon, it was a weapon that could *think*.

Artificial Intelligence had been around for centuries but this was the first weapon system to be certified to operate fully autonomously – at least in the Coalition. It was proving to be a great way to boost battlefield numbers without risking too many lives.

'Beautiful aren't they?' JT said as he walked up, snapping Aaron back to reality.

'Sure are! How many does it take to operate one?' Aaron enquired.

'Two... pilot and sensor operator... or none when in auto mode. We just program the mission parameters and the AI does the rest. They can also run in swarm mode... basically one acts as controller and the rest follow the leader's orders.' JT moved to the nearest rack and ran his hand over the Dart's skin. 'If only she could cook.'

'Sometimes, nephew, you worry me,' Aaron joked. 'Let's get back and help with the load out.'

JT smiled. 'We can't bring Valiant in here... there's not

enough room in this bay. We need to pick her up in space.'

Aaron knew he was right. Condor was a large vessel for this bay and had very little clearance – just another annoying thing to slow them down. The load out was progressing well and seemed ahead of schedule. By the time JT and Aaron returned to the shuttle bay, it had been cleared and the Darts were secured in their racks. The control hub had been secured in the auxiliary hold and engineers were connecting cables and other feed lines to it.

'Sir,' Dianna greeted Aaron, 'we are almost done. We have a couple of racks to finish in the yacht hangar and that's all. The engineers can keep working on the hub in transit, so we will be ready to pick up the Valiant in about an hour.' She was immensely proud of her engineering staff as they had proved themselves time after time to be among the best in the business. 'Simon has done the preliminary calcs for the drive. We only need to confirm when we actually have the full load.'

'Well done, Lieutenant, excellent work!' Aaron said, congratulating his chief engineer. 'Now JT, you better get back to your ship and get ready to bring her aboard.'

'Yes Sir! JT saluted and went straight for the exit.

Aaron spoke into his communicator. 'Commander Albrect.'

'Here, Sir.

'Kate, how soon will we be ready to leave?' Aaron asked.

'Now Sir, Condor is prepped and everything is in the green. We're just waiting for the order.'

'That'll come from our engineer... as soon as they've finished we'll depart.' Aaron started to exit the shuttle bay and called back, 'Dianna, let the bridge know when you're ready.'

Fifty seven minutes later, Dianna notified the bridge that she was ready for departure and acting first officer Katherine Albrect began the process of leaving the dock. Fifteen minutes after that Condor sliced quietly through the dock force field and turned towards the rendezvous point to collect Valiant.

The process of fitting Valiant into the cargo bay was very tedious as there were literally only a few millimetres clearance between the edges of Valiant and Condor's hold entry, but the skill of both pilots was equal to the task. Twenty minutes later Valiant was secured inside Condor's main cargo bay. As a safety precaution, she was almost totally powered down with only life support and gravity left functioning.

Simon Holm had selected their first jump point and with all cargo secure, Condor initiated its displacement field and sped away. Half an hour later they reached the first jump coordinates. Simon did his calculations for the fifth time before programing the new drive console.

'Ready as I'll ever be Captain,' he nervously announced.

Aaron smiled. Simon was a perfectionist when it came to his job. 'Good enough for me... punch it!'

Simon tapped the icon on the console before him and initiated the jump. Unlike displacement drive, the new jump drive didn't use an artificial worm hole – there was no sensation of motion at all. The jump drive dropped the ship into sub space allowing it to cover vast distances in the blink of an eye. The deeper they dropped, the quicker the trip; the interdependent relationship between time, speed and distance becoming irrelevant. To the uninitiated, it looked as if space simply folded back onto itself, although this was a physical impossibility. The depth of this jump equated to one light year travelled in normal space every one minute. Given that the maximum theoretical time for human sub space endurance was unknown, each jump was timed for thirty minutes – for safety – meaning a 30 minute trip covered 30 light-years of distance.

While there was light refracted and diffused in a displacement worm-hole, the jump drive was executed in the total darkness of sub space with nothing visible outside the ship. With no sensation of movement – no visual references and ship sounds normal – there was no indication that they were travelling anywhere. This could – some psychologists thought – have a damaging effect on the human mind and the main reason why trip durations were limited with normally at least twenty minute intervals between jumps.

Having some time to spare, Aaron consulted JT on the condition of his crew. They were all busy making preparations to the hub or the ROV's and nobody had noticed what had taken place; so Simon moved the next jump up. With only enough time taken to calibrate the drive, Condor jumped again; this time 50 light-years.

Fifty minutes in total darkness didn't go unnoticed this time, but still it created no problems. The last jump would take them 1.5million kilometres past their target but they would arrive behind an asteroid belt. With any luck, this would mask the drive signature from Cordoba Blue's sensors.

***

The man sitting in the command chair of Rhapsody wasn't tall, average height with long grey hair and a full, but well-trimmed grey beard. His eyes were a steel blue and his mouth was fronted by thin cruel lips but most noticeable were his hands. These were small – much smaller than one would expect on someone of his stature – more like a child's hands. His fingers were long and thin but in proportion, they looked elegant and feminine, their appearance gave the impression they could do no harm.

Eugene Sarclan was one of the most brilliant minds ever created by the human race, but flawed, completely lacking empathy or compassion. A classic sociopath, Eugene cared only for himself and his plans, and had no interest in who was injured or killed in their achievement.

At this moment, he was extremely pleased with how the operation was going. Reports from his operatives confirmed the dispersion of the coalition fleet; for the duration of this operation, they would be relegated to an observation force only. Cordoba Green was ahead of schedule and so was he; the unloading of passengers had taken less than the five hours his advisors had planned for.

He sat admiring the functional beauty of the bridge. Albrect had built a beautiful ship and it did seem a pity it had such a short life in its designed task, but then his needs were far more important than any others. He glanced at the view screen. The timer showed fifty one minutes and forty seconds since they left Blue. Yes, things were going very well.

A sudden but slight vibration was felt beneath his feet. He stood, puzzled. Before he could demand an explanation, a second vibration rumbled through the ship moments before inertial dampening failed. He fell from his chair as the ship yawed violently and dropped out of displacement.

'What the fuck was that?' Sarclan screamed.

The chief engineer scrambled back to his console and

frantically scanned the ship's systems. 'We've lost the forward deflector array!'

'Crap, where's the back up?'

'We've lost that too, that was the second vibration.' The engineer barked commands for repair crews to investigate.

Sarclan was fuming. 'Get it fixed *now*!' he hissed.

'Crews are already on their way, but we need to stop the ship.' The engineer's voice was quaking. 'Without the forward deflector, we will get hammered. Tactical, can you sweep for micro meteorites or any other debris that we might hit?'

'Sir,' the reply came from the nav station, 'we have dropped out of displacement into a relatively empty sector fortunately, but it does have a large amount of debris and space dust, including meteorites. I agree, we have to stop till repairs are made.'

'*Fuck, Fuck!* All right... all stop! Angle the remaining deflectors to give what cover we can to the forward section. And someone find out what's happened... *now!*' Sarclan stormed off the bridge into the Captain's ready room.

With all the commotion, nobody noticed the small flashing amber indicator in the lower left corner of the communication console. One of the safety features built into all starships is an emergency transmitter; one that automatically begins transmitting an emergency signal instantly after what is called an Extinction Level Failure – an ELF. Unplanned dropping out of displacement and losing deflector function are two such events, so Rhapsody's emergency system began to transmit location and details of their situation. No one noticed the indicator until Sarclan stormed back into the bridge.

'What fucking idiot missed the emergency beacon?' He glared at the young woman manning that console. 'Shut it down *now!*' She leapt to action and cancelled the transmission, but the damage had already been done.

The operator was visibly shaken. Young, no more than thirty years old with blonde hair, she had a pretty face with large blue eyes, eyes that were now filled with terror. 'Sorry Sir, I missed it in all the excitement.' She had a large red welt on her forehead where she had been thrown against the rear bulkhead when the ship yawed so violently.

She was about to continue when Sarclan waved her down, his hand resting on the butt of his side arm. 'Enough... the damage is done... no doubt the Coalition has received that emergency transmission so we need to get busy on repairs.' He paused, his steely gaze roaming the room till he found his next target. 'You on the sensor console, what's our sensor status?'

Another woman, older than the comms officer, made eye contact with Sarclan and replied, 'Full sensor capability, Sir.'

'Good, continue maximum range sweeps till we are under way again.'

'Sir,' she responded.

'Now listen up, all of you,' Sarclan barked, 'we are dead in the water. Until we have deflector capability, we can only manoeuvre slowly so we are sitting ducks and I don't intend to be caught here like this. You are all here because you are the best we have, so think, and find a way for us to get out of this mess! Any ideas, no matter how crazy it seems, we'll look at them, understand?'

'Yes Sir,' the words came from every one almost exactly at the same time.

Sarclan smiled; satisfied he had got the message across. Inwardly he was seething at this delay – timing was everything in this operation.

He turned to his first officer. 'I'm going to the deflector array... maybe I can encourage a quick solution.' The officer just nodded mutely. Having been with Sarclan for many years, he knew just what that could mean and felt sorry for the repair team.

The scene in the deflector node was one of total chaos. The air was thick with ozone and smoke from the explosion. There had been several fires when the repair crews had arrived and these were now almost extinguished – fire aboard a space ship is one of the most feared of all situations. Fire destroyed, consumed oxygen and gave off toxic fumes, making it the worst possible scenario that could happen in a sealed and finite environment.

The last fire was being put out as Sarclan entered the node, flanked by two guards. The chief engineer – one of a handful of Albrect employees kept on board – was surveying the damage as Sarclan approached. 'Well, chief, what's the verdict?'

The chief engineer Warren Parsons stood to confront Sarclan. A large man, he was taller than most and towered over Sarclan. His body was very well muscled and his large hands' sported callouses from years of hard work. He had been the chief engineer since the ship's construction began and he knew every component of her. He stared down at Sarclan.

'I would say someone doesn't like you very much,' Parsons said through clenched teeth. 'Whoever did this was either very lucky or they knew a great deal about this ship. They managed to take out both the primary and backup power bus systems as well as destroying the changeover relay.'

'Ok, so the saboteurs were very good... but how long to fix it?'

'It can't be fixed, there's too much damage. Look for yourself.' Parsons moved aside and pointed to the remains of the bus system. There was not much left, the coveralls had fallen across the main bus with a much greater effect than Anton had considered. The main bus had vaporised instantly and the resulting fireball had fused the outgoing conduit into one solid mass of composite and metal.

The instant this happened, the main breaker had tripped. A few milliseconds later, the automatic change over relay had operated and switched all deflector array power to the backup bus system. With the backup bus system already bridged by the other coverall, the change-over relay closed onto an equally large fault with similar catastrophic results. Sarclan could see the damage and knew the engineer was right.

'Alright... if this can't be fixed, tell me how you are going to get our forward array back on line?'

Parsons could see that he had no choice – Sarclan wouldn't accept any other option than getting the ship under way.

'The only way is to run a new power supply to the array. To do that we need to install new cables or a bus system to bypass this mess, then bridge that into the power system. The problem with that, however, is that the forward and lateral arrays share a common power source. We will need to take the lateral array offline to complete the connections.'

Sarclan held his hand up for Parsons to stop. 'I don't care what has to be done, how fucking long till we can get moving again?'

The look in Sarclan's eyes froze Parsons' blood. He had been in many situations, came up against many hard cases in his life but he had never seen such malevolence in eyes before. 'Five or six hours at least,' he replied in a subdued voice.

'You have four, so I suggest you get moving.' Sarclan turned and stormed out of the node, followed by his two guards. They took the elevator to the bridge and the damage was now very visible through the elevator's clear sides. The centre portion of the ship was a large hollow tube, inside which ran a myriad of smaller tubes and conduits carrying power and services to every part of the vessel. The conduit for the forward array had buckled and ruptured just forward of the explosions, damaging several conduits around it, some of which were now leaking fluids and gas into the main space. Sarclan could see a couple of crews dressed in hazard suits were already working on this problem. Attitude aside, Sarclan was confident Parsons could cope with the emergency.

They had just reached the bridge when another vibration was felt through the ship and alarms started to scream. 'What now?' Sarclan shouted to no one in particular.

'Hull breach on level ten... I'm reading a massive depressurisation in sector 4!'

Unsure who made the announcement, Sarclan scanned the room trying to find the source. Finally his gaze settled on the woman manning the sensor console.

'Are we under attack?' he yelled.

'No Sir, the breach was initiated internally,' she said as the alarms were silenced. The sensor operator had control of both internal and external sensor systems. 'It appears that a cabin view port was breached. The decompression caused a twenty metre section of the hull to explode... bulkhead doors have now closed and the area is secure.'

'Get a remote out there so we can see just how much damage we have!'

Sarclan stormed to the command chair and sat down. 'Where is fucking Korder?' He fumed. 'Someone find the security chief!' At this outburst, the Bridge crew went into overdrive. Looking busy was the only way to avoid a tirade – or worse – from Sarclan.

The duty engineer started a remote inspection drone but its hatch door wouldn't open so he re-routed it through the ship to the main airlock. The drone was not very large – about three metres in length and two in diameter – so routing it through the ship was relatively easy. Finally it was approaching the airlock when Sarclan asked, 'Where's the fucking remote?'

'Just about to enter the main airlock,' the duty engineer replied. 'We had some issues with the drone's exit hatch so I thought it would be quicker to do this than try to rectify the hatch problem.' He emphasised his success by switching the drone's vision to the main viewer. 'In case you want to see the damage Sir,' he explained.

'At last, someone who thinks... what's your name.'

'Teague Sir, Jack Teague,' the engineer replied.

'Well then, Mr Teague, let's get this thing outside and see how badly the ship is damaged.'

The main airlock was large enough to fit several drones, so Teague easily manoeuvred it inside. As he disengaged the drive, set the motion dampeners and began to close the inner door, Teague noticed a small, intense flash in the upper left section of the inner seal on the outer door; so did Sarclan.

'Mr Teague, what was that flash?'

'Don't know.' Teague's reply was quiet. It worried him that the inner door was taking an eternity to close and he had a very bad feeling about what he had just seen. Due to their size and for passenger safety, the inner doors were timed to close in sixty eight seconds. This never varied, except in the event of decompression, when they would close instantly. Half way closed was their weakest point and the door had just reached this point when the outer door seal failed.

What happened next was spectacular. The outer door was torn off its mounts by the explosive force of the pressure difference between the vacuum of space and the air pressure in the ship. It also ripped a large section of the surrounding hull away. Fortunately, the inner door held and rolled instantly to its seated position, sealing the breach. Teague fought hard to regain control of the drone and bring it back to the airlock. The damage filled the view screen.

Sarclan turned to the duty engineer. 'What the fuck!' 'Get the chief engineer here at once! Teague, continue to check the damage then go to the other site and survey the damage there. We need to know how bad we have been hit... and will someone please locate the damn security chief!'

Chief Engineer Parsons made the bridge in double quick time; he knew the results of a Sarclan tantrum and didn't want to be on the receiving end. First Officer Hiro Nakamura pointed toward the ready room as Parsons entered the bridge and relinquished control to the second officer so he could join them; he beckoned Teague as well. They found Sarclan sitting at his desk pouring over the damage video from both sites. He barely looked up as the others entered before he barked, 'Parsons, look at this!

Parsons watched the video from both damage sites and his blood ran cold.

'Teague, can you enhance this area?' Parsons pointed to the top right of the view screen. 'Just this area,' he said as Teague worked the console and the area of interest now filled the screen. 'What're the stress readings?'

Teague looked as if he had just seen his own demise and answered quietly, 'Seventy percent over max.' He looked only at the console, fearful of being singled out as the culprit.

'So, just rig a fucking force field and get us moving!' Sarclan shouted.

'It's not that simple. You may be one of the smartest people ever but sometimes you sure can be dumb. The stress levels show a major flaw in the structural integrity of the hull, something no force field will fix. This ship needs a dock to complete repairs. Nothing can be done out here.'

'Bullshit! Just weld some patches and we can get going. We're on a strict timeline!' Sarclan screamed.

Parsons moved Teague away from the console and started to work on it. It took him ten minutes – while Sarclan fumed at his desk – to superimpose additional information on the screen.

'Take a look at this,' Parsons said as he pointed to the screen. 'What you have now is the damage overlaid with the stress readings. If you take a good look at it you can see where the major stress issues are.' He pointed to the screen and, using a laser pointer, indicated the area of concern.

'You can see the extent of the stress fractures... they reach half way around the fucking hull. If you place much more force to these areas, the whole hull in this section will fail.

The result will be catastrophic... the ship will tear apart. I would say either the person who planted the device had intimate knowledge of the ship's construction, or they had damn good luck on their side. So, if you want to kill everyone on board and fail in your venture, just ignore me and do what you fucking well want!'

This was the last straw for Sarclan. He leapt to his feet and drew his sidearm; as he raised it, Hiro Nakamura stepped between the two men. 'Eugene, stop!' Nakamura shouted.

Nakamura and Sarclan had been together since they were forced to leave Earth many years ago. He had always been Sarclan's right hand man – the go to guy to get things fixed. In addition, he was a skilled engineer himself.

'What Parsons says is correct,' he said. 'We can't proceed without proper repairs.'

Sarclan was now shaking with rage. So many years of planning, so many years of intrigue, so much resting in the balance – his whole life's work was now hanging by a thread! Even so, he knew the engineer was right. His rage started to dissipate and he re-holstered his weapon, taking a deep breath to regain his composure.

'Yes, you're right. Parsons, what do you suggest?'

'We return to Cordoba Blue,' Parsons suggested. 'They have facilities we could use to make repairs... but at best, we can only manage displacement two. Any more will be too dangerous.' He looked over to Nakamura who nodded in agreement.

The reality was now sinking in. Displacement two to Blue would take around sixteen hours. Displacement two to Green – their ultimate destination – would take weeks. Blue was the only option.

'Agreed,' Sarclan's voice was heavy with resignation. 'How long before we can start?'

'I need another three hours to have the deflector working. While this is happening, Teague can shore up the hull as best we can. I would say a total of five hours.' Parsons' tone demonstrated that he was giving his best estimate and wanted no opposition.

Sarclan nodded and replied 'then you better get started.' Teague and Parsons left the room to start the process. Sarclan stared at Nakamura. 'How did this happen? We scoured the ship for any operatives and found nothing... what did we miss?'

Nakamura shook his head. 'I think Korder had some suspicions, but we just can't find him. Could he be a traitor?'

'No, Korder has nowhere else to go. Every authority in the galaxy is after his head... we're his only hope of survival so where is he?' Sarclan voice conveyed his concern. 'Trace his movements... find him!'

Nakamura was about to leave when Sarclan spoke again. 'We may need some assistance. Maybe it's time for our coalition friend to earn his exorbitant fee.' He waved Nakamura away and opened a small case attached to his belt.

As the door closed, he brought the device to the desk and activated it. The technology from Nileros was an advanced communications system that allowed real time communication over distances never before contemplated. With it he could securely contact his various operatives almost instantly – the tyranny of galactic distance negated by the device. He didn't actually know who the contact at the other end was, but so far his actions and information had been worth the vast price he had paid.

The call was answered – audio only as always. He started to discuss his situation and requirements and, by the end of the conversation, Sarclan was satisfied that things were not as bad as he thought. He smiled and reached for a glass – time for a drink. He had just added a good amount of brandy when Nakamura's voice interrupted him.

'Eugene,' Hiro said, 'we have found Korder... he is in a bad way. The doctor is on his way now.' As usual Nakamura's report was short and to the point.

'What do you mean, in a bad way?'

'Don't know yet. He is in a small security room tied to a chair. It appears he has been beaten and possibly poisoned. The doctor will know more in a few minutes.'

This news caused some concern to Sarclan. Korder was not someone who could be overpowered easily. Sarclan had watched him in action and always thought Korder could handle anyone without raising a sweat. For him to be overpowered and tied up was serious.

'Nakamura, can you get a security feed from the room?' Sarclan had a feeling that this was not all it seemed. A couple of seconds later his main monitor was filled with the sight of Korder tied to a chair in the centre of the room, he had clearly been interrogated with some prejudice. Something wasn't right and Sarclan could feel it. As this thought was coalescing in his mind the doctor entered the room and began examining Korder. What was he missing? He enhanced the image concentrating on Korder, but the doctor was in the way.

'Nakamura, get the doctor to move to his left... something is wrong.'

Nakamura repeated this to the doctor who complied. Sarclan enlarged the image again and saw something on Korder's right wrist – a watch? But he always wore a wrist watch on his left. The doctor's hand moved to the device as it seemed to be caught in the bindings.

'No!' Sarclan screamed, but it was too late. Anton's incendiary device activated and Korder, the doctor and three guards in the hall were engulfed in a huge fireball. The monitor went blank.

'Nakamura, seal that area!'

Nakamura was already on it. He sealed the section and flooded it with carbon dioxide to kill the fire.

'Nakamura, I want every person on this ship accounted for *now!*' Sarclan shouted.

'ir, we have an incoming message from Albatross,' the comms operator called.

'On the main viewer,' Aaron replied. The screen flickered and the face of Steve Harris appeared.

'Heard you might need a bit of a hand,' he said. 'I'm in the vicinity... how can I help?'

'I'll send you the coordinates. How soon can you get here?' Aaron glanced across to the Nav station and saw Simon already transmitting the coordinates of their destination to the other ship. The screen went blank for a moment then Steve's face reappeared, 'probably about two hours, why?'

'Tell you what, meet us there and we'll fill you in. I might even buy you a drink.'

'Deal,' the screen faded and the stars began to reappear.

'Simon, how long to our next jump coordinates?'

'Ten minutes... we'll be at the target site in just under an hour before they arrive.' Simon seemed relieved, having another ship was always going to make things better.

***

An hour later, Condor had arrived at the coordinates and everyone settled down to wait for Albatross. Allen Grainger sent a message that a trader vessel had been diverted to the location where the emergency signal from Rhapsody had originated. It should arrive within the next hour and it would be able to give them real intelligence about what had happened. There was also a private message from Damien Albrecht for Aaron.

Aaron left the bridge and listened to the message in his ready room. It contained information about the contractor he had on board Rhapsody together with a frequency and code to use to communicate with him. Aaron filed the information – someone on the inside might be a great help.

Finally Albatross arrived. She was now stationary beside Condor and Greg Lewis – First Officer on Albatross – requested clarification from Condor's shuttle bay.

'You want us to dock where?'

Lateral airlock number three, Condor replied.

Steve Harris, Captain of Albatross, shrugged and nodded to his number one. It had been a long time since either had needed to use a soft dock system but, if that was what was needed; they were up to the task. It took ten minutes to locate the docking ring and complete the manoeuvre, but finally they had a green light and proceeded to board Condor.

Aaron met them at the airlock door.

'Sorry for the drama but our shuttle bay is rather full at the moment. It's good to see you both again... follow me.' The three walked down the passageway, Aaron filling them in on the situation as they walked.

Finally they reached the main conference room and joined Condor's senior officers, JT and his First Officer. Aaron pointed to the welcoming coffee tray and food. 'Better get some now... it may be a while till the next chance.' When everyone was seated – each with a steaming mug and a plate of food – he continued. 'I've filled Steve and Greg in on the situation. Dave, what's the sensor sweep show?' Dave Carter stood and switched the view screen on.

'Seems that Rhapsody had some sort of catastrophic failure and executed an emergency displacement shut down here,' he indicated a spot on the star chart on the screen. 'Shortly after this, there were two explosive decompression events; from the debris analysis, we think a view port in one of the cabins failed and also shortly after that, an airlock had a similar failure. It would appear that there's significant structural damage to the hull.' He zoomed in on some of the pieces of debris; there was a substantial amount and some of the pieces were quite large.

Greg Lewis interrupted. 'What are the chances that these failures were from manufacturing defects?'

Dianna Holland answered. 'Virtually zero,' There was silence in the room as this sank in.

Dave continued. 'They were here for around half an hour before they engaged their main drive and started on this course… the only possible destination is Cordoba Blue. Interestingly, we believe they reversed their course. The only assumption is they sustained damage to their forward deflector array… that's one of a few reasons for a mid-displacement shut down and explains why they're reversing.

They continued on this course for two hours when it looks like, from the signature decay, that they must have repaired the deflector and engaged the displacement drive at very low power, probably no more than factor two.'

Dianna took over. 'The damage we believe they suffered was well calculated. It limits their options and speed and, if they have the sort of damage the debris suggests, they need a heavy repair facility and Blue is the only one close by. Although it was converted to a resort, it still maintains a healthy repair business and has the only dock capable of housing Rhapsody. So, we can conclude with some certainty that's their destination.' As she concluded, JT's communicator chimed.

'Captain, we have a comm from Earth.'

'On the main screen,' Aaron replied. The screen went blank and the star chart was replaced by Sam Grogan's face.

'Gentlemen,' Grogan began, 'we received your message and concur with your assessment. We also received a communique from an Eldoran ship. It seems they have been watching Cordoba Green... six KL10n cruisers also left there about the same time. Our conclusion is they are heading your way, probably to set a perimeter around Blue. The communique also included news from other realms that others... Galdorans I believe... are mobilising so Sarclan may be expecting some other assistance.

'It is imperative that we destroy Rhapsody... without it he has nothing to execute his plan. Grainger agrees, and will send you confirmation independently. We would prefer Blue was spared however, if necessary, you must consider Cordoba Blue as collateral damage.' He paused to let this sink in.

'You know the alternative if Sarclan succeeds. But there is another issue... Alan Dean. It appears that our Captain Dean is Sarclan's man in the coalition. He commandeered the Otamah and has taken Wilson and Morris hostage. We believe he's trying to reach Sarclan, so he may turn up there.

'Captain Abraham,' this time Grogan was addressing JT,

'you're authorised to take whatever measures necessary to stop Dean and release the hostages but they are *never* to reach Sarclan, do you understand?'

JT's face paled. His immediate superior had just ordered him to destroy a Coalition ship and, if necessary, kill the two highest ranking officers in Space Corps.

'Sir, you are authorising lethal force on the most senior officers on the Corps... is that correct?' he asked.

'Correct,' Grogan continued, 'in accord with standing Presidential order, Delta X-ray 0158 issued by President Malik today, I am. A copy of this directive has been sent to your secure file and placed on your permanent record. Any fallout will be on my head, not yours.'

The screen changed and Allen Grainger's face appeared, 'Aaron, please understand this. I have read the directive and agree with its authenticity but it only covers coalition forces. Freebooters cannot take any deadly action against Dean. You can assist to disable the ship if required... as I believe it poses a direct threat to our society... but in the worst case scenario, it must be by coalition forces... confirmed?'

'Confirmed... so much for being apolitical,' Aaron's replied bitterly.

'I agree, but we must abide by this,' Grainger responded.

Grogan's face reappeared. 'I have contacted a number of our ships and they are heading back at maximum displacement. It will be at least twelve hours before any appreciable numbers are available so you guys are the only hope. What's your timing?'

Aaron and Dave conferred with JT and Jarad.

'It will take the cruisers at least seven hours to reach Blue. They have already been travelling for two hours, so we have five hours before we have company. We are only an hour from Blue so we have a two pronged strategy planned.'

Before Aaron could elaborate, Grogan interrupted. 'Good... now get going and good luck... Grogan out.'

'Ok, what's this two pronged plan?' Dave asked.

Aaron smiled. 'At displacement two, how long till Rhapsody reaches Blue?'

'Three hours, why?' Dave asked.

'If we assume they are desperate to complete repairs, they will run the risk of being without cover for a couple of hours. After those cruisers arrive we won't have any chance of getting through.' It only took Aaron a couple of minutes to outline his strategy.

'Are you serious?' JT asked when Aaron finished.

'If anyone has a better idea, please speak up!' Aaron fired back. The question was met with silence. 'I thought not. I agree this is a bit thin, but what else can we do? The only unknown is Dean. Where is he heading and how much firepower can he bring? But, that will be your problem JT. Now, if we agree, we have a lot of work to do and not much time.'

The first part of Aaron's plan involved getting Valiant out of the main hold – a delicate task that took twenty minutes to complete before they could commence preparation of the drones. They had to be prepped and modified for the task in hand – this took another hour. All the prep work on Condor was complete and the transfer of a secondary control hub and twenty drones to Albatross was under way. One hour and fifty minutes after they started all was ready.

JT, Aaron and Steve stood at the airlock door.

'See you two later,' Aaron shook both their hands, 'Just don't be late.'

Considering the magnitude of their task, the mood was light. Steve went through the airlock and JT to the shuttle bay. Ten minutes later, the three ships split up and headed for their respective places. The die was now cast.

Condor's place was behind a small planetoid – the one that had been mined out by the Cordoba Corporation for its incredibly rich diamond fields; its hard irradiated cobalt outer shell would still mask any drive signature very effectively. Aaron immediately launched a number of micro probes to scout the area. If their calculations were correct, Rhapsody should be here in fifty five minutes – Albatross and Valiant should arrive ten minutes later. All this was based on their perception that Sarclan would reinsert very close to the station to reduce the amount of time the ship would be in normal space, and thus limit its vulnerability. If they were correct, they would have only ten minutes max to destroy it.

'Not much time and lots to do,' Aaron thought. He was unsure about the next part but had agreed to it nevertheless. Albrect had requested – and Grainger had insisted – that on arrival he should release a probe to transmit a message. It was to be a coded message from Albrect to his contractor on a very old frequency, one that was no longer in use. Although Aaron thought it useless, he complied. Little did he know, but this message would prove to be one of the best actions in the whole enterprise.

***

Anton and Janice had secured a suite in one of the upmarket areas of the resort. His notoriety had allowed them to skip most of the formal identification process with his name and credit rating proving to be more than enough for the concierge. It always amused him that there were very few recorded images of him anywhere but his credit identity was always enough to get whatever he wanted.

They were sitting on the balcony overlooking a recreation of Venice when he felt an itch behind his left ear. It felt like a spider trying to crawl out of his skin, something he had not felt for many years. He excused himself, pleading they needed more champagne, and went inside. He reached up and pressed gently behind the offending ear. Instantly a scratchy voice echoed in his head. It was a short message asking him to transmit back on this system, he complied and, to the astonishment of both himself and Aaron, they were now talking. It only took a few exchanges for both of them to become comfortable with the situation.

By transmitting the message, Aaron triggered another message on his own comm system. This time it was Damien Albrect who quickly informed Aaron who was on the other end of the discussion – the infamous Doctor. Albrect's comm was brief and both Aaron and Anton heard it. He quickly explained who the Doctor was and why he had engaged his services. His final request was that they work together to solve the situation. Albrect's communication ended and Anton and Aaron continued for another few minutes, agreeing on a very sketchy plan.

Janice had busied herself reading the very extensive room service menu, building a wonderful meal in her mind but Anton's return scuttled that idea.

'Better get your working kit on... we're back in the game.'

Anton's booking on Rhapsody as a Platinum passenger had, fortunately, included his own Butler so, in the confusion of a hasty disembarkation of all passengers, it was assumed that he had forgotten to collect his belongings and, as part of the Platinum service, his Butler had packed and arranged to transfer his luggage to Blue. As soon as his disembarkation had been confirmed by the very obliging security officer, he had been informed that his luggage was in storage. The first thing he did, after they had secured their room, was to have his luggage retrieved.

Now with some of his toys back, Anton was greatly relieved. While reloading his special belt, he filled Janice in on the communication he had received, including a strange code word from Crompton for her.

'Mother love,' said Anton with amusement. 'I just love the silly codes you spooks come up with.'

'It means that I am to assist you, not kill you.'

Janice's comment stopped him in his tracks. Of all the people he had come up against in his career, Janice was the only one he believed actually had a chance of doing that. His expression showed his thoughts.

'Don't worry... I will make sure that rather cute arse of yours gets back intact. The code also meant I am to follow your lead, so what's the plan?'

'Well, we have a simple task,' explained Anton. 'Rhapsody is returning... seems our work was rather effective, she needs the dock facilities here. All we have to do then is get to the dock area, disable, or destroy whatever we can, and wait for the cavalry to arrive. Oh, by the way, we have a full thirty minutes from now to do it.'

'Are you serious? Do the others have any idea how fucking big this station is? We'll be lucky to get half way in thirty minutes... did you consider that?'

'Have you studied the schematic of this old station?'

Anton enquired.

Janice shook her head and walked through the door to see him studying the station schematic.

'Here's our ticket, Commander.' He stood back to allow Janice to see what was on both the screen and the chair.

The screen showed the transport layout of the station and, highlighted, was a special security transport pod. On the chair was a security officers uniform, complete with her ID card and rank insignia.

'You're still an active security officer. In fact, you're probably the most senior Rhapsody security officer on this station... I believe that only the late Major Korder outranked you. So, in your capacity of senior security officer, you're going to the dock to oversee the arrival of Rhapsody. I've already inserted clearance into the stations computer. It may be a little basic, but the system seemed to accept it so, Commander, I think you should get dressed and be quick about it.'

'You really are full of surprises... where did you get this?' She asked indicating the uniform. She quickly removed the elegant dress she had purchased earlier.

'I liberated it while you were trying on clothes... I just thought it might come in handy. The ID card I kept from the ship. 'I must say, I prefer you in what you just covered up.'

'Thank you, but it might prove a little distracting at the moment.' She picked up her side arm, something she was amazed that Anton had been able to procure. Satisfied with the look, she opened the door, 'just one thing... why am I taking you?'

Anton smiled. 'Give me a break; I haven't got all the details. You may need to fill in some blanks.'

'Oh, I do love your works in progress.' She led the way to the nearest elevator. 'Going down?' she asked with a wicked smile as the doors closed.

'Maybe later, we have a job to do now,' Anton fired back. Adrenalin was starting to infiltrate his system, heightening his senses and priming his body for action.

It took seven minutes to reach the security transport pod. The clearance that Anton had inserted into the control computer was accepted and they quickly boarded. It sped towards the dock area, Janice trying desperately to come up with some plausible reason she would be taking one of the galaxy's top Geophysicists with her – unfortunately she could find none. She feared Anton's gung ho attitude may prove fatal to them both.

Even at speed, it still took a full nine minutes to reach the dock, leaving them only fourteen minutes to delay Rhapsody's entry to the repair facility. As the doors slid open, they were greeted by a Cordoba Corporation security guard who demanded to know what business they had in this area. The clearance Anton had generated for her was quickly accepted but Anton was another matter. The guard blocked his path, demanding to know why he was here.

Anton stared at the guard. 'My dear fellow, do you know who I am?' The guard did not, so Anton continued, pompously. 'I am Anton Alvaris, Doctor Anton Alvaris... Chairman of Omnicron. I was, unfortunately, a passenger on Rhapsody before they marooned us here on this god forsaken lump of metal.

'Omnicron, is working with the Cordoba Corporation to terraform a couple of nearby planetoids, to restart the local mining industry. So, while I am forcibly detained here, I thought it might be a good time to inspect the repair facilities, in case we need repairs to our equipment. The good Commander here, offered to allow me to accompany her.'

'Now,' and here Anton looked purposefully at the guard's ID badge, 'Officer Stanton, I deal personally with Luigi Cordoba, so if me being here causes you concern I suggest you get on that comm system... I believe Luigi will be on Stratos Major at this time of year... and ask him if I should be here.' Anton's tone left the guard in no doubt that he was displeased at being questioned.

The very mention that he should call the head of the Corporation obviously filled the man with dread. 'My apologies Doctor Alvaris; we had heard that there was going to be some development around here. I didn't know your company was involved... please continue.' He stood back and allowed them to leave.

Janice was furious at all this but she held it in till they were out of earshot of the guard. 'One day your bluff and bullshit will get you killed!'

'Hang on,' Anton said. 'First, I do deal with Luigi... Omnicron is involved with Cordoba in three projects at the moment and second, I have had some initial discussions regarding some possible development in this general region. I learnt long ago that the best lie is one that has a fair degree of truth in it so, while there was a great deal of bluff, there really wasn't that much bullshit. Now, what's next?'

Anton recalled the dock schematic he had recorded earlier via his ocular implant. He had marked three possible sabotage points that could be mistaken for industrial accidents or carelessness of the workers and time was ticking incessantly by as he scanned the dock. Finally he found what he was looking for.

'Let's split up here.' He handed her one of the miniature explosives from his belt. 'Fifty metres to your right is the main switch room, place this on the main power conduit… it doesn't matter which one. There are two, one incoming and one outgoing, either will shut things down, at least for a while.' He surreptitiously fingered the icons on his wrist watch. 'That'll go off in five minutes, so get going,' and then more loudly for anyone listening, 'and thank you Commander, I can find my own way now.'

They parted and headed in different directions. Janice walked quickly toward the switch room giving the impression she was simply inspecting the facility. It took her three minutes to reach the target and to give it a quick visual inspection. She placed the tiny device on one of the conduits as she walked past and continued on her way without stopping.

Meanwhile, Anton went to a different location. Delaying Rhapsody from docking was what was asked of him and he could only assume that external forces wanted more time to attack. What he hoped was they could offer two different failures that would facilitate this delay and his target was the dock anchoring system.

While there was an artificial gravity generated on the station, something as large as Rhapsody required extensive anchoring. If there was even a momentary failure of the gravity system, the damage that something with Rhapsody's mass could do was monumental. Anton's plan was to disable it but the anchoring control room was constantly manned and guarded.

His route to the control room was monitored visually so he needed to divert attention somewhere else. Below he saw an opportunity. Workers were transferring some type of fluid and, from all the protective clothing; he knew it was something volatile. He removed one of the small studs from his belt, quickly set the timer and dropped it through the open railing on the walk way; it dropped into one of the open drums they were syphoning the liquid from. Anton increased his pace. Ten seconds later, the tiny device ignited and the liquid exploded into flame.

A huge fireball shot up through the walk way, barely missing him. Anton broke into a run, trying to appear panicked. He ran straight to the anchor control room entrance, now blocked by the two guards. Their attention was not on the seemingly small frightened man running toward them, but more on the fireball. It went straight up and engulfed the control room of a huge overhead crane. The control room exploded and further enraged the fire. Anton reached the anchor control room, gasping for breath.

'Doctor Alvaris?' One of the guards enquired, 'quickly Sir, in here!' The guard operated the security lock in the entrance door and ushered him inside. 'You'll be safe in here.' Unwittingly and in his haste to protect one of his corporations' chief contractors, the guard had given Anton access to his target. He glanced at his watch, one minute till Janice's device detonated; he hoped she'd gotten clear.

Another guard came over to Anton. 'Doctor Alvaris!' He held out his hand.

'Do I know you?' Anton questioned, his body preparing to attack.

'No, Sir. The guard at the pod station alerted us to your visit. I am sorry you had to be here when this accident occurred,' the guard apologised. 'We have a great safety record. In fact, this is the first problem we have had in over two years.'

Anton quickly scanned the room and located his target.

'I fully understand dear fellow. We go through the same things with Terraforming. You set up the system... the most dangerous phase... and nothing happens. Then, years later, something totally out of the blue happens and everything goes to hell. I am just glad I could get in here. By the way, what is all this for?'

'This controls the anchoring system. Here, allow me to introduce you to our shift supervisor, she can explain the system better than I can.' He beckoned to one of the others who came over to them. The woman was quite tall and carried herself with the air of someone who held authority. The guard introduced them and she began Anton's guided tour. As they walked round the room, she explained the operation of each station with great pride, finally approaching the target Anton wanted.

'This station is our master. With this, we oversee all the anchor points and distribute any loads or forces equally, ensuring the security of the vessel while at the same time, minimise the energy requirements. Even minute fluctuations in the security of the anchored mass can equate to quite large increases in power consumption.'

'I am impressed,' Anton looked at her security tag, 'supervisor Coulter. 'You obviously take great pride in your job... I might have to try and steal you from Luigi.' While he was genuinely impressed with her dedication, he felt that flattery would be the best way to get her to drop her guard. 'Do you think I might sit at the station and see first-hand how you operate?'

It worked, and she asked the console operator to vacate his chair and Anton sat down. While she was explaining the station to Anton the room was suddenly filled with the screams of alarms.

'What's that?' Anton tried to sound terrified.

'Just sit there Sir, I'll see what the problem is.' Coulter went to the console opposite and began interrogating the system – just what Anton needed. He quickly removed another small stud from his belt and attached it to the side of the console's icon pad. This one would not explode, well at least not in a violent way. It contained a small transmitter that interfaced with the computer. Once the interface was complete, it inserted a virus into the computer system that would only become active if the system it infected completed a specific command. The trick now was to get someone to enter the command he needed. Coulter was very busy so Anton beckoned to the operator to return.

'Just a small question, how does this system coordinate all the others... it seems like a stand-alone to me?' Anton pleaded ignorance well.

'Simple Sir. Here, let me show you.' Anton rose to allow the operator to resume his seat. He called to two operators to his left. 'Let's do a simulation for the Doctor, guys!'

They agreed and started the process. It only took moments for them to start the simulation. 'We use these simulations to keep us on the ball. We don't get much call for the system now, but every now and then, like today; we get an emergency that requires us to anchor a large vessel so we need to be ready.' He explained the process and they ran through a typical twin anchoring simulation. Finally they passed control over to the master, unwittingly giving the virus the command it would require should Rhapsody return and enter the dock.

Coulter returned just as Anton secretly removed the stud.

'You certainly came on the wrong day... we had a problem with the main door supply, old conduit failed. Anyway, we have repair crews on the job and we should be able to receive Rhapsody in a couple of hours, tops. I'm sorry but we need to finalise preparations.' She didn't need to say more, Anton thanked them and went back to the guard.

'Sir,' the guard addressed Anton, 'Commander Barker is waiting down below; I'll accompany you to her.'

'Thank you, I must say this has been a most exciting visit.'

'Yes, we normally don't have any issues, but it seems we were destined to show you how we respond to these emergencies.'

'I must say I'm impressed with how your people handled the situation. I won't have any worries when we need to send our equipment here. Thank you.' Anton shook his hand and left the room.

***

A few moments after Aaron and Anton had concluded their communications, Aaron called for his bridge team's attention.

'It appears that we have a couple of assets on that station. They are going to try to delay Rhapsody's docking so we can have more time to have a go at her but, we still don't know what the capability of the station is, so we need to be a little cautious. We have a ten minute window before the troops arrive so here is what we need to do.' He continued for a few more minutes filling in details of their battle plan.

With the secondary hub now aboard Albatross with twenty drones, Condor's twenty would have to carry out the main attack. The plan was simple: ten drones had been programmed as a sort of decoy with special sensor generators to fool Rhapsody's sensors into the belief they were a force of much larger vessels. They had been despatched and were laying dormant waiting for the command.

The twenty remaining Darts had been stealthily flown through the asteroid field and spread out in a line on the far perimeter. Powered down to minimum, they effectively had a sensor signal of a small irradiated asteroid, like most of those around them.

Unfortunately Condor would have to stay concealed – at least until the initial attack had been completed – because of the control hub. The drones had been programmed with the schematics of Rhapsody and the main targets; the displacement drive and main power nacelles attached to the rear of her. The drones AI would quickly learn what was needed and, if Condor must enter the fight, they could be quickly transferred to autonomous operation and continue their mission. The flight of eight Darts on Albatross was being held in reserve – their target was Blue. If it looked like Rhapsody was going to be able to break through, the Darts were to inflict as much damage on the docking area as possible.

The second phase began when the other two ships arrived; all would converge on Rhapsody and, using the drones, give Valiant time to use her main weapon. The belief was that Slingshot was the most effective way to stop Sarclan and everyone hoped it was true. Now, with five minutes until the estimated time of Rhapsody's arrival, activity ceased and everything was in position. The minutes ticked slowly by when the old comm signal again energised.

The brief message told Aaron what had happened and he spoke to his crew, 'It seems our compatriots on the station had some success. Rhapsody will be delayed for a couple of hours while repairs are made to the dock entrance.'

That was music to the ears of the hub commander, Captain Radchak. He had demonstrated his mastery of the drones many times and had been the obvious choice for the job. JT had enthusiastically agreed, remembering the demonstrations Radchak had given on the range on a number of occasions.

Piloting a drone was not as easy as some thought; with no physical input, a pilot's *sixth sense* was acutely missing. To minimise this, each pilot and sensor operator sat in a simulator, their heads and faces hidden by the virtual reality equipment. Vast amounts of data were instantly transferred from the drone to the two operators in the simulator and, while it was only a digital representation of what the drone was doing, it did give some of the *feel* back to the crew.

As if on cue, Rhapsody reinserted into normal space, albeit a couple of hundred thousand kilometres further out than expected. She showed the results of travelling without adequate deflector coverage and even with reshaping and extending the lateral fields; the front of the ship had sustained considerable damage. Also, the results of the explosive decompression on levels ten and fifteen were amazing — how she had managed to stay together was a mystery. Two huge sections of the hull were missing, obviously the only thing holding it together were force fields — this was a major repair job.

Condor was on continuous communication monitoring and soon had the correct frequency and protocol for Sarclan's comms. It was clear he was not pleased at the thought of delays. His words were less than complimentary and he demanded two things: he wanted any and all of their defensive forces despatched immediately to cover his ship; and that the station commander find out what actually happened. Eugene Sarclan didn't believe in coincidence.

'Captain,' Solomon's voice called over the comm unit, 'What defence do they have?'

'We really don't know but, what we do know is they have some mark one darts… very old and only ten of them… about a dozen armed shuttles, again old and… ' Aaron was frantically searching a database, 'there is a record of some drones being sent here only a few weeks ago.'

'Great! If they aren't already prepped and spun up, it will take them at least twenty minutes to get ready,' Sol sounded excited. 'We need to go now! If we can convince Sarclan that we are friendlies, we may get close enough to disable his displacement drive.'

'Your call Sol,' Aaron answered.

Sol surveyed his team: forty people sitting two abreast in their simulators.

'Ok Ladies and Gents, let's party!' He then pressed the execute icon on his console and started the battle. The twenty Mark 4 Dart Remote Operated Vehicles – drones – began a sequential power up and, while this took more time, it would mask where they were – after all, they were supposed to be despatched from Blue. The power up only took a few extra minutes and the twenty drones were on their way. They formed a cone formation and sped toward Rhapsody just as three large armed shuttles exited Blue's main hangar.

The two groups merged with the shuttles taking the lead – so far the ruse was working. The five minute it took for drones and the Rhapsody defence group to meet was essential for the drone's operation. They constantly updated information from sensors, both on board and from the remote probes Aaron had launched. Condor had also begun to generate a dampening field, disabling communication from Blue and enabling her comm officer to imitate Blue's system.

As the drones arrived, Sarclan ordered Blue to have them form a close shield and the larger shuttles to stand off deeper, effectively giving him a two layered defence, exactly as Sol had hoped.

'Ok team, now we start to earn our pay,' he commented as his fingers ran over the icon pad of his console. Suddenly sensors on Condor and Rhapsody went into overdrive as more ships appeared in the area. To the rear of Rhapsody, a very large signature was detected which matched a Coalition Alron class battle cruiser. No sooner had it appeared when two more signatures were detected flanking Rhapsody, this time they were identified as Morgan class frigates. Almost immediately, the signals faded and as Sol hoped, Sarclan took the bait.

Pandemonium broke out on the bridge of Rhapsody. The appearance of the three new ships was something unexpected and the equally sudden disappearance indicated to Sarclan that they had some sort of cloaking device, similar to his old Krell KL10n's.

'Someone get a line on those fucking ships! Blue, get more ships out here **NOW**!' Sarclan screamed into his comm unit. 'Turn those drones around, form a defensive shield between us and those ships!'

The last command was just what was needed, the drones immediately obeyed Sarclan's order, except three that were aft of Rhapsody. These were slightly different from the other seventeen drones – they had a heavy Thermionic charge attached to their main reactors. Their job was to completely disable Rhapsody and with a wicked smile on his face, Sol pressed another icon.

'Suck on this Sarclan.' Immediately, the other seven drones momentarily appeared on the sensor screens, again imitating much larger vessels.

Sarclan was trapped, or so he thought.

'How the fucking hell did these get here? I thought our Coalition agent had sent them elsewhere?' At the same time, Captain Solomon Radchak initiated his final act in this drama. He sent the three drones surging toward Rhapsody at full power.

'Shit!' was all Nakamura could yell as he desperately worked on the icon pad. 'Eugene, those ships are decoys, the real threat is from the drones.'

'Bullshit! The drones are from Blue. In any case, they can't hurt something this size.'

Nakamura was furiously working on the console before him, watching the small dots on his screen getting ever closer to Rhapsody. The first drone began firing all its weapons at once, the energy release fatally overloading the defence grid at the rear of the ship. Again, Rhapsody's design helped the attackers – the rear of the vessel was very lightly shielded and quickly failed.

The drone slammed into the main engine nacelle, with devastating result. The entire nacelle was torn apart and Rhapsody lost all motive power and began yawing violently. If it wasn't for the inertial dampeners, everyone on the ship would have been flung around like rag dolls.

The second drone sped toward the displacement drive nacelle, all weapons firing, but the trajectory was bad and the last remaining defence pod at the rear of Rhapsody opened up with spectacular result. The drone vaporised in a massive brilliant white flash.

'Go to displacement, Nakamura, go to fucking displacement!' Sarclan shouted, over the shrieks of multiple alarms.

'We can't, the displacement field would tear the station apart!' Nakamura yelled in reply.

'I don't care... just get us out of here now!' Sarclan's tone was maniacal and his hand was resting on his side arm. Nakamura leapt from his console to the engineering console, backhanding the operator out of the way, his expert fingers working quickly on the icon pad. The indicators started to show increases in the core flux as more plasma was fed into the field generator. A few more seconds was all he needed – just a few more.

Sarclan watched in horror as the third small dot sped toward the displacement nacelle, its weapons firing incessantly; suddenly it seemed to change course. At the same time the last rear defence pod indicator blinked and went dark – the displacement nacelle was intact.

'Now Nakamura, now!' he screamed.

The displacement field was building. He could see the tell-tale shimmering in front of the ship, but failed to notice one ship, then another, appear behind him.

aliant reinserted into normal space just behind the battle.

JT had charged the Sling Shot while in transit but he now saw his quarry starting to initiate its displacement field.

'Guns fire, shoot the bastard!' he commanded.

Helen Tradeski – as usual – was at the weapons command post. She had very little time to gauge any of the sight before her. It took a few seconds for the sensors and targeting systems to re-adjust to normal space – after exiting the worm hole. She would only have one chance and she knew it had better work. She manually lined up the target and tapped the initiate icon. Immediately, three seventy five millimetre projectiles leapt from the ship at point nine light speed.

Rhapsody was beginning to shimmer, indicating she was entering the displacement field when the first projectile struck. It missed the displacement nacelle but impacted just ahead of the main drive nacelle attachment point and simply blew the main drive off Rhapsody. The second slammed into the main hull slightly off to the left of the displacement nacelle and blew a hole clear through the hull. The third, a few milliseconds later, found its target just as Rhapsody was starting to become transparent. The result was immediate

– Rhapsody's displacement field immediately collapsed as the nacelle disintegrated – the resultant force thrusting her toward Blue.

The destruction on Rhapsody was massive – all main power was lost, including dampeners. The ship was yawing and rolling violently and anything that was not securely tied down was being thrown around the ship – crew members were slammed into the sides of their stations with deadly results. On the bridge, Sarclan had managed to resume his seat and fastened his restraints. A young crew member flew toward him, frantically grabbing the side of the command chair, her eyes showing relief that she had managed to stop herself.

Her relief was short lived as Sarclan smashed her fingers forcing her to let go. Her screams filled the room until she crashed into the forward view screen and the sound stopped. Nakamura watched the scene in horror. Now that the gravity system had failed, the young woman's body was thrown around the bridge again and again each time the ship moved violently and a bloody trail followed her. Two more crew lost their grip and suffered a similar fate; he turned his face from the carnage only to look at the view screen. Filling it was the hull of Blue and there was nothing that could be done – four seconds later Rhapsody of the Stars slammed into Cordoba Blue with incredible force.

The impact fused the ship and the station, their outer hulls melting into one another forming a new homogenous mass. The bridge was seventy metres back from Rhapsody's bow which offered it some protection. When the ship finally stopped, it was only three metres from Blue's hull. As if by some grotesque twist of fate, Sarclan and Nakamura had survived but the rest of the bridge crew were now no more than a bloodied pulp. Nakamura stood, dazed and horrified at the scene before him.

'Nakamura, we live to fight on. Come on… the escape pods are still operational!' Sarclan yelled as he opened one of the escape pod doors. 'We can use these to get onto Blue.' Nakamura shook his head and stumbled toward the pod closest to him. He opened the door and climbed in just as he heard Sarclan's pod exit the bay. Nakamura followed him and they both dropped toward the station.

***

Petra confirmed the ship's status, quietly confident that all had gone to plan. Everything was ok, the ship now operating in true sub space.

'Well done, Man-Nix,' Mondrac complimented her. Tocmal chirped in, 'This little ship handles very well.'

They now had seven minutes till the next insertion which would take them through to the eleventh realm – from there another two jumps, and just over four hours, to the tenth realm and Tocmal's home planet of Reglaos. Petra re-calculated the next jump and programmed the nav computer. Seven minutes later, the little yacht glowed as the jump drive activated and reinserted into the eleventh realm. It was instantaneous with no sensation, just the transition from total darkness of sub space to a star filled vista of the realm's normal space. They were travelling at 0.5 of light, and had 46 minutes before their next jump. Again, Petra programmed the nav computer and sat back.

'I think we have time for some coffee before we jump again. Mondrac, you take the con and I'll rustle up a brew.' She stood and looked over to Tocmal who was nodding as best as he could, he had developed quite a taste for coffee.

She returned ten minutes later with a large pot of coffee, milk and three mugs. She placed these in the dispenser beside the command chair and poured each a brew: black for Mondrac, white for herself and black with eight spoons of sugar for Tocmal. They sat quietly, enjoying the coffee and a few minutes of down time.

She watched Tocmal drink his coffee. Reglaons didn't have a mouth instead, they had a tube like organ that they ingested their food with and, with liquids it worked similar to a straw. She had developed a deep fondness for the little guy with his very brusque, businesslike manner. Deep in her psyche she knew he and his people would be strong allies and firm friends.

Tocmal had been tasked with running the sensors and tactical array of the yacht, more for something to do as it was capable of automatic operation. Suddenly, the Bubble energised and they all leapt to their stations. The image cleared and stabilised with Junior at the centre. Ahead of the ship were three smaller shapes and behind them were two more.

'Tocmal, can you identify them?' Petra asked.

'Galdoran fighters I believe you call them,' he replied. 'But they cannot operate this far out on their own.' What passed for fingers on the end of his four arms flew over the console more effectively than Petra thought possible. 'They must have a mothership close by.' The tactical hologram showed the five small vessels converging on the yacht.

'Shields,' Petra called and Mondrac, who was at weapons control, raised the ship's defensive shields, at the same time energising the weapons systems. 'How long before they are in weapons range?'

'Twenty five of the units you use,' Tocmal replied. Petra added this to the jump timer on her console.

'That's a difference of six minutes between then and our next jump.'

The problem they faced was one of space/time-disruption – they had mapped their trip to coincide with a number of things, primarily arriving on Reglaos at a certain time. If they changed their insertion points, they changed everything and by huge margins – they were trapped between the proverbial rock and a hard place. They could jump now – but that could mean hundreds of light years difference in their planned insertion into the tenth realm – or they could continue and fight their way to their programmed point. Petra had a hard decision to make.

'Mondrac, I thought only Eldora had access to inter realm drive?'

'Correct, in a way. The eleventh realm has always been a barrier; it is very hard to navigate. That is why we Eldorans have been the only ones to achieve it, why?'

'Well, if that's true, how did our friends get here?'

'Good question Man-Nix,' Mondrac spoke quietly. 'Either they have somehow gained access to the drive and navigation technology, or some Eldoran clan has sided with them. Regardless, not a good situation and this is the second time we have encountered them in this realm.'

Tocmal interrupted. 'They are trying to contact their mother ship... I have generated a blocking field, but it won't hold for long.' Petra's mind was racing, what would Aaron do? Then she remembered the story of JT's action at Zyralin 4, a wicked smile crossing her lips. She reached the controls and increased power to full. The nimble little vessel surged forward, the gap between the forward ships and the yacht closing rapidly – timing was everything now.

'Mondrac, are the rear weapons energised?'

'Yes, Man-Nix. What are you doing?'

'A little thing I call the Zyralin manoeuvre, courtesy of one John Thomas Abraham the fourth. We are closing now at a combined speed of one point four light, correct?'

'Correct.'

She consulted her console and did a few calculations. 'In exactly six minutes and twenty seconds, we will jump to displacement six point five for four milliseconds. When we reinsert, fire the rear weapons at these coordinates... fire everything, got it?'

'I understand, but what do you hope to accomplish?' Mondrac asked.

'I'm sorry, no time to explain... you just need to trust me here. If this works, we should give them a little surprise.' Petra busied herself energising the displacement drive, setting it for an instant insertion, something she had never done before. In fact, the only person she had ever heard of doing it was young JT – she just hoped it worked.

A third timer appeared on her screen adding to: the other two. One timer was for their next jump insertion, the other for intercepting the three ships in front of them and now this last one was for the time to displacement initiation.

'I have set the weapons coordinates as you asked and tied the firing sequence to coincide with the displacement field collapsing. I don't think I can react fast enough to do it myself,' Mondrac informed her.

'Twelve seconds,' Petra called. They could see the enemy

clearly now through the view screen, their ships getting bigger each second and closing at almost four hundred and twenty thousand kilometres a second. The forward shields glowed as the Galdoran ships fired. 'Don't return,' Petra commanded. 'Three seconds... two... one'

What happened next seemed to be in slow motion. The Galdoran ships became almost transparent, the stars behind them appearing to merge with the small vessels – as though they were in two places at the one time – in front of the three fighters and behind them.

To Mondrac, it felt like being suspended in time and space – a very strange feeling. Almost instantly, the forward vision changed and the three Galdoran ships were no longer there. At that exact moment the rear weapons all fired at once.

All four torpedos found their targets, two impacting on the ship to the port rear quarter of the yacht vaporising it instantly. The ship to the starboard quarter was hit directly on its main reactor nacelle, losing all power. The blasters and disrupters concentrated on the central ship, its shields flaring a brilliant white before collapsing and allowing the directed energy from the yacht's weapons to deliver the killing blow. The yacht had not escaped unscathed. Its shield capacity was down to forty percent, too low for any more encounters without recharging; but the exchange had left the Galdorans with a bloody nose and three less fighters.

Tocmal stood in silence, observing the carnage they had just wrought. Finally he spoke 'If this is A-Bra-Ham's pleasure craft, it will be interesting to see what his battle craft can do.'

This brought a chuckle to them all. They were still on course but were now going to reach their insertion point earlier than expected. Petra slowed the ship trying to compensate for the extra distance they had just covered. The Bubble showed the two remaining Galdoran vessels slowing at the debris field, finally stopping. 'I am sorry, they just contacted their mother ship; the field was not strong enough.'

'Doesn't matter now… we'll reach our insertion point in a few seconds; it looks like we will reach the Tenth earlier than we wanted to,' replied Petra indicating the last timer, now showing six seconds. The jump drive powered up and the yacht vanished from the eleventh realm.

The sub space jump between the eleventh and tenth realm took the yacht only thirty five minutes but when it arrived they couldn't recognise any of the programmed reference points. Tocmal started to scan the sector, widening his search each cycle. It took a good fifteen minutes till he finally looked up, his head shaking.

'Not where we should be, not by one hundred and twenty parsecs,' he groaned. The early jump had caused them to arrive in a totally different part of space to where they intended. 'What can this vessel maintain in hyperspace?'

Petra thought for a while. 'Displacement twelve for extended periods, possibly a little more.' She was racking her brain, trying to remember if Kate had told her anything else on her shake down flight and totally forgetting the increased capabilities the Reglaon engineers had given the ship on its last visit to the realm.

Tocmal started doing the maths, the buzz and clicking coming from him not being translated by Petra's enhancements. After ten minutes of feverish activity he lifted his head.

'This is a disaster. We will need to run at displacement six for almost twenty of your years to reach Reglaos. We have to use the jump drive, it is the only way.'

Petra started her own calculations and soon had an answer but not one anyone wanted to hear.

'Our problem will be fuel: the yacht only has a small antimatter generator and the jump drive uses energy in huge amounts. So far our jumps have taken almost seventy two percent of our supply. We could jump once again but we would not have enough reserves to complete the journey and then, if we run into any more Galdoran welcomes, we'd be in deep shit. She's designed as a pleasure boat not an interdimensional warship.'

Mondrac stood and paced around the small bridge, finally speaking.

'How long to generate sufficient antimatter for our journey and for any possible altercations we may have on the way?'

Again both Tocmal and Petra worked at their consoles. The main source for making antimatter was hydrogen atoms, stored in an inert form and the generator converted it to antimatter plasma which was used to power the ship's energy and drive systems. The only other source was free hydrogen atoms that can be found in space – it was possible to collect these and feed them into the generator to fuel the conversion. To complete their calculations, they needed to know what free hydrogen was available and this varied greatly throughout space. Tocmal sent his sensor findings to Petra who fed them into her console. The answer was worse than expected.

'In this region, we would need nearly four days at full production to replenish our fuel,' Petra announced, 'there's just not enough free hydrogen here.'

While all this was happening, Mondrac was searching

through the scans that Tocmal had made when they arrived. Finally he leaned back, a smile on his face. 'Please check this. Seven light years on heading three zero four by zero two seven, there seems to be a hydrogen rich nebula... can you both confirm?'

Petra and Tocmal consulted their consoles again and agreed. 'If we used the jump drive, we could be there in moments. Given the concentrations of hydrogen there, how long to re fuel?'

Petra was already working on this and had her answer quickly. 'Six hours to full supply.' She returned her attention to the console and programmed the jump into the ship's nav system. The drive powered up and they disappeared again, reappearing a few minutes later exactly on target. She immediately started the generator and opened the intake hatch, extending an ionising force field to capture the hydrogen – nothing to do now but wait. Tocmal busied himself with the sensors, gathering as much data as he could on the surrounding nebula.

'We have not penetrated this far from Reglaos. I would like to take back as much information as I can.' His clicks, buzzes and wheezes sounded joyful. Petra went to check the generator and the plasma storage. The hydrogen was more abundant than they had predicted so their stay would be shortened by at least an hour. Feeling very pleased, she returned to the bridge where Tocmal was still recording sensor scans. Two hours later, he started clicking furiously, the sounds too fast for Petra to decode.

'Slowly, please Tocmal,' she requested.

'My apologies but I think I have found a Galdoran outpost here in our realm,' he repeated slowly, 'Even after the Mother Queen warned them, still they defy our laws.' Petra paralleled her console to his and reviewed his findings.

The readings were from a small M class planet, at the extreme limit of their sensors. There could be a mistake but it did seem that there were energy signatures that were very similar to Galdoran ships and faint life signs on the planet. Petra called Mondrac to the bridge to confer the findings.

'Why out here?' he mused. 'There is nothing for them to gain.' He shook his head. 'Unless... ... .' His voice trailed off as he again began to enhance the sensor scans.

'If they have inter-realm drive capability, why would they need to work with a nut job like Sarclan?' Petra asked.

'Man-Nix, as you have found out, travelling between realms takes incredible amounts of energy. I don't think they have the technology they need to fully exploit your realm, but, if there was a permanent breach, or a gateway... well... that is another matter altogether. No, I think they need this Sar-Clan more than he needs them.' Mondrac finished and stared at the screen. After quite some time, he asked 'Man-Nix, how is the power conversion going?'

Petra switched her console back and replied. 'Great, another thirty minutes and we'll be at full capacity.'

'Good, I think we shall need it. I have been studying the signatures from those ships: there are five smaller vessels, probably Malor class mainly used as transports. They pose no real threat to us, but there are two very large units, probably Klarim class battleships, with no other purpose than war; now these we should avoid at all costs. They would, as you say, swat us like a fly. Also, they have sensors that are far more powerful than ours so if we can see them from here, they will see our energy trail as soon as we leave this nebula. Tocmal, can you please calculate the jumps needed to get us back to Reglaos from here? We may need to get back urgently.'

Tocmal set about the task. Petra sat quietly, watching her companions and reflecting on how much had changed in only a very short time. Her day dream was shattered by the proximity alarm screaming over the bridge.

'What is that?' Mondrac cried. The sound was so insistent no one could ignore it.

Petra was back at her console, frantically searching for the cause of the sound. There, only five thousand kilometres off the port quarter, was a small spidery looking craft; she put it on the main viewer.

Tocmal's clicks and buzzes increased. 'It's a Galdoran sensor probe. They send them out to patrol when their ship's are stationary. So far, it has not detected us, but if it gets any closer, even our hull coating may not hide us.'

'They may be scanning the nebula, as we did, as a source of energy. It may not even be searching for a vessel.' Mondrac watched the small craft. 'Man-Nix, can you slowly collapse the force field? If it detects our collection of hydrogen, or if it detects a sudden change in the ionisation field, it will investigate, and we do *not* want that.'

Petra busied herself at the controls. Slowly and deliberately she lowered the field, at the same time reducing the chamber's intake. She was trying to make the whole event as seamless as possible.

'Man-nix, how much energy do we now have?' Mondrac asked.

'Just over ninety five percent.'

'I don't think we will get much more... our little friend seems to have taken an interest in us.' Mondrac pointed to the probe which was now moving slowly but deliberately toward them. 'I am also detecting an increase in the energy output on one of those large vessels we saw. I would suggest that now is a good time to leave.' Tocmal worked the nav console and sent the data to Petra, who programmed the jump drive.

'I am not an expert in nebula science, but what is the make-up of this one? Hydrogen we know, but what would happen if we jumped in here?' Petra was concerned. Her initial readings had shown large areas of methane and oxygen as well as hydrogen. If they were all combined with a concussive event, who knows what might happen. Her gut told her that she should clear the nebula before engaging in doing anything, so she compensated the insertion parameters. She didn't wait for an answer and initiated the docking thrusters – cold pressure jets. The yacht started to move slowly toward the edge of the nebula. 'What are the readings outside?' she called to her companions.

'Hydrogen falling, some methane but negligible oxygen, you are now safe to engage the main drive.' Mondrac confirmed. Petra initialised the main drive and the ship leapt forward. At the same time, she directed a low yield shot from the disrupters at the probe. She hit it, but too late – it had already sent its data back to the mothership.

'I detected a displacement initialisation. I think they are coming to investigate.' Mondrac called.

Petra watched the timer counting down.

Three... two...

'Stop, do not jump!' Mondrac called.

Petra hit the cancel icon less than a second before the drive activated. 'Please tell me you have a good reason for this?' she asked.

Mondrac switched his console screen to the main viewer. There before them was the distinct image of an Exodus Gate. 'I think we now know why they have defied the Mother Queen. We have found the location of their other gate.'

'Mondrac that may be the case, but if we don't get out of here it won't make any difference.'

'Yes, but I would like a closer look at this if that's possible.' Mondrac put the feed from his console onto the main screen.

Petra fed the coordinates into the nav system, calculated a course and programmed the displacement drive. 'This will get us to within one million kilometres and give us an instant jump window,' she said as she initialised the drive.

Seventeen minutes later Junior rematerialized at the programmed location, fortunately behind a small lifeless planetoid. Immediately, Petra launched a sensor probe, programmed to head toward the gate. Very slowly, she moved Junior out from behind the cover. The gate came into view – even at this distance it was impressive. Mondrac worked at his console, not even looking at the structure. Tocmal searched for any Galdoran craft and located another twelve.

'Galdoran scum, we will show you what happens when you defy us!' Tocmal buzzed.

As he spoke, the inner ring of the gate started to glow, indicating it was preparing to initiate a worm hole. The centre transformed to a translucent fog and three ships came through. Petra had the recognition program working on the identity of them, as a bad feeling started to fill her body.

'This can't be right?' She spoke to no one in particular and re-confirmed the findings. 'Not possible,' she said, shaking her head before turning to Mondrac. 'Two are Krell... old KL10N cruisers. The other is one of the coalitions' newest ships, the Otamah. What are they doing here?'

'I don't think we can wait to find out,' Tocmal indicated toward the Bubble. Their probe had been detected and two Galdoran cruisers were following its drive trail, directly toward them.

'I agree,' Petra said as she engaged the jump drive. Moments later Junior vanished, leaving no trace for the Galdorans to follow.

Their insertion went smoothly as they entered sub space. Another uneventful twenty five minutes and back to normal space for seven and a half minutes and back into subspace for the last and longest jump – forty eight minutes.

'I do not... what are your words... feel *right*.' Tocmal announced.

Mondrac went to the small creature. 'Are you unwell?'

'No, nothing like that... this has been too easy. That cruiser must have known we were there and, if they can jump between realms, they can follow us now. No, I think we should be ready, but I don't know what for.' Tocmal's warning sent the hairs on the back of Petra's neck into a vertical stance; he was right, it had been very easy. She leapt into action. Shields could not be raised in sub space but weapons could be energised and shield generators brought to standby. Thankfully the yacht had a basic absorption field, and the storage system was almost empty. That would allow them to safely absorb just a few energy blasts.

'Tocmal,' Petra called, 'can you bring up the space where

we will materialise?' He busied himself and finally let her know it was ready. 'Put it in the Bubble.'

Tocmal had been an extremely quick learner and had adapted to the alien controls very easily. The Bubble changed and coalesced into a view of where they would re-enter – just over four million kilometres from Reglaos – much too far if there was a welcome committee. She studied the scene for a while before starting calculations for the displacement drive.

'Tocmal, do your people have anything like our communication system?'

The small insectoid rubbed one of his arm appendages against his head and answered. 'Yes we do have something similar.'

'Can they receive things like our burst transmissions?'

'Yes, but we will need to structure it correctly... give me your message.' Tocmal replied.

'We only have ten minutes.' Petra busied herself writing the message.

Tocmal worked at a blistering pace, reconfiguring the main transmitter and eight minutes later announced, 'That is the best I can do. I have no way of testing it, but it should work.'

Petra sent the message to him already translated to his language. He read it and buzzed a little, 'you are a most ingenious companion... and certainly imaginative.' He entered it into the system, 'ready to transmit.'

'The instant we re-enter... Ok?' Tocmal nodded his understanding.

'Here we go... re-entry in five, four, three, two, and one.'

With a minimum of disturbance, the small vessel appeared

in normal space, but only for an instant as Petra engaged the displacement drive. The couple of seconds in normal space was too much – there arrayed before them were four large Galdoran warships. As one, they opened fire, a massive barrage that would have destroyed any ship, given the time to hit it. The barrage wasn't accurate – the enemy had no way of knowing exactly where they would re-enter. But with that amount of firepower unleashed, accuracy was not important – one of the shots had to hit. And it did, or rather four did. The first three were negated by the absorption field but the fourth caught the ship just behind the bridge. Even with the new Reglaon coating, the hull distorted under the impact. The damage was not enough to stop her from entering the displacement field, but bad enough to know they needed help and a good repair dock.

All Petra could hope for was that Tocmal's message got through and would be acted on. She sealed all bulkheads and energised an emergency force field to reinforce the hull. The displacement trip was a dangerous gamble – they would re-insert only a few thousand kilometres from Reglaos. She told her companions of her decision and they agreed – she silently hoped that the Galdorans had not taken the planet over.

Mondrac read her thoughts. 'Don't worry, our friends may be small but they are ferocious fighters. They have never been invaded and rarely defeated in battle. I don't think Galdor would be foolish enough to tackle them openly.' As they re-inserted, they were surrounded by vessels of Reglaos – the largest less than half the size of the Galdoran ships, but still several times larger than the yacht.

Tocmal was buzzing and clicking over the comm system.

'Man-Nix, please follow that vessel moving in front of us;

it will guide us to the repair dock.' They fell into formation and followed the lead ship toward a large mushroom shaped station in geosynchronous orbit. As they approached, the side of the station opened and what appeared to be an arm extended toward them and began unfolding – it formed an enclosure that Petra remembered from her last visit. She cut power and a tractor beam caught the ship and moved it carefully to the now complete dock.

An umbilical snaked toward the yacht and with remarkable accuracy, aligned and connected to the external power port in the nose. 'We studied your power system and connections when you were last here. We thought it would be good if you could have a place to recharge and resupply when you visited... we just didn't think it would be so soon.' The clicks Tocmal made were his closest approximation of a chuckle.

The dock structure now fully enveloped the yacht and, as soon as it had sealed, an atmosphere was generated and dozens of Reglaons were swarming over the hull. Tocmal issued instructions with a great deal of theatre and finally turned to Petra.

'Man-Nix, our engineers believe they can repair your ship, but it will take some time. I think we should leave and allow them to work.'

'How long will it take?' Petra asked.

Tocmal thought a while, 'In your time about eight hours, maybe ten. While that is happening, we should meet with our leaders to understand what has happened while we were away.' His suggestion made sense – the presence of Galdoran war ships in this realm was a great concern.

Petra and Mondrac agreed and followed their small companion out the airlock. She took a few minutes to view the damage. It was quite extensive, far more than she had first thought. A large portion of the top of the hull was buckled and deformed, if it weren't for the new coating, Petra didn't believe the ship would have survived.

'Seems every time we come here our ship is damaged,' Petra mused.

'We should go and let our crew make the repairs.' Tocmal turned and led them to an airlock at the end of the dock; mated to it and waiting for them was a shuttle. As soon as they entered, the door closed and the shuttle left the dock for the planet's surface. Petra looked up out of the shuttle's clear canopy she could see the dock and surrounding it were twelve large vessels.

'That seems a lot of protection for our little yacht,' she commented as she touched the clear cover above her head.

'Our leader ordered it so,' Tocmal replied. 'We do not want anything to happen to you while you are under our protection.'

'Tocmal I need to get to our embassy urgently,' Mondrac insisted. 'The information I have is now critical. I must send a message to the Twelfth Realm.'

Tocmal realised his friend was very serious and instructed the pilot to land at the Eldoran Embassy. 'Why the urgency; after all, we know the location of the gate... we will mobilise our forces and destroy it.'

'No!' Mondrac shouted, 'We cannot destroy it, it is too late for that. We must capture *both* gates: the one here and the other in the Twelfth Realm.'

'Why? If we destroy it, it will stop the invasion,' Petra pointed out.

'For the moment,' Mondrac added, 'but we have just seen

that vessels are coming from the Twelfth Realm. How many have gone through? How many of Sar-Clan's vessels are already here and how many of Galdor are on the other side? No, we must capture them if we have any hope of restoring the balance.' His voice was both pleading and affirmative, but his logic was sound.

aaron dropped his comms interference field and JT hailed the station.

'Cordoba Blue, this is Captain JT Abraham of the Coalition Space Corps. Stand down all your weapons systems. Comply, or I will open fire.' Strong words, but they had the desired effect.

Captain Abraham, this is Station Commander, Shar Stevens, a female voice replied. *We have no operational weapons... all shuttles will comply with your orders. Please, we are in a mess here, can you assist?*

JT confirmed their assistance just as another four Freebooter ships materialised. Aaron conferred with the captains of the newly arrived ships and they formed a deep cordon around Blue – the drones formed a roving barrier closer to the station. He was satisfied that they were secure enough to start a rescue operation and, more importantly, confirm Sarclan's fate.

His efforts were interrupted by JT. *Aaron; Sarclan's six cruisers are here.*

Aaron checked his readout and ran back onto the bridge. The Bubble confirmed JT's report: now showing the six old converted KL10n cruisers heading toward Blue.

'Open a channel', Aaron commanded, 'and hail them.' Though old, these ships were still very formidable and, with the current situation, could easily change the outcome of this battle.

Freebooter vessels, this is Captain Garrick of the Sedition cruiser Eugene... stand down or be destroyed! Sarclan's vanity was evident, naming this ship after himself. *As you can see, we are much more than a match for you. Stand down or we will open fire.*

Aaron's heart sank a little at this. They had very little chance of doing anything more than inflicting a small amount damage if they fought on, but he was damned if he was going to surrender.

A new voice came over the comm system: one of Sarclan's agents on Blue who inadvertently gave them the reprieve they needed. *Garrick be careful... they have several cloaked Coalition cruisers supporting them.*

Sol's ruse was still working it seemed. There were now only three of the drones still on station as decoys. Aaron decided to run the bluff again. He instructed Sol to make the cruisers appear. As commanded, three large vessels appeared on the Sedition sensor screen – just as quickly they disappeared – then the drones were moved to another location to reappear again. The sensors on the Sedition ships only saw a number of larger signatures appearing and just as quickly disappearing, reinforcing the illusion that they faced a much larger and more powerful force.

'Now, Captain, what were you saying?' Aaron responded. 'I suggest you power your weapons down, or face the consequences. Those are only a few of the ships now targeting you... your choice.' He waited, the seconds ticking by. 'Your decision, Garrick, I am tired of waiting.'

This was the most dangerous bluff Aaron had ever played and, just as his nerve was starting to waiver, another much larger signature appeared in the Bubble. Now Aaron smiled and initiated the internal com. 'Sol... now might be a good time to let him see a few more of our cruisers.

Sol repeated the sensor trick, this time increasing the drone's false signature to give the impression they were powering weapons. Seconds ticked by while everyone waited.

'Decision time, Garrick... power down or be destroyed, your call.'

Garrick responded *Agreed Freebooter, we are powering down*.

As one, the six cruisers dropped their shields and began powering their weapons down. Suddenly, a new voice screamed over the comm system.

Garrick you fucking idiot, this is Sarclan! They have no cruisers. Those images are only drones... destroy them all!

At the sound of that voice, Garrick and the other commanders began to reverse their power down order. It was now or never for the Freebooters. As soon as the cruisers had arrived they had been designated as targets and each was assigned to a specific Freebooter ship.

As one, they commenced firing on the Sedition vessels. Without the advantage of full shields, the Sedition vessels were vulnerable but, even with reduced shield capacity, they remained a formidable adversary.

JT directed a full spread of torpedos at his assigned ship followed by three shots from the Sling Shot. Six torpedos sped toward their target — two were destroyed by the shields but the other four got through.

Two torpedos impacted close to the bridge exploding in spectacular fashion though causing little actual damage. The other two caused minor breaches in the upper hull plating, damage which was easily contained. The Sedition ship returned fire, but Valiant was already at speed and easily evaded the attack.

The three anti matter charges from the Sling Shot were a different matter altogether – they impacted at the rear upper section of the cruiser's hull with devastating effect. The main power system was compromised and a large section of the hull was vaporised. The cruiser was now powerless and nothing but a drifting hulk.

Condor was engaged with Garrick's cruiser and had moved into a better firing position. Aaron ordered a full spread; his blasters and disrupters opened up and simultaneously six torpedos were launched. At half the speed of light, they smashed into the depleted shield of the ship. The resulting explosions were spectacular, but did no damage. Garrick returned fire and Condor's shields blazed in defence.

'Shields at ninety percent, absorption bank now at twenty percent,' Dave Carter called out.

'Dave, hit them again before they can fully raise their shields,' Aaron commanded.

Condor returned fire with another full spread including several shots from the plasma cannon, this time with better results. The torpedos were again stopped by the shields but the difference this time was that they overloaded the shield generator and it shut down.

Dave kept the blasters and disruptors firing; an almost continuous stream of raw energy smashing into the cruiser's hull. It was the discharge from the plasma cannon that turned the tide. Even with its thick plating, the hull of the cruiser could not withstand the onslaught. Hull plates buckled and finally collapsed. A large section of the port side exploded and opened a massive breach in the hull.

On board the cruiser it was chaotic, crew rushing to seal breaches, fighting fires, and the screams of the injured echoing in their heads. Bulkheads were sealing and fires were being controlled.

Garrick was screaming at his weapons officer. 'I don't care what the consequences are, fire the damn torpedo!'

The weapons officer complied and a sleek torpedo leapt out of its launch tube and flew toward Condor. The impact was massive. A huge brilliant white fireball blotted out everything else.

Dave Carter looked at his console. 'Shit, what was that?' 'Shields down to twenty percent, absorption bank at one hundred and ten percent. We need to drain some energy... another hit and we'll be history.'

Multiple alarms were screaming and consoles indicated a number of system warnings, Condor wasn't having the fight all its own way.

'Hit that cruiser with everything... don't stop till it's destroyed!' Aaron commanded.

Dave complied and Condor returned fire again.

Aaron looked to his engineer, 'What just hit us, Dianna?'

Condor was now firing continuously, all the energy from its absorption battery diverted back through the blaster and disruptor banks. Dianne turned to Bill Croaker and together they worked the console, desperately trying to identify the weapon that had almost destroyed their ship.

Croaker called out. 'Trisidium charge… that was a Trisidium charge… our shields can't withstand another!'

The massive amount of energy now slamming into the cruiser was taking effect. The plasma cannon scored another two massive direct hits and more of the cruiser's hull was breached.

Suddenly the old cruiser started to yaw violently, all control now lost. She was dead in space with her main power gone and all weapon systems off line, but still Condor kept up its continuous barrage. Finally Aaron called a halt, realising that there was no point in wasting any more energy. The old cruiser was now just another piece of space junk.

Elsewhere the battle was more even. Both sides had lost two ships but the remaining cruisers were now back to full power and the tide was starting to turn. JT had inflicted some damage on another cruiser by using the same tactic he did at the range, but now they were using a random shield modulation and they were hitting back.

Valiant had one advantage: manoeuvrability — she was quick and could turn on the spot. But, she had one weakness: she was using energy at an alarming rate. If they didn't conclude the battle soon, they'd run out of reserves.

The old cruisers, on the other hand, had a huge generating capacity and just needed to hold out long enough for victory. It wasn't such an issue for the other Freebooter ships. Their endurance was legendary but they were not built as battle ships and the massive firepower of the cruisers was taking its toll.

Albatross hailing Condor… come in Condor. Steve Harris's voice rang out over Condor's comm system.

'Condor here, what's your situation Steve?' Aaron replied.

Not too bad, but we need to finish this soon if you get my drift? Steve sounded concerned. Albatross was twenty years older than Condor and due for a complete refit when she returned to Argos. Aaron knew her limitations too well. He also knew that some of the other Freebooter ships would be in the same situation.

The sedition cruisers had realised that the advantage was turning in their direction and re-grouped. They formed a tight star formation allowing them to interlink their shields, making them almost invulnerable – at least to the weapons assailing them.

***

The old comm link that Aaron had used to contact Anton crackled in his ear. *Mr Abraham, it seems things are not going too well. What can we do to help*?

'Doctor, I really don't know,' Aaron replied, 'Hang on… Sarclan appears to have survived… he's just sent a message from the station. Think you can find him? It might give us a chance.'

'We'll have a quick look and see if he wants some visitors. See you soon,' Anton replied. He turned to his companion. 'Come on Janice, we need to invite ourselves to the control room and have a chat with Sarclan.'

Luckily, Janice and Anton had been in the security pod when Sarclan's ship had impacted the station; as it ran through the centre of the sphere, it was undamaged in the crash. Anton consulted the schematics of the station; the main control room was in the upper hemisphere of the station, well away from the crash site.

'Quick, back into the pod, we've another fifty floors to cover!' He pushed Janice back into the waiting pod and closed the doors, entered the deck number into the control panel and the pod sped away.

'Ok Doctor, what happens when we get there? Do we just knock politely and ask Sarclan to come quietly?' Janice's voice was filled with sarcasm.

Anton thought for a moment. He checked his gear and took two grey throwing knives and hid them under the cuff of his shirt sleeves. 'Not a bad idea, but I don't think that'll work.'

'Really,' Janice was becoming annoyed at his flippancy. 'Anton this is serious, we need a *plan*.'

Anton smiled and replied, 'Don't worry, I've got one. You're still a ranking security officer so, what if you caught the saboteur who damaged the dock? Where would you take him?' He didn't wait for a reply, 'Straight to the boss himself... Sarclan. I will be your prisoner. We gain entry to the control room, take down any security guards and capture Sarclan. What could be easier?'

'Probably walking barefoot on the sun,' she retorted, but she knew he was right. It may be thin but it was simple and might just gain them access – there was no time for anything else. The pod had just stopped at the control room exit. Anton Alvaris might just be the most exasperating person she had ever met – how he'd survived this long, she didn't know.

There were two guards outside the control room. Janice handed her security ID to one of them who moved to a console mounted in an alcove to one side of the corridor. It seemed to take ages before the guard came back and gestured to his companion to let them in. The door opened and Janice pushed Anton through. Inside there were: another two guards with side arms only; the station commander and two assistants; Sarclan; and Nakamura.

Sarclan was sitting in the station command chair and Nakamura was working at a console to Anton's left. Two guards were flanking Sarclan in the centre of the room.

The room itself was divided into three levels: the lower was for minor operations and vacant at the moment; the second level was mainly for engineering and operations staff and was manned by the station commander and her assistants only. The room usually held thirty people but only seven were visible. Anton didn't like the set up – too many unknowns – but they only had this one chance.

'So, Commander Barker, you have apprehended the saboteur?' Sarclan rose as he spoke, the two guards moving to either side of him. They were about ten metres from Anton and Janice. Anton glanced across to Nakamura who was still busy at his station.

'It would seem that you have done a good job. How did you find him so fast?' Sarclan asked.

The question stunned Janice for a second and she desperately sought a viable answer.

'Seems strange to me,' Sarclan continued, 'you took him to the dock, used your security pass to give him access and then left him to do his work. Finally, you were able to apprehend him but only after he had done the damage. As I said, seems you have done a good job, Commander, except that the main damage to the doors was a long way from where he went. I do not believe in coincidences... you are both saboteurs. Guards, kill them!' He shouted.

Both guards went for their side arms, but Anton was quicker. With deadly accuracy, the two knives he had hidden in his shirt sleeves flew from his hands. The closest guard was hit in the left eye, the one hundred and fifty millimetre blade shearing through his frontal cortex and killing him instantly.

The second blade was for Sarclan but the remaining guard leapt in front of him, taking the knife deep in side of his throat. It sliced straight through his carotid artery, deep red blood suddenly spurting from his neck. His hand flew to his neck and he spun around, knocking Sarclan off his feet just as Sarclan fired his weapon at Janice.

Although he was falling, Sarclan managed to get his shot away. The energy bolt impacted the bulkhead to Janice's right. The blast threw her back and spun her to the left into the wall – she fell to the ground, motionless. Just as Nakamura took aim at Janice, Anton drew his own weapon and fired a full power burst. It hit Nakamura in the chest, blowing a fist sized hole clear through him – he was dead before he even knew he was shot.

Sarclan had regained his feet and was running for an exit door on the other side of the room. Anton fired again narrowly missing. Sarclan reached the door and slipped out.

Anton jumped across to Janice and bent down to check her pulse just as the door opened and the two guards entered. They hesitated for a second, trying to comprehend the scene that lay before them.

Anton rolled away from Janice and fired two blasts. Both guards were standing in the doorway, only a metre from him. Neither guard ever knew what hit them.

Anton moved back to Janice, feeling for her pulse again. There it was, faint but regular. He gave her a quick examination. She had a large gash to her forehead and a large contusion was forming on her neck. Her left shoulder seemed at an odd angle. Anton moved it gently and could see it was dislocated.

'Better to do this now while you sleep,' he mumbled as he took her arm in his right hand and placed his left hand on the joint. He moved both hands in a way he'd been taught on one of his training schools and the joint snapped back into position. It would be very sore for a few days, but that was all. Slowly she started to regain consciousness. Anton pulled a small cylinder from his belt, snapped the top off and waved it under her nose. The acrid smell penetrated her stupor causing her to convulse and push his hand away.

'What's that fucking stink?' she cried.

'You're welcome,' Anton replied, 'just a little old remedy.'

'Get it away from me!' She pushed him back with her right arm. 'Ahhh!' She reached up and gingerly touched her aching shoulder, feeling for any damage. 'Did someone shoot me?'

'In a manner of speaking, yes; the only real damage was when you slammed into this bulkhead and dislocated your shoulder, but don't worry, I put it back in,' Anton said, trying to sound reassuring. It didn't work.

'Sarclan, what happened to him?' Janice was trying to get to her feet.

'He got away,' Anton admitted as the station Commander came toward him. He raised his blaster to warn her, but it was not necessary.

'Please, lower your weapon, we're unarmed,' she pleaded as she raised her hands. 'We aren't part of this... we work for Cordoba. Can I help?'

'Yes, where does that exit go to?' Anton pointed to the

door Sarclan used to escape.

'Nowhere, it's just our rec room, just some lounges and the food dispensers. There's no other way out.'

Slowly Janice regained her feet while Anton scooped up her side arm and handed it to her.

'Can you hold the fort while I go and have a quiet chat with mister Sarclan?' He asked.

Anton winked and walked toward the door across the room. He paused at the entry, listening for any movement; hearing none, he moved closer to inspect the door.

Unfortunately it was a sliding unit, thus negating his preferred kick and enter tactic. He stood at the side and reached for the door catch. As his hand passed the sensor the door slid into the wall. Two flashes from a blaster inside confirmed that Sarclan was still alive and not in any mood for conversation, but he thought he should try anyway.

'Sarclan, throw down you weapon and come out, there's no other way!' He was rewarded with two more blistering shots. Sensing he had no options, Anton slid four studs from his belt.

Two were the exploding type, but with a lower yield than those he used in the dock. The other two were miniature gas canisters – deadly within five square metres – so in the sealed room Sarclan stood no chance but Anton needed to make sure the door was closed before they went off. He fingered the icons on his watch, setting the gas canisters for ten seconds then decided to give Sarclan one more chance to surrender. He waved his hand in front of the door sensor – the door opened. A barrage of blaster fire slammed into it and the wall it slid into. The door buckled and stopped, totally jammed in its housing.

'Shit!' Anton swore. He picked up the two gas canisters and deactivated them and set the explosive studs for contact detonation. This would be messy but there was no other way.

'Last chance Sarclan!' he shouted and was rewarded with more blaster fire, this time hitting several of the control consoles. Anton heard the sound of a power cell being dropped out of the blaster – this was his chance. He leapt past the door, throwing the charges into the room as he went. He rolled as far away from the door as he could and, just as he slid behind a console, there was a muted explosion, then another.

The wall into the rec room was buckled and breached in two places. Flames shot out of the room and licked at the control room ceiling. They died just as quickly as the fire suppression system kicked in and the rec room was flooded with CO_2, killing the flames, and any oxygen breather that may be inside. An emergency force field activated as part of the fire suppression system, containing the flames and CO_2 in the rec room.

Anton stood and walked to Janice and the commander. 'How long will that force field stay up?' he asked.

'Until the fire is out... probably no more than ten minutes,' she replied.

'Good, nothing to do but wait,' Anton said as he sank to the floor, suddenly feeling very tired.

***

JT swung Valiant back toward the four enemy cruisers. At the same time, Aaron and Steve moved into opposing positions. They had synchronised their attack to the second, all firing at the same time. Albatross was equipped with a plasma cannon, like Condor, and Valiant had her Sling Shot. The combined energy hammering at the cruisers shields was incredible. Surely something had to give — nothing could withstand this sort of barrage indefinitely. But no one had unlimited energy. Valiant was down to reserves and could only keep this assault up for a few more minutes — Albatross was in no better shape.

Aaron reluctantly gave the order. 'Call off the attack.'

While they had succeeded in reducing the Sedition ship's shield effectiveness, it still held. 'We need to try something else.'

Freebooter vessel, this is the Commander of the Sedition force. Withdraw and we will let you live. As you have seen, you don't have the firepower to hurt us. I will not make this offer again. You have sixty seconds to comply.

The voice echoed on Condor's bridge and Aaron slumped in his chair. The commander was right. They had thrown everything at the Sedition ships, without success. If they withdrew, at least they could fight another day.

'Sir,' Phillip Harper called, 'we are being hailed on the secure channel!'

'Put it through,' Aaron commanded.

The view screen flickered and filled with a Krell face. *Freebooter, Abraham. Emperor Dokad would address you.* The face faded and was replaced with Dokad's image sitting in a huge command chair wearing the imperial Krell battle dress.

'Emperor?' Aaron stuttered.

Yes, my friend... Emperor. I will explain soon but first, could you use a bit of a hand? Dokad smiled from the screen. The image disappeared and was replaced with the Sedition blockade.

Suddenly, behind, above, below and to each side of the four ships, five huge Krell vessels de-cloaked. They were at least twice the size of the old KL10n units facing them. Dokad's voice returned over the open channel

Sedition vessels, this is Admiral Dokad, Emperor of the Krell. Drop your shields and disengage your weapons. You have ten seconds to comply. The answer came violently with all four cruisers firing as one. Their weapons had no effect and Dokad hailed them again. *I gave you the chance to survive, so be it.*

Harper called to Aaron. 'The Sedition ships, they're firing but their shields are dropping... are they mad?' As if to answer his cry, the Dokad's ships fired again with spectacular results. All four Sedition ships exploded almost simultaneously.

Anticlimactic was the only way Aaron could describe how he felt. All the effort, all the sacrifice and it was now over.

Captain Abraham, a Krell voice sounded over the comm system, *The Emperor asks that you attend him on his flagship. We will send a shuttle for you.*

Aaron shook his head and turned to Kate. 'Looks like I have an audience with Emperor Dokad. You have the con Number Two.' As he walked past the sensor station, he noticed Harper furtively working at the console. 'Problems, Mr Harper?'

'No Sir,' Harper stuttered. 'In all the confusion, I didn't ask if I should record the signature of those ships, so I did anyway.' He looked worried. Had he overstepped his authority?

'Never know when that will come in handy. Good job!' Aaron patted him on the back as he walked past, entered the transport pod and selected the shuttle bay. As he did the old comm system crackled into life, again. *Mr Abraham… the Doctor here.*

'I hear you, Doctor,' Aaron replied, a wry smile on his face. By now he knew who the mysterious Doctor was, but the pretence was still being played.

I have some news, good or bad depending on your point of view. Sarclan is dead. The news shocked Aaron; he had hoped they could capture him. At least that way they might find out what this was all about.

'Are you sure?' Aaron blurted out.

Yes, I am standing beside his body now, well, what's left of it that is. What do you want me to do with it? Anton asked.

Aaron's mind was in turmoil – they would need proof – that was for sure. 'Place it into a stasis casket,' he decided. 'We'll need to take it back for formal identification.' Whether necessary or not, it seemed a good idea.

OK, I'll make the arrangements… you can collect it when you're ready, Anton replied, cutting the link.

Aaron arrived at the shuttle bay just as the Krell shuttle entered. It was a very sleek looking craft, with an oval body, short wings and a tall tailpiece. Mounted on the top of this was a menacing looking plasma projector – one of the Krell Navy's best weapons. No doubt there were more weapon ports that Aaron couldn't see. It settled to the deck and a door dropped silently down. He walked up the inbuilt stairs and the door closed behind him.

The Krell officer who Aaron had seen on the view screen now stood before him, 'Welcome Captain Abraham,' he said. 'I am Captain Kaddin, commander of the Emperor's flagship… please sit.' He gestured for Aaron to take the seat opposite him. 'You certainly gave a very good account of yourselves… I am impressed.'

'Thank you Captain, we are most grateful. Your arrival was well timed; we were getting our butts kicked,' Aaron admitted.

The shuttle was different to any Krell unit Aaron had seen before – less utilitarian and more stylish. The seats were very plush and covered in dark blue leather. From the inside, the walls seemed transparent – an illusion achieved by covering the whole structure with view screens, giving the impression of sitting in space and not in a shuttle.

'Do you find this disturbing?' Kaddin asked. 'I can turn the screens off if you prefer.'

'No, the view is fascinating. It's something I never expected from a Krell design.' Aaron replied.

'Like this shuttle, the cruisers we arrived in are a new class of vessel – larger and more powerful than anything we have ever built before. While at the same time, our designers and engineers were tasked with adding some aesthetic appeal to their work. If you look at the screen above and to your left, you get a good view of the Emperor's Flag Ship.' Kaddin pointed to the screen. Aaron was enthralled.

Krell naval architecture had always followed function as the main design criteria, leading to some very sturdy but somewhat ugly ships. Yet the ship he was looking at now was anything but. Gone was the old boxy design. This ship was sleek, smooth and big. The forward section had a slight concave curve to it with what seemed to be a semi-transparent wall running almost the whole width. The underside seemed to have a massive container type section attached to it.

'What you are looking at here is an idea we actually took from you,' Kaddin explained. 'That section you are looking at is removable. We can change the mission profile of these ships simply by changing the container section. Anything from a full battle group complete with fighters and ground troops, to a full medical facility, can be configured in a matter of a few hours. The Emperor's ship currently has four divisions of ground troops, complete with all support systems,' he smiled, obviously very proud of his command.

'Impressive… very impressive,' Aaron agreed.

Kaddin spoke into the intercom at his side. 'Pilot, please do a full circuit of the ship for the benefit of our guest.' The pilot acknowledged the order and changed course.

They flew directly toward the centre of the forward section giving Aaron a good view of the massive weapon's port, then the pilot dove down under the ship and towards the rear. Here the forward concave design was more pronounced with the engineering and power nacelles forming part of each side of the vessel.

Kaddin continued. 'We use a system similar to your Gravitron drive for our *in space* operations and the whole outer skin becomes an integrated displacement field projector, thus eliminating our old, and somewhat ugly, displacement spears.' The shuttle climbed up and over the rear section and decelerated to approach the shuttle bay doors. Again, a departure from usual Krell design, the entrance to the shuttle bay was flush with the rest of the hull – the doors now unsealed to allow access. The pilot settled the shuttle into its docking bay and completed his power down process before opening the door.

'Please, Captain,' Kaddin indicated for Aaron to exit before him.

Aaron was left in no doubt about this being an imperial ship. Two full squads of imperial guards formed either side of the gangway and turned to escort Aaron and Kaddin as they left the shuttle. They walked down the passageway with guards on each side, until they reached a transport pod. Here, Aaron and Kaddin entered alone, the pod sealed and sped off with their escort left at the door.

The journey took only thirty seconds and when the pod doors opened, another guard detail was waiting to escort them. They snapped to attention and saluted smartly as Aaron and Kaddin exited the pod, and turned as one to face a door in front of them, it opened vertically allowing them access to the room it formerly concealed.

The room was large; with the ceiling soaring high above them softy glowing to light the room. In the centre was a raised dais with a replica of the imperial throne on it. Sitting here was Dokad, resplendent in the purple and gold uniform of the Emperor. Standing in a semi-circle behind the throne were the leaders of the thirteen Krell clans that made up the Imperial Council, all in full ceremonial dress.

As protocol dictated, Aaron dropped to one knee and bowed deeply as did Kaddin.

'Please... stand my friend,' Dokad spoke to Aaron, before turning to address the assembled Council. 'Let it be known that I owe this human the debt that cannot be repaid; without him and his crew, I would have been murdered in the recent rebellion. At great risk to himself, Captain Abraham transported me to safety. I owe him my life.'

Aaron was stunned by this comment, but said nothing as Dokad continued. 'Members of the imperial council, our Empire and the Coalition face an imminent threat, a threat that could end our way of life. As your Emperor, I believe that we should continue to work with the Coalition to end this threat but, because of recent events, I ask for your support. How say you in this matter?' He paused and waited for the assembled leaders to reply.

The assembled clan leaders huddled together. There was nothing of the usual heated debate that the Krell Council was famed for. Moments later, one member stepped forward and spoke for all.

Lotarik, head of the Glanak clan and senior assembly member addressed his Emperor. 'Emperor Dokad, we of the Imperial Council support your request and we will commit whatever forces we have to assist in the ending of this threat. I am forced, by honour, to report that one of my lesser clansmen was the instigator of the attempt on your life and that he, Ga'dok, has been apprehended and is now on his way to Mortuk. His band of rebels has been neutralised.' Lotarik finished and bowed to his Emperor. The mention of Mortuk brought a collective shiver to all. Mortuk was the Krell prison planet and no-one ever left Mortuk. A sentence there was forever.

'Thank you Lotarik,' the Emperor replied.

At the same time, the throne started turning to face the council and a table rose out of the floor. It was a crescent shaped unit with Lotarik opposite the Emperor signifying his position as head of the council and chief advisor to the Emperor. 'Please sit, Captain Abraham... would you bring us up to date on the current situation?'

'Of course, Emperor,' Aaron relied. 'Before I commence, I understand you have ground troops aboard,' he paused as the Emperor nodded. 'May I humbly ask that you send a security force to the station to assist with securing any remnants of hostile forces that may be there?'

Dokad immediately called an aide who left with instructions to despatch the necessary forces and for them to work under the command of Commander Janice Barker.

As soon as the aide departed, Aaron continued. 'I thank you for your assistance. The situation, as we currently see it is this: the threat of a Trisidic fuelled breach through sub space has, largely, been neutralised. Fortunately, due to the destruction of Rhapsody, the rebels have no large ships to transport the fuel. Now it appears that Sarclan has been killed so it would seem that the immediate threat to our space has been removed.'

'You don't seem convinced, Captain,' Lotarik commented.

Aaron eyed Lotarik cautiously. Krell intrigue could be very dangerous and he didn't know where the power play that had brought his friend to the role of Emperor was going.

'You are indeed astute, Lotarik. Call it a warrior's hunch, but it all seems too easy. We were a small force that appeared to win victory too quickly.'

Lotarik smiled. 'Well said, Captain. I also feel this way... as though we are missing a vital piece of the puzzle.'

Aaron felt that familiar buzz in his head. 'One moment, please.' He stood quietly for almost a minute before speaking again. 'I have just had a communication from an Eldoran vessel... it will be materialising close to us very soon. Emperor, may I ask for your weapons systems to be placed on hold?'

Dokad nodded and indicated to an aide who spoke into his comm unit then replied, 'It is done.'

Aaron continued, 'my friend and emissary from Eldora, Jok-Tar; begs your permission to attend you and address the council.'

Dokad replied. 'Of course... we would welcome the opportunity to finally meet with an Eldoran. Please activate the main view screen.'

The view screen was actually a three dimensional hologram – similar to the Bubble Aaron had on his ship. It glimmered into focus in the centre of the table. A few seconds later, a faint glow was detected at a position very close to the Krell task force. The hologram immediately focussed on that point and displayed a huge white orb slowly coalescing into a solid shape – Jok-Tar's ship.

The attention in the room was focussed totally on the new arrival. It was the first time any of them had seen an Eldoran vessel and Jok-Tar's sense of drama was evident. The ship initially appeared as a small globe, totally round and white, no windows or any external protrusions, no obvious form of propulsion and no visible weapon ports but, as the image coalesced, it took its true ovoid form.

Aaron's mental link activated again and he spoke to the assembly.

'Jok-Tar requests permission to come aboard Emperor.'

'Granted,' Dokad replied and Aaron relayed the message. All eyes were on the hologram, waiting to see a shuttle, but none materialised. There was a sudden but minute feeling like a static electric charge and a form materialised beside Aaron. Jok-Tar had arrived.

'My apologies for the dramatic entrance, Emperor of the Krell, but I have very important information to discuss. I am Jok of the clan Tar, one of the ruling clans on Eldora and I come in peace and friendship.' Jok-Tar bowed deeply to Dokad who stood and replied with a shallow bow as befitted his rank.

'Please, Jok-Tar, deliver your information,' Dokad asked.

'We have been observing the structure of what you call Green… there has been much activity with many vessels leaving. We traced these to a point three parsecs from Green, where they entered one of the gates and disappeared… we believe to the Tenth Realm.' Jok-Tar placed a small golden disk on the table, activated it and the hologram changed. It now showed a different location. 'I took it upon myself to go to the location and these are the images from that visit.' The images displayed one after the other, all of the same old gate.

Aaron was puzzled. Something wasn't right with the gate – he just couldn't identify what. 'Can we enhance these images?' he asked.

Jok-Tar stared at the disk and the image changed.

'Did you take any ambient radiation readings?' Aaron asked.

'Yes, there was a background Trisidium emission,' Jok-Tar answered.

Aaron studied the images intently. It was another council member Krodan who spoke.

'I have used these gates but I have never seen one that was so dark. It is like looking into a black hole.'

'That's it!' Aaron replied. 'Normally, the centre of a gate is light and mostly a bluish white in colour. This one however, is black-and a deep *absence-of-all-light* type of black… just like a black hole. The gate is focussed into sub space. There must still be another portal operating in the Tenth Realm and by focussing the sub space fields and inter-linking them, they form an interdimensional… or inter-realm portal.' Aaron thought for a while. 'Emperor, how long will it take your ships to reach that location?'

Dokad motioned to his captain, who answered. 'At maximum displacement, six hours, Earth time.'

Aaron turned to Jok-Tar. 'Can you take any vessels on your ship?'

Jok-Tar thought on this proposal. While his ship was big, these new Krell vessels were much bigger. 'Only one of these ships... and even that will be straining our resources.'

Dokad held his hand up for quiet. 'Captain, what are you two discussing?'

Aaron knew he had no choice but to tell the gathered Krell about their new drive system. This was not something he wanted to do, but it was now unavoidable.

'Emperor, as you know, the Eldorans have a drive system that allows them to travel through sub space. Jok-Tar's ship and Condor can travel from here to the portal site in a very short time. Using standard displacement drive, it will take six hours. If we can put one of your ships in his, we could arrive at the portal with enough firepower to stall any incursion – at least till reinforcements arrive. We simply can't allow the Galdorans to gain any sizeable foothold. There is one issue... we don't know how Krell physiology will react to this drive system.'

Jok-Tar interrupted. 'This is true Emperor. At this juncture, we have still to agree on terms for Freebooters to release this technology. Initially, we needed to ascertain if the system would cause any injury... so far, Humans seem to be compatible. But your race, we do not know.'

Dokad stared intently at Jok-Tar and Aaron. 'I understand, but if we can use this technology to intervene in this situation, I for one, am willing to shoulder the burden of any risk.' As he finished, an aide entered the room and handed a comm tablet to the Emperor. 'Seems that Green has also been pacified by Coalition forces and, now that we have troops on this station, we are free to tackle the next problem. When do we leave?'

'Emperor, to keep this site secure, I would suggest you leave one of your ships here with most of our vessels. The others I think should head out to here as soon as possible,' Aaron pointed to the portal site in the hologram. 'I'll take Valiant and as many of the drones as we can on Condor… your ship can travel with Jok-Tar's vessel. We should be ready to depart in about an hour, agreed?'

Both Emperor Dokad and Jok-Tar nodded. 'Captain Kaddin, if I could impose for a shuttle back to my ship?'

Kaddin smiled. 'I will have one prepared immediately.'

Jok-Tar turned toward Aaron. 'I will go and prepare my ship. Emperor, I will send word when we are ready to bring you aboard.' He touched the small round device that was round his neck and activated his transport. Jok-Tar vanished.

Dokad rose and walked to Aaron. 'Captain, your friend is full of surprises.'

Aaron nodded. 'He never ceases to amaze me either, but please, I don't seem to be up to date with things. A couple of days ago you were an Admiral, and now you are the Emperor. Also, when you arrived, the Sedition cruisers seemed to drop their shields. What happened?'

Dokad laughed. 'I will walk with you to your shuttle and explain all on the way.'

Dokad's explanation was concise and to the point. He had left the Abraham compound with President Malik and Admirals Wilson and Morris. While in transit to Perth, a communication from the Krell Embassy on Earth was sent to him. It contained a cryptic message that an Imperial shuttle was waiting at the Perth space port and his presence was required by Imperial decree. Dokad knew he couldn't refuse and arrangements were made.

The shuttle conveyed him to the outer reaches of the solar system and to an Imperial task force – the same one that he now commanded. Once there, he learned the Emperor had recently died and that he now had the endorsement of the old Emperor's sons to be named as successor to the Emperor. As the entire imperial council was on the task force, the ascension protocol was enacted and Admiral Dokad became Emperor Dokad.

'It was that simple my friend. I tried to contact you but you and your first officer had already disappeared so I attempted to contact President Malik only to discover he was locked down in your brother's compound. I also found out that Wilson and Morris had disappeared. So I did the only thing I could. I set about cleaning my own house, and the rest you seem to know.

'So what do we do now? Jump over to this displacement gate site and destroy it? That should close this issue. As for the shields on those old ships well, shall we just say that the Emperor has certain information that he can use in situations like that.'

'Point taken... now all we can do is try and finish this and destroy the gate as soon as possible,' Aaron answered.

'Well, here we are at the shuttle bay. I will wait for your friend to contact us and we will be away.' Dokad smiled as he held out his hand. 'I meant what I said, Aaron. You did save my life and that can never be forgotten. We will be seeing a lot more of each other in the future.'

'It's an honour Emperor, and I'll look forward to it.' Aaron
took his leave and entered the shuttle.

T he shuttle landed at the Eldoran Embassy and Mondrac disembarked.

'Do not wait... this may take a while. I will join you again when I have completed my task.' Tocmal agreed and the shuttle resumed its original flight plan.

Mondrac was greeted by the Ambassador. 'Greetings Mondrac,' he announced. 'Everything is ready my friend.' They took an elevator down to the lowest sub-basement level – over two hundred metres underground.

While all Eldorans are telepathic, the link was strongest in those genetically related: father to son, brother to sister. Mondrac was only half-brother to Jok-Tar's sire so, to make contact through realms – especially to the Twelfth Realm – was difficult enough but the distance of the genetic relationship between Jok-Tar and Mondrac made it even more difficult. For this reason, Mondrac needed to be away from other minds or the telepathic interference created would block his thoughts. The embassy had the necessary isolation chamber.

The sight of the isolation chamber greeted them as they exited – a bleak, foreboding sight. The purpose of the chamber was exactly as its name implied, to completely isolate anyone inside from any outside influence and interference. It was a perfect sphere made of a dark grey substance that gave it a malevolent appearance. No windows or entry ports were visible and it hovered effortlessly half a metre off the floor, adding to its sinister facade. An entry slowly materialised and Mondrac turned to his companion.

'Thank you, Ambassador,' he said as he entered the chamber.

'No thanks necessary, Mondrac. There are four guards in this room and another six in the lobby and the elevator has been locked off... you will be secure,' the Ambassador replied.

An isolation chamber made the user totally vulnerable and the trance like state needed for the communication could be dangerous. He entered and sat on the curved floor, immediately in front of him was a stand that held a strange webbed headpiece. He removed his clothes, donned the headpiece and lay down as the entry port closed and sealed. This was the worst part for Mondrac as he was voluntarily surrendering his safety to others – something he rarely did. As he lay down, the light in the sphere slowly faded. He calmed his mind and slowed his breathing, starting the ritual used for so long by his people.

As his mind cleared, his breathing became shallower as he was beginning to enter the trance. Inside the sphere, gravity was slowly reduced until finally, Mondrac's body floated free in the exact centre of the chamber. There was total darkness, silence and no sensory input from touching the floor, even the temperature was adjusted to match his exact body temperature – there could be no distractions now.

It was dark inside Mondrac's mind as well as in the sphere as he slowly dropped deeper into the trance. He started to visualise a tiny point of light and he concentrated all his being on this luminescent spot. His mind began calling his brother's name.

He concentrated on the name "Edrac-Tar" increasing his concentration and building in intensity until it was almost a scream in his mind. For what seemed like hours, he kept this concentration, screaming his brother's name across the multiverse.

***

On Eldora, Edrac-Tar sensed something like an itch in his head and it bothered him. He was trying to decipher the plans for a new construction of another ancient Earth building but couldn't concentrate – the dammed itch was becoming a nuisance. Suddenly, he heard Mondrac's voice and instinctively knew what the itch was.

Eldrac-Tar leapt up from his desk, sending plans flying in all directions.

He ran as fast as he could to his isolation chamber located deep under his home. He was breathless as he entered the room and activated the chamber.

Brother, I am coming, he thought, knowing that there must be some very serious reason for this contact. He flung his clothes off and entered the chamber, placed the head piece over his head and lay down. It took a full twenty minutes for him to reach the trance state where he could contact Mondrac. The contact was as real as if they were standing together. In his mind, he was standing facing Mondrac who spoke – just a few words and a set of coordinates.

'A-Bra-Ham, Jok-Tar, do not destroy... capture.' Mondrac repeated it over and over until Edrac-Tar held his hand for it to stop. He knew this was taking a great toll on his brother and broke the connection knowing that at the other end,

Mondrac would now return from his trance.

He also knew he was not strong enough to contact Jok-Tar alone. He sent a telepathic call for Jok-Tar's birth mother to join him – only together could they hope to reach their offspring – and Edrac-Tar had a feeling that time was very short.

Fortunately, Batir-Tar had seen her clan Sire running toward the chamber room and had followed him, concern for the safety of her offspring rising. She opened the chamber and saw Edrac-Tar on the floor. She quickly disrobed, donned a head piece and joined him. They sat facing each other, legs crossed, their knees and toes touching. They both reached out and spread their fingers allowing their finger-tips to meet, thus joining into a single mind.

Together they descended into the trance, and repeated the ritual, first finding the tiny white dot of light, then concentrating all their being on it. Finally they began calling the name of their offspring, Jok-Tar, repeating it over and over till it too, built into a telepathic scream.

In the Twelfth Realm Jok-Tar was busy, trying to accommodate the large Krell ship in his hold area, a task that was proving extremely difficult. He felt something in the depths of his mind, an annoying something that he couldn't quite understand, but it was distracting. He tried to lock the annoyance out of his consciousness and solve the problem at hand.

The annoyance began to recede as he put more effort into the problem. Dokad's ship was too large to be accommodated on the Eldoran vessel, so he was working on a system of tethers that would allow him to secure it as an external extension to his ship. The last problem was now being resolved and finally he had a solution.

On Eldora, Eldrac-Tar and Jok-Tar's birth mother broke the telepathic link. Exhausted by the effort, they collapsed on the floor of the chamber. Batir-Tar slowly sat up. 'We have failed, my Sire. We could not make contact. What shall we do now?'

Eldrac-Tar slowly rose, 'I do not know. I do not have the strength left to contact Mondrac. We must send a message to the embassy. I hope it will reach him in time.' Slowly they re-dressed and left the chamber.

***

Tocmal and Petra had taken the shuttle and were in a meeting with the Mother Queen. The sensor data from Junior had been downloaded and was displayed on the view screen above everyone's heads.

Tocmal was addressing the group. 'As you can all see, the Galdorans have defied our Mother Queen's directive. Not only have they built a second portal, they are using it. Ships are being transported in both directions. Now what stage they are up to, we do not know, but this clearly shows they are now capable of moving between the realms.

'Mother Queen, Officers of Reglaos, this is a deliberate act of war and must be met with utmost force.' As Tocmal completed his speech, the doors opened and Mondrac entered. The Mother Queen recognised Mondrac and asked him to speak.

'Mother Queen, delegates,' he began, 'what Admiral Tocmal says is true and very concerning, but one thing must be understood: we cannot destroy the portal, we must capture it. I have sent word to Eldora and, hopefully, they have been able to contact the Twelfth Realm and advise of this.' There was a muted murmur that began to fill the room as others disagreed. One of the officers stood and spoke to Mondrac.

'Mondrac, this threat is not in your realm, it is in ours. It is Reglaos who must decide on the course of action and I, for one, say we should destroy this apparatus. End this threat now.'

Mondrac studied the speaker, General Zastril, Commander of Reglaos Army. 'General, in most circumstances I would agree but consider this. How many Galdoran ships have been sent to the Twelfth Realm: one, ten or one hundred? And while this is not the concern of Reglaos, what has been sent here *from* the Twelfth Realm? We see here four battleships, equipped with weaponry we may not understand. How many of these have been sent here? How much Trisidium has been sent here to power the portal? These are the questions that are far more relevant.' Mondrac paused to allow his words to settle in the minds of his audience.

'If we destroy the portals, we lose the ability to return foreign things, or retrieve items that have been erroneously sent from this realm. No General, we must capture the portals,' Mondrac concluded and sat down to the right of the Mother Queen.

The Mother Queen hesitated, listening to the growing rumble of discussion filling the room. Knowing Mondrac had started something she knew **she** would have to resolve, she beckoned him to her side. 'My friend,' she asked in hushed voice, 'you are absolutely certain this is the best course for us to follow?'

'Yes Mother Queen... absolutely,' Mondrac replied and resumed his seat.

The sound of the heel of the royal sceptre being slammed

into the floor stopped further discussion.

'Officers of Reglaos,' the Mother Queen's announcement broke the silence, 'we will follow Ambassador Mondrac's advice. Admiral Tocmal, you will devise a plan to capture the portal and neutralise any Galdoran or Nileran presence in our realm. But make no mistake about my orders. They have started a war, but we Reglaons shall finish it.' With the decision made, the meeting was over and the Mother Queen left the room. Tocmal called a number of the other officers to him, their conversation too fast for Petra to decipher.

When they broke up, Tocmal came back to Petra and Mondrac. 'We have the start of a plan, come with me.' He led them out of the room and down to a landing pad, to his waiting shuttle.

Taking off immediately after they boarded, the shuttle climbed swiftly as Tocmal began to explain. 'We are going to one of our bases. We have decided to send in a small force to gather more information. They will be well away by the time we reach our destination. I just hope you're right old friend.'

'Tocmal, I can see no other option,' Mondrac replied, gravely.

Petra tuned the discussion out and concentrated on the scenery flashing below which was green and lush with no signs of the magnitude of the population of the planet. She was thinking how it almost seemed too perfect when suddenly the craft started to lose altitude and speed – they had arrived at their destination.

The base was similar to the one she had visited before, with an entry via a tunnel into the side of a mountain. Petra was fairly certain that this base was in the opposite direction from the city, but it was just as vast. They went to an observation area where once again the immensity of the base staggered her. Over 300 metres below was a huge number of large space ships – thousands were parked there. Tocmal saw the puzzled look on her face.

'What troubles you Man-nix?'

'I'm not troubled, as such, it's just the size of the base. There must be millions of Reglaons here; it's difficult to grasp the scale of these operations.'

Tocmal clicked and buzzed; his version of laughter. 'Yes, we may be small but we do tend to do things on a grand scale. It has helped keep us safe for many years. Now follow me, we must see what information our reconnaissance force has found.'

Petra followed him down the long corridor. About half way, Tocmal stopped and opened a door. They entered a dimly lit room full of consoles and view screens. Over 100 Reglaons were present and each seemed to have an individual task, they barely noticed the newcomers enter.

'This is one of our main control rooms... there are another three exactly like this,' Tocmal explained. 'Each one is monitoring the same things but from different perspectives. We have found this works extremely well for us.'

One group was making more noise than the others and Tocmal moved closer, the screen showing the presence of a number of Eldoran ships disgorging Galdoran vessels from their interior. Tocmal shook his head. 'Seems Mondrac was correct... some Eldorans have taken another side. This is very unfortunate.'

'Why unfortunate?' Petra asked.

'Eldora has always been neutral, only observing conflict,

never entering or assisting in any inter-realm actions. This however,' he gestured to the screen, 'this is something totally new and unknown.' He turned to one of the operators and issued an order. 'I have asked for Mondrac to be brought here; we need to solve this puzzle before we proceed.' He led Petra to a viewing area at the rear of the room where they sat in human chairs in company with several of the Reglaon units. Thy waited silently for Mondrac, Petra's mind whirling as to the implications of what she had just seen.

Shortly after, the door opened and in strode Mondrac. He stood and looked at the display before moving back to Tocmal and Petra. 'I was afraid this might happen. Those ships are from clan Kyos, a lesser clan with great ambition. The Ambassador has received a briefing from Eldora on this matter. It transpires that Rogan-Kyos, the clan sire, has chosen to support Galdor and Nileros in the conquest of the Twelfth Realm. Eldrac-Tar has called a meeting of the Eldoran Council. Until I receive their decisions, I cannot do anything overt to stop this action.' His voice was filled with sadness. 'I have informed the Mother Queen of the situation and she has granted me my freedom.'

'You mean you can't help us?' Petra cried.

'Not overtly. I can assist as an individual, but I can't implicate the council until they have met and issued instructions. You must understand,' Mondrac explained, 'nothing like this has happened for millennia, we have no precedent to follow. Kyos has always been a problem. Rogan-Kyos styles himself as an ancient feudal lord from Earth history. His territories are large but he has minimal influence with the council. This act may be his first move in trying to usurp power on Eldora.'

'So we now have the Twelfth Realm as target of Nileros, Galdor and now parts of Eldora?' Petra interrupted. Her anger was rising, this was not what they needed – more adversaries.

'Then it is good that we stand together, Man-Nix.' Tocmal stated firmly. 'Together we will overcome all this treachery. Now, Mondrac, our ships have launched a number of probes. Can you assist in deciphering the data?'

Mondrac smiled. 'Of course, where do you need me to go?'

Tocmal called one of the operators over and instructed him where to take Mondrac. 'Have no fear, Man-Nix. There may be a few minor clans that dissent over this, but we still have the Tar clan and most of the council with us. This incident will be of little consequence to the outcome.'

They sat and watched the unfolding scenes for half an hour, until one of the operators informed them that Mondrac wanted to see them. They quickly made their way from the control room to one of the science stations located three levels below.

'As they entered the room, Mondrac blurted out with great excitement, 'I think we have had a breakthrough!' We have confirmed how they are using the portal. Come with me.'

Mondrac quickly led the way into another room filled with all manner of equipment. In the centre was a very large view screen with four Reglaon scientists standing in front of it. They waited for Mondrac to re-join the group and, as they began to run a stream, he said, 'both of you watch carefully... see if you can see what is happening.'

The screen showed the portal and several of the Galdoran ships around the periphery – the centre of the portal was totally black and devoid of any light. The screen split to allow two images, both of the same portal but from different distances. They watched for what seemed like an hour and then the centre of the portal flared blue and white, but only for a second. The close image showed nothing else, but the image recorded from further away suddenly showed a ship materialising, as if from a displacement re-entry.

Petra was first to speak. 'I don't get it. Why is a ship re-entering normal space such a big deal?' It made no sense to her. The ship had materialised nearly half a million kilometres from the portal, but it was just a normal re-entry.

'That is what we thought when we saw it,' Mondrac explained. 'First, we believed this was just a supply or patrol ship returning to the portal site, until we analysed the complete picture. Look, we will run it again very slowly.' The scene was replayed almost frame by frame, this time showing much more. When the portal flared blue and white, the slow motion showed something coming through it – nothing solid, more like an energy burst – then a few seconds later the ship materialised.

'That's not possible,' Petra almost whispered.

'We thought the same,' Mondrac agreed, 'until we started to run our own simulations. It all makes sense, now. I will try to explain. There are two portals; one in the Twelfth Realm and one here. In effect, they are doors to the Eleventh Realm; setting them up allows the entry and exit point into sub space to be very close together in astrometric terms. The problem is that all the portals can do is open one side of the door – basically open a door to the next realm and no more. But, by using the ship's displacement field, they are able to convert the portal's fields into a bridge between them. I don't know why we didn't think of this ourselves. It is brilliant and totally negates all the problems we have faced with the Eleventh Realm.'

Petra considered what Mondrac had just revealed. 'So to use the portal, we just need to initiate a worm hole? How can we do that without a reinsertion point?'

Mondrac smiled. 'Excellent, you start to see the problems! You are correct, without a predetermined exit location a worm hole is dangerous. We also believe that to use the displacement field and portal together, the fields of both must be set at the same resonance. To do otherwise, the consensus is that any ship would be vaporised as it entered the portal's field. We haven't been able to isolate the correct frequency as yet.'

'Do the ships start and re-enter at the same point?' Tocmal had been silent so far but now wanted some answers.

One of the Reglaons answered him, 'yes Admiral, always from the same point... why?'

Petra saw where Tocmal was going with this train of thought and entered the conversation. 'Then there should be some sort of beacon or signal buoy for the ships to fix their entry and exit points on. Can you check around the location where the ships all reinsert?' The technicians started to scan the area requested.

'Also, could you use one of those probes to tag along with the next ship and analyse the field harmonics?' Tocmal asked. 'How often are they sending ships through?'

'One every standard interval Sir,' the scientist replied.

'Then get a probe ready and let's see what we can find out.' Tocmal turned to Petra. 'Are all your scientists like this, ignoring the obvious and spending huge amounts of time on the obscure?'

Petra smiled, 'pretty much.'

'Admiral,' a scientist exclaimed, 'there is one ship moving into the insertion point now! I have a probe ready.'

'Then send it in!' Tocmal almost shouted.

The probe was small enough to be ignored by the Galdoran sensor system. It effectively had the signature of a small rock – all they could do now was wait.

The probe approached the ship – the operator keeping it in the area that seemed to be the weakest sensor point – cautiously moving it closer and closer till finally it was inside the ship's deflector field. Next, he attached the probe to the ship's hull via a narrow band umbilical field and sat back to wait. All this time, the small probe was sending data back to Reglaos which included: the ship's deflector, defence and displacement field operation, frequencies, harmonics and any changes to these.

'Set it to scan for any beacons at the exit point!' Petra cried, fearing they had overlooked the obvious, again. One of the techs quickly entered the commands to the probe.

'I am seeing changes in the displacement field and it's intensifying,' one of the scientists exclaimed. This indicated that the ship was preparing for a displacement initiation, but it was still stationary – usually a ship would be at flight speed before initiating the field.

'Recording the field data,' as he said this, the ship started to rapidly accelerate. The displacement field increased and the frequency and harmonics began to almost dance, constantly changing. As the ship approached the portal, everything changed as the displacement field stabilised and matched the portal's harmonics. Then the two fields acted as one with the ship and probe disappearing from the screen.

'The probe is programmed to detach from that ship as

soon as it materialises on the other side. Then it will try to identify the next ship to come back through, attach itself to that ship, and return, recording all the time,' the Reglaon scientist explained.

'So how many ships have they sent both ways, and how many personnel have they also sent through?' Tocmal asked.

Mondrac answered. 'We do not know. We know that four ships came from the Twelfth Realm and two have returned, but we have no data on how many have gone from this side. I think they are still testing it.'

'Suggests to me that they don't have full confidence in their system... would you agree?' Tocmal ventured.

'More along the lines of making very sure that the system can be trusted,' Mondrac answered. 'Remember that this technology is from the Twelfth Realm and I don't think either Galdor or Nileros want to sacrifice their people to prove it works.' He turned to the scientists now pouring over the data from the probe, 'any ideas?'

The lead operator answered. 'Yes, we believe the frequency and harmonic fluctuations were part of an identification protocol to make sure only authorised ships can enter. A signal was received just moments before the displacement field finally settled to a fixed frequency. Unfortunately, we have no idea what was in the signal, only that one was received. We may know more when the probe returns, but it will take time.' He returned to his display and continued working.

Tocmal was getting impatient. 'Mondrac, we need answers! We have many ships already in the field and we must start our main operation. I need to know what we are facing, and I need to know very soon.'

'I am sorry, my friend. 'But we cannot rush this, we are entirely at the mercy of our adversary… they are calling the shots at this stage. Come on, we simply must let these people do their job.'

Before they had even left the room, the lead operator called, 'The probe, it's back! Another ship came through almost immediately and it was able to attach to it.' He was smiling, clicking and buzzing wildly. 'All life signs are good… human life signs.'

'What?' Petra exclaimed. 'Show me the ship.' The ship was brought up on the main screen. 'That's a Coalition Frigate… why is it here? How many crew?'

The console operator worked the controls before answering. 'Twenty… five on the bridge, the others in what I would assume is engineering and weapons control. But there are two in a small room that seems to be very heavily secured with force fields.'

Petra shook her head. 'That'd be the brig… where we hold prisoners… but a crew that small makes no sense. Normally a ship that size has a crew of five hundred… twenty is only a skeleton or maintenance crew. That ship is definitely not going to battle, but why is it here?'

The lead scientist was clicking and wheezing with great excitement – Petra couldn't understand anything he was saying. Tocmal saw her dilemma and started to translate.

'It seems that our probe has some very interesting data. He believes they can have an identification program for you within an hour, and they have isolated the beacon signal. We will be able to use the portal after all. What we need now is our third crew man.' He turned to Mondrac. 'Care to come with us?'

'Where to?' he asked.

Petra answered. 'We are going through the portal and back home.'

Mondrac smiled. 'Well, I suppose there is very little else I can do here, so a short trip might be in order. When do we leave?'

'Now,' Petra answered. 'Can we leave the probe attached to that ship?'

Mondrac looked puzzled. 'Yes, but why?'

'That ship is an enigma and I don't like enigmas. I am particularly interested in who the prisoners are. Tocmal, when the battle starts, can you have that ship captured?'

'Understood, Man-Nix, I will make the arrangements immediately,' Tocmal answered.

It only took them a few minutes to reach the shuttle, Tocmal had it kept ready for immediate departure. Tocmal wasted no time in contacting Reglaos command centre and arrangements were made to capture the alien ship. They reached the main command centre in record time and their journey started. The pilot had broken every rule in the book regarding atmospheric flight, but he earned Tocmal's gratitude. He was given ten minutes to prepare to take them to the repair dock where Junior was waiting, while Tocmal made final arrangements for the coming venture.

Mondrac was contacted by the Science Institute. They had the ID program completed and wanted to transmit it to their ship. Petra accessed Junior's comm system and authorised the transfer. Everything was now as ready as it could be.

Well, now it's up to lady luck Petra thought.

'Just have a little faith, Man-Nix. Our small friends are very resourceful and skilled... if they are confident, so am I,' Mondrac replied.

'That's not what I'm worried about Mondrac. From what I heard at the Science Institute, this interdimensional, or inter-realm bridge works like this: first the portals set up the dimensional breach on each side; then the ships displacement field joins the entry portal field and initiates the bridging field. The final phase is when it matches with the opposite portal and completes the bridge and we just fly through. Is that correct?'

'Yes, that is a good description Man-Nix,' Mondrac replied enthusiastically.

'What happens if the opposite portal is shut down – or destroyed – while we're in transit?' Petra asked.

'Man-Nix, I have contacted Eldora to send a message to Jok-Tar requesting they capture the portal, not destroy it.'

'But what if the message didn't get through or the powers in our realm disagree?' Petra replied.

Mondrac suddenly looked scared. 'That would not be good. You are suggesting that if A-Bra-Ham and his compatriots have discovered the other portal, they may be trying to destroy it?'

'That is exactly what I'm saying. If they succeed while we're in transit... well, I don't want to imagine what would happen... Regardless, I think we should get underway urgently.'

She called Tocmal on the comm link. Tocmal took her call and returned to the shuttle urgently. He hadn't considered the scenario she and Mondrac had just mentioned. The shuttle left the bay as soon as the door was closed and headed straight to the repair dock where Junior was waiting.

The shuttle settled into the dock bay and the three exited as soon as the door opened. They walked quickly down the service gangway and into the yacht. Petra took her place in the command chair and commenced the start-up procedure. Tocmal went to the sensor and tactical station and Mondrac to the engineering and communications role. He contacted the dock commander and received permission to detach. Petra needed no additional encouragement, immediately disconnecting all tethers and umbilicals.

'Ok boys, are you ready?' She asked excitedly.

'Ready,' Mondrac replied.

Petra reached the safety mark in record time, programmed the nav computer and engaged the displacement drive. Junior entered the worm hole and started on its most ambitious journey yet.

Reglaos had sent 2,000 ships to intercept the Eldoran vessels; their mission was to stop any more Galdorans entering the Tenth Realm. A further 1,000 had been despatched to the portal site which, strangely, seemed very lightly guarded with only 200 ships in total and only 75 identified as battle class vessels. Caution was still prudent so Junior reinserted 700,000 kilometres from the portal.

'Man-Nix,' Tocmal said, 'I have sensors showing a line of four Galdoran vessels waiting for the portal, no... three now... one has just accelerated through the portal event horizon. More are joining the line... probably the ones being delivered by Clan Kyos.'

'Ok. Tocmal, your ships need to start their attack now! If they can disrupt the line to the portal, it may make our approach easier.'

Tocmal opened a channel to the fleet commander and buzzed and clicked his commands. Immediately, the first wave of the fleet initiated their displacement drives and disappeared toward the portal. Petra entered the coordinates that had been selected for her and they entered their own displacement field.

'Mondrac,' Petra called, 'Now we see if that identification program will work.' She touched an icon on her display and the program took over. 'If this doesn't work, we'll know very soon.' She tried to sound flippant, but her voice betrayed her and her concern came through as she glanced over to Mondrac. 'Maybe time for a little faith?'

They reinserted into normal space three minutes after the attack had begun. Already there were casualties on both sides, but the Galdoran vessels had been caught off guard and were suffering more. Petra noted four that were seriously damaged. They were heading into the portal flight path and a group of Reglaon ships raced past them and started to engage two of the Galdoran ships in the line.

They didn't stand a chance. Not being ready for the attack meant the Galdorans ships were sitting ducks, and the Reglaons took the advantage seriously. In seconds, both ships were drifting without power and the Reglaon attackers showed no mercy.

Mondrac was right, Petra thought, *they may be small but they are ferocious*. She felt a wave of relief, and felt very glad they were allies and not adversaries.

'I have a new program from Reglaos… what do you want to do?' Tocmal cried out.

'Send it to the nav system… they must have isolated the beacons,' Petra replied, hoping she was correct. If not, then

Junior had no exit coordinates and could end up anywhere.

'The program is taking over,' Mondrac announced. 'Whatever happens now, we are committed.' The ship in front of them accelerated and disappeared into a displacement field.

'Point three of light speed and displacement field intensity of six point eight five.' Tocmal read out the sensor data. Petra initialised the Bubble and Tocmal fed the data directly into it.

The three stood watching. There was nothing they could do now except watch and wait. Junior started to accelerate and they felt the displacement field start to build.

They watched as the portal loomed closer and closer, accelerating all the time, the blackness of its heart deep and foreboding. Just as they were almost on the portal, the program kicked in. The view screen flashed a brilliant blue white and they were through the first portal.

15

It took Aaron nearly two hours to gather all the available drones and secure them.

While frustrating, it proved an advantage as the bulk of the Krell force would already be closer to the gate site. He contacted Jok-Tar who was having issues fitting the Emperor's flagship into the hold of his ship, instead opting to attach the two ships by tethers, allowing the two ships to be enveloped in the jump drive field as one unit. In all it took three and a half hours before they were ready to depart.

They finally engaged the jump drive and disappeared at about the same time Petra and her companions were joining up with the Reglaon fleet. Fourteen minutes and twenty five seconds later, the two ships materialised one million kilometres from the gate. Immediately, Aaron opened the main hold doors and Valiant dropped silently out of Condor's belly.

In the drone command centre, Sol prepared his crew. Twenty drones were prepped and ready – they would not be used unless absolutely necessary. There was an atmosphere of expectation and a little trepidation – no one knew just what they would have to face.

On the bridge, the feelings were the same. Phillip Harper

and Ensign Croker were engrossed at their sensor stations, trying to locate any adversaries. Croker's fingers flew across his console as he refined his search.

'Got something Skipper!' he exclaimed, 'feeding into the Bubble now.'

The hologram in the Bubble changed and now the gate site showed three additional images – Galdoran cruisers arranged in a twelve, four and eight o'clock pattern around the gate one hundred thousand kilometres from its periphery, giving them a complete field of fire coverage.

'Jok-Tar is hailing us Sir,' Simon called.

Aaron replied and the attack plan was decided. Condor would take the ship at twelve o'clock, Dokad the one at eight and Jok-Tar was left with four o'clock. Valiant would stay attached to Condor until they were close enough to detach unseen; its goal was to disable the Gate power system and render it useless, stopping any invasion in its tracks.

'Dianna,' Aaron called to his chief engineer, 'tie Valiant to us as close as you can. We need to look like a single ship, so make sure they stay tied till we need to separate.'

'Aye Sir,' she replied as she huddled with Colin Anderson, her junior engineer. They discussed ways of securing Valiant and finally decided to erect a force field around Valiant and secure it to Condor's docking ports.

Once this was done, Aaron gave the order to begin the attack. The three vessels parted company and immediately powered up their weapons, accelerating toward their targets. The Galdorans were already at a high alert status holding their positions which gave them a complete covering field of fire.

***

The Galdoran in command of this small group hailed his other two ships. 'Now it begins.' His voice boomed exultantly from the comm systems. 'Hold your position... reinforcements are already in transit. We will soon crush these fools and complete our annexing of this realm.' He sat back in his chair. 'Strategy Master, do you have a solution to this?'

To his right, a female Galdoran stood. 'Yes, Commander, their attack is simple... they have split, one vessel for each of us. We have three additional ships in transit that will arrive as we engage the enemy... they will not be a match for us.' She resumed her seat.

Galdoran hierarchy dictated that a Commander should be in an elevated position on the bridge, emphasising their status, so all Galdoran bridges were constructed with the commander's station no less than one metre above every other station. These were arranged in a line across and in front of this position, allowing the commander to see all of his bridge crew all of the time.

'Good. Hold your fire till they are almost on us... then fire everything. We will end this debacle very quickly.' The commander had a reputation for arrogance but, in the past, had always been successful in battle so his decisions were never questioned. The console in front of him displayed the approaching ships; he studied it and placed a mark on the screen, in front of the approaching ships.

'Weapons Master, this is your firing point, make certain the other ships do the same.' The mark was just five thousand kilometres in distance from them, much closer than the weapons master wanted.

Obviously, he thought, *the commander believes the intensity of our initial barrage will destroy the attackers.*

'Yes Sir,' the Weapons Master replied, unconvinced as to the wisdom of the decision. But, unwilling to contradict his Commander, he sent a coded message to the other ship's weapons masters with his Commander's instructions.

***

On board Condor, Aaron watched the distance between the adversaries close — less than 200,000 kilometres now. 'Ship status?' he asked.

'All power systems at full capacity, absorption banks at minimum, shields at maximum. We're as ready as we can be Skipper,' Dave Carter answered.

Aaron continued to watch the decreasing distance between them. Suddenly he sat bolt upright, the glimmer of an idea coalescing in his mind. He hailed the other ships. 'I don't have time to discuss this but I have an idea. We are heading straight at the Galdoran ships and I bet they will wait till the last second and then hit us with everything they have. Frankly, I don't like those odds for Condor... she isn't a battleship.' He quickly explained his idea and on receiving unanimous agreement, called out to his navigator. 'Simon, change course and head straight for the centre of the gate. At ten thousand kilometres, we break away and run up the face of the portal... JT will detach and attack the power station. Job finished!' He didn't wait for an answer as he saw Simon's hands working the controls and felt Condor change course violently.

***

'*What!*' the Galdoran Commander screamed. 'What are they doing?' The trace on his screen changed and now all three attackers were heading directly at the centre of the portal. The strategy Master considered this before answering.

268

'They seem to be in an attack formation... all their weapons are charged. I think they are trying to disrupt the portal field... that would be disastrous for our ships already in transit.'

'Fire now!' the Commander ordered.

The Weapons Master hesitated. 'It is not possible. They are now below our field of fire... we are unable to target them.'

'Navigator, break from this position, give me a firing solution.' The Commander was angrier than anyone had seen him before – the strange tactic his enemy had employed had taken him totally by surprise. He felt his ship accelerate and change attitude, his screen tracking its movements. At the same time, the three enemy ships had again changed course and he noticed the other two Galdoran ships had not moved.

His target had changed course into an attacking position giving it a much stronger firing solution. Then, to his total dismay, he saw something else, a smaller vessel, detach from the first – now he had two targets to contend with.

Good... I will destroy both of you! This thought screamed in his head.

Condor fired its forward torpedos. The five units sped towards the Galdoran vessel, each impacting harmlessly on the shields.

'Did I not tell you?' The Commander yelled triumphantly to his crew. 'Their weapons are useless against us. Return fire!' The weapons Master did his best but the angle was not good and Condor had again changed course, using the shadow of the Galdoran vessel as cover. What they didn't see was where Valiant's surreptitious manoeuvre was taking her.

Valiant had moved quickly into firing position and sent a triple burst from the Sling Shot at the enemy ship. Condor's torpedos did their job well. The impact of the torpedos gave Valiant time to log the shield frequency of the Galdoran ship. The three balls of encased antimatter were almost undetectable until they flared white and broke through the shield defence. All three impacted the Galdoran vessel's hull, instantly vaporising a large section each. Over half of the vessel's hull was destroyed, all power failed and it was only a matter of minutes before every Galdoran on board was dead.

***

'Great work, JT!' Aaron yelled into the comm system. 'Now, destroy the portal power station.' As he said that, another Galdoran vessel came up in the Bubble.

'Seems we have another that has just come through,' Kate called. 'What now?'

'How are the others doing?' Aaron asked.

Kate studied her console before replying. 'Emperor Dokad has inflicted serious damage on this adversary, but Jok-Tar is still fighting hard though not making much of an impression on his target.'

'Hail the Emperor's ship,' Aaron called.

When the Emperor replied Aaron spoke. 'Emperor, we have a new adversary, one just came through the portal. Can you take him? We're no match for these Galdoran vessels but I believe we can finish yours off and help Jok-Tar.'

Of course, my friend, the Emperor answered as his ship broke off the battle to head toward the new threat.

Condor changed course and entered battle with the damaged Galdoran cruiser. She had lost half her shields, but her weapons were still formidable. Her commander seemed very competent, constantly manoeuvring to protect the part of the ship where the shields were weakest. Twice Aaron tried to attack that point and twice he was repelled.

'Damn, this guy is good,' Aaron commented. Then he made a decision and opened a channel to Sol. 'Solomon, are your drones ready?'

'Affirmative, Captain,' Sol replied, eager to join the fray.

'Good, time to go into battle. Here's what we do.' Aaron quickly laid out his idea – Sol agreed and started launching the drones. At the same time, JT was making his first run at the power station. He fired a full spread of torpedos and waited till they impacted on the shields.

'Did you get the shield frequency Guns?' JT called.

'Sure did… programming containment field harmonics now.' It took her only a couple of seconds to do this. 'Firing Sling Shot!' Helen announced as she sent another triple burst towards the Gate. This time, the three antimatter balls impacted on the shields, the resulting explosion temporarily overloading Valiant's sensors rendering her blind.

'Got it,' Helen smiled. It took a few seconds for the screens and the Bubble to reboot before the result of their attack was clearly visible. 'What, no damage?' she said in disbelief. 'That can't be… I know we hit it!'

'Hang on a second,' Greg Holgate the Tactical Officer called as he poured over his console. 'Very clever, they are using a shield generator with a random harmonic oscillator.'

'So, how do we defeat it?' JT asked.

'I don't think we can,' Amy Rodregas, Valiants' engineering officer replied. 'The only way I think we can even make a dent in it is to increase our antimatter yield… but it will be difficult.' We're only a small ship so our ability to generate the sort of yield we need may be impossible.'

'So, how much bigger can we go?' JT asked.

Helen and Amy conferred. 'We can double that last shot,' Amy declared, 'but we need to be much further away or we'll be collateral damage. We better warn the others.'

JT gave everyone their tasks. 'Ok you two get it happening. Jarad, call the others and let them know what we are doing. Colin, see if we can boost our shields and Holly, give me a course and flight plan for getting us clear.'

***

No-one in the Twelfth Realm was aware that the first shot JT fired had any an effect. For a micro second, the power supply to the portal was interrupted just enough to lower the field intensity. On board the yacht, Tocmal watched his sensor readout. 'Man-Nix, something is wrong.' He sounded worried.

'Tocmal, talk to me,' Petra called.

'There was a small disruption to the portal field... one moment,' he said, as he manipulated the sensor console. 'No, this is not good, there seems to be a reverse shock wave coming.'

'Where, coming from where?' Petra voice had and edge of mild panic to it. 'Put it in the Bubble so I can see it.'

Again Tocmal worked feverously at the controls.

Petra watched as the Bubble's image changed. Now she could see the approaching shock wave. 'Mondrac, can you calculate the intensity?'

'No, all I can tell you is this is huge,' Mondrac replied. 'There is a great amount of energy in that wave. Our friends in the

Twelfth Realm must have begun attacking the portal. I will re-route power to reinforce the aft and lateral shields, but I don't know what effect this will have on the portal. If the shock wave hits that, we are in trouble.' Mondrac worked the controls to enhance the selected screen generators.

'Mondrac how long to re-insertion and how long before that wave hits us?' Petra asked.

Mondrac looked at his console. 'Thirty seconds to re-insertion, eighteen to the shock wave. Man-Nix, I don't think we can survive that shock wave.'

Petra watched as the seconds ticked by. She had a solution but it was risky. She reached to her left and selected the manual control icon, touched it and her station changed. A control pedestal rose out of her chair, control stick to the right and engine and displacement controls to the left.

'Man-Nix, what are you doing?' Mondrac's voice was wavering.

'Hopefully, not killing us,' she replied as she took the controls in hand. At five seconds to impact she selected the maximum displacement setting then at two seconds she engaged max displacement and the yacht's field increased exponentially. 'No Aaron, don't fry my arse now,' she whispered, 'we're so close.'

The shock wave hit two seconds later, violently throwing the small vessel around just as it burst through the portal. The sight was awesome. A huge brilliant white energy ball spat out of the portal, almost engulfing Valiant – the shock wave throwing all adversaries off their course.

The bridge on Junior went dark as all power shut down – Petra leapt to Mondrac's side and they started to reinitialise the ship's power and systems. Very slowly, circuits started to reset. Power nodes cleared overloads and came back on line; like a wounded warrior, Junior was coming back to life.

'Tocmal, start hailing on Coalition and Freebooter frequencies; we need to stop this attack,' Petra said firmly. It would be a few minutes until their allies knew where they were, but the attack needed to be halted immediately.

Mondrac smiled and said 'It would seem that you have saved our arses. An interesting solution... exciting and inventive... I see why your species has developed so quickly. Well done.'

Valiant had fared a little better than Junior – being out of the direct path of the energy wave – but still suffered a multi system failure; Amy was working feverously to get everything back on line.

'How long, Amy?' JT enquired.

'A few minutes, no more,' Amy responded.

Jarad stood by his Captain's chair. 'What was that? Did we do more damage with the first attack that we thought?'

'Don't know. Colin, what can you see?' JT called.

Colin Bryant was desperately trying to get the sensors back on line, with little success.

'At the moment nothing... wait one, the system is finally rebooting,' he replied. 'Seems that the others weren't hit as badly as us, they are still attacking their targets.' He transferred the data to the Bubble. 'In front of you now Skipper.'

The Bubble cleared and there, in front of JT, was the battle scene. Aaron and Jok-Tar were now both attacking one Galdoran cruiser – Aaron had successfully left one drifting powerless. Dokad seemed to have an advantage over the new arrival and in total control of the battle – but they were all still too close to the portal.

'Jarod, did you advise them to move away?' JT asked.

'Yes, and they all said they would comply, as soon as they finished their battle – except for captain Abraham, who said he needed to help the Eldorans,' Jarod replied.

'Fucking typical, he's just like my father. Open a channel.' JT commanded. Jarad gave him the signal that the channel was open and JT hailed Condor.

'Captain, you need to clear the area before I fire. This yield has never been used before, so we don't know what will happen. The same goes for Jok-Tar and Emperor Dokad… please disengage and leave now.' He waited for a response.

'Ok. We'll finish this run at the target before we withdraw,' Aaron replied, 'we only need about twenty seconds.

'We also will comply.' The response was from the Krell Flagship, and Jok-Tar agreed to the same time frame. Everyone now had twenty seconds to break off their battle and depart the area.

'Finally… Helen, when can we fire?' JT called.

'A few more seconds Skipper,' she replied. Helen and Amy made the final adjustments and double checked the settings. 'Ok, we're ready. Spinning up three new charges… this will take a bit longer.' Everyone waited while the system generated the three charges. At just over one hundred millimetres in diameter, they would deliver more than double the energy previously released.

'Course entered Sir,' Ensign Morgan called; confirming that their attack and escape flight path was programmed into the nav system. JT studied the Bubble – it was clear on their flight path. It also showed the current state of battle.

Jok-Tar's adversary had taken a multitude of hits and had sustained terminal damage. Aaron was in the final stages of his last run while much further out, Dokad's battle had ended with the Galdoran cruiser dead in space. All three were in the process of disengaging.

Satisfied with what he saw, JT issued the command. 'Ok, commence attack run.' This was relayed to the other ships and Valiant accelerated towards the portal.

'Thirty seconds till fire point,' Helen called, 'Initialising Sling Shot.' The first step to firing the Sling Shot was to power the gravimetric field. This would propel the antimatter spheres to almost light speed and direct them to the target. 'Fifteen seconds.'

***

On Junior, it was a flurry of activity as they desperately worked to establish contact. Mondrac showed signs of desperation, something Petra didn't believe an Eldoran could experience. Desperately she started hailing the other ships.

Condor Junior calling any Coalition or Freebooter ships… please respond.

She was rewarded with silence.

Again Petra repeated the hail, desperation clearly evident in her voice.

Condor Junior calling any Coalition or Freebooter ships… please respond.

Jarad called to his Captain 'Skipper, we are being hailed.' He put the call on the internal bridge comm system.

Condor Junior calling any Coalition or Freebooter ships… please respond.

'Ten seconds,' Helen called.

'Condor Junior this is ECS Valiant... what do you want?' JT responded.

JT, this is Petra, please do not destroy the portal... repeat... do not destroy the portal, do you understand? Petra's voice pleaded over the comm.

'Five seconds,' Hellen called.

'Helen, hold fire. Petra, where are you?'

We're approximately five hundred thousand kilometres from you on heading two-five-seven by one-three-six, Petra replied.

Greg Holgate focussed his sensors on the point. 'Nothing, Skipper, I can't see anything,' he replied.

'Petra, if this is you why can't we detect your ship?' JT asked.

On Junior, Petra was at a loss. They should have shown up on Valiant's sensors. It was Tocmal who gave her the answer. 'The resin coating, remember it masks us from their sensors.'

JT, it's too complicated to explain now, just watch and you will see. Petra loaded one torpedo. *I will detonate a torpedo fifty thousand kilometres from my location.*

JT was glued to the Bubble and, sure enough, it showed an explosion at the location indicated.

Did you see that? Petra's voice sounded eager for his response.

'Yes we saw, but why do you want this portal left intact?' JT could see Condor speeding toward Petra's location. 'We need to stop any more of these coming through.'

'No, that is being taken care of on the other side. Just wait

so we can explain in person. She was pleading with him. *'Please, many lives depend on this.'*

'Roger that, but we will keep our weapons on target just in case.'

On Condor, Aaron set course for the location he heard Petra give JT, despite his own sensors showed nothing. Ten minutes later – according to the nav computer – Condor was only a few hundred kilometres from the Yacht, but still no sensor readings. Aaron was concerned. 'Petra, do you have your transponder shut down?' He asked.

Sorry, Petra answered as she energised the transponder circuit; *we had to come through the portal without being recognised.*

Aaron saw the transponder signal come on in the Bubble. Cautiously, Condor closed to within one hundred kilometres, just close enough for the transponder beacon to be detected visually. The sensors were still registering empty space. 'Got it, I see that Tocmal's resin still works, our sensors still can't see you.'

'Well, hold your position and we'll come to you.' A relieved Petra replied.

'By the way Number One, do you remember how to park that thing?' Aaron asked flippantly.

'Of course, Captain. Which orifice would you like me to park it in?' Petra replied with a not too subtle hint of sarcasm.

Aaron just laughed. 'You'll need to use a docking port, the hangar's occupied.' He turned to his navigation officer, 'All stop please Simon... number two; you have the con. As soon as they are secured, regroup with the others.' Aaron stood and left for the pod doors, 'and we aren't in any particular hurry.' Everyone on the bridge smiled as he ducked into the transport pod.

Petra gently eased the yacht to align with the docking ring and completed the docking process. She tested the result and found the seal to be effective. As she opened the access hatch, she could see Aaron anxiously waiting behind the airlock inner door. Mondrac had also noticed and called to Petra.

'Man-Nix, Tocmal and I need to check something… in engineering, I think. Yes… we will be in the engineering space.' He beckoned for Tocmal to follow and the little insectoid creature dutifully followed. 'They need to be alone for a bit,' he whispered to Tocmal as they hastily left the bridge.

'If it were me, I would need a long time alone. You must be getting old, Mondrac,' Tocmal replied, the clicks and buzzes indicating a chuckle.

Petra left Aaron fidgeting for a few more moments, till he finally spoke, 'permission to board, Number One?'

Petra opened the airlock and replied. 'Permission granted Captain.'

Aaron climbed down the access ladder and quickly entered the bridge; she met him at the door and flew into his arms. Their lips met in a long passionate kiss. Petra finally broke free, almost gasping for breath.

'I must go away more often if this is the greeting I get.' She offered her lips again and they were eagerly accepted. This time, there was less desperation and more emotion, more tenderness. Finally they broke apart. 'I never want anything as close as that again.'

'What, you didn't like my kiss?' Aaron sounded deflated.

'No, the re-entry; you nearly fried us when you attacked the portal! If JT had fired his second volley, I have no idea where we would be or even if we would be alive.' She paused and called her companions back to the bridge.

'I was thinking we could take a few minutes, you know, to re-acquaint?' Aaron suggested.

'Darling,' Petra replied, 'when we re-acquaint, I want a hell of a lot more than a few minutes! So, until we sort this mess out, cold showers might be in order.' Aaron knew she was right and agreed just as Tocmal and Mondrac returned. He greeted his friends and led them through the hatch into Condor.

'*Captain to the Bridge*' the words echoed through the ship.

'On the way,' Aaron replied as they entered the transport pod. 'What's the flap, Kate?' Aaron asked as they left the pod and walked onto the bridge.

'Sir, something has just come through the portal... Jok-Tar is investigating,' Kate replied, and turned to Petra. 'Welcome back, Number One.'

Petra smiled back to her friend. 'Thanks, Kate. Believe me; it's good to be back in one piece.'

Jok-Tar hailed Condor, announcing that the object that came through the portal was a communication drone of Eldoran origin and gave instructions on how to access it. Unfortunately, only Jok-Tar's ship and Condor had the technology to utilise the system so they arranged for the others to come aboard for a briefing. As they were securing the drone, the four other Krell cruisers arrived. Emperor Dokad arranged for their Commanders to be brought up to speed and asked Captain Kaddin to have them form a perimeter when they were briefed.

Once everyone was comfortably set up in Aaron's private lounge, Jok-Tar initiated the comm link. Almost instantly he was rewarded with a response from his Sire's ship and Eldrac-Tar's image filled the view screen. After the customary Eldoran greetings, he brought everyone up to date with developments in the inner realms.

The battle for the Tenth Realm portal had been brutal, with considerable losses on both sides. In the end, the Galdoran commanders capitulated, knowing they were outnumbered and out gunned – any further resistance would have been both futile and suicidal. He also gave them a long account of how they tried to capture the Coalition vessel that had been sent through. It had fought very hard to try and escape but something had gone wrong on board and their drive systems shut down.

It appeared there had been a mutiny by some of the crew, unfortunately resulting in all but one being killed. One person had used an escape pod and ejected before the final battle. The pod had been retrieved and the occupant placed in a stasis compartment until his identification could be confirmed. The Kyos vessels had retreated back to the Fifth Realm where they were immediately impounded by the Eldoran Council.

Rogan-Kyos, sire of the Kyos Clan, had been arrested and would face the council for judgement. The punishment for his actions was severe; if found guilty, he would have all his lands and assets confiscated, his Clan would be dispersed and Clan Kyos would vanish forever. Would it come to that, no one knew. It had been many thousands of years since any Eldoran had been subject to Council censure and Eldora was entering a new phase of existence.

Eldrac-Tar inserted an image on the screen; an image of the person in the stasis tube.

'That's not possible,' Aaron called out. 'He's dead!'

'Yes, I am afraid the escape pod was damaged and his life expired before we could get to him,' Eldrac-Tar replied.

'No, you don't understand. I saw this man's body on Cordoba Blue… he was killed in the battle there,' Aaron replied.

'I do not understand… how could he be killed in a battle two days ago and also now in our realm?'

'Good question, but the body you have and the one we have in stasis are the same man… Eugene Sarclan.' Aaron's mention of the name caused silence to fall in both realms.

Eldrac-Tar broke the silence. 'So this is the person responsible for all this death and destruction? But how can he be dead in two different places?'

'I don't know, but we will find out. Please keep his body in stasis, we'll collect it soon.'

As the conversation ended, seven Coalition cruisers entered the portal zone, including one carrying Admiral Grogan. A shuttle was sent for him and he was soon sitting in the lounge with a mug of Mondrac's brew in his hand.

'I must say, this is the best coffee I've ever had,' Grogan said as he took a deep draw from his mug. Aaron, JT and Dokad quickly filled Grogan in on what had transpired in both realms, including the issue of the two Sarclan bodies.

Once again the comm system announced a new call, this time from Malik on Earth. Sam Grogan took the call and brought the President up to date on the situation, including the discovery of two Eugene Sarclan's, and the bodies of Admirals Wilson and Morris.

It was revealed that Wilson and Morris were the prisoners on board the Otamah. Dean had held them as insurance, should he need to negotiate his future. Unfortunately for him, they had escaped from the brig and disabled the ship. Sadly they had both died in the fire fight with the dissident crew.

'Please confirm your last statement Admiral,' Malik asked.

Grogan repeated his statement. 'Yes Sir. Admirals Wilson and Morris were killed in action and it seems we have two Sarclan's. We'll need to examine both bodies to sort this out.' Everyone agreed and a time for the transfer was arranged.

The only other issue was that neither Zarof nor Nefaris could be located and it transpired they had used the portal to transfer to the Twelfth Realm two days previously. Eldrac-Tar had persuaded the Galdoran commander to furnish them with details of the ships they were travelling in and this was transmitted to the Coalition vessels. Grogan ordered a search for these two ships and four of the coalition force was despatched to this task.

Malik spoke again. 'Admiral Grogan, as you are now the most senior officer in Space Corps, I am promoting you to Fleet Admiral and giving you total command of our armed forces. You may choose your other senior officers when we finish mopping up. As for now, I would like to meet with the leader of Reglaos, on their home world.'

Arrangements were made for this first state visit by the leader of the Coalition with one proviso; Aaron and Petra were part of the delegation – the Mother Queen insisted on this. Aaron agreed but also negotiated that Prime Grainger and Emperor Dokad join them. Finally, full agreement was reached and a meeting was set for two days' time.

It was decided that the Krell flagship would be the best vessel to use for this journey. Not only was it larger and more comfortable, it was also much more powerful and could withstand more of a beating should anything go wrong with the portal transit, Petra's memory of her first transit still fresh in her mind, had insisted.

Grainger had arrived the following day and was briefed on the up to date situation. He brought a supply of translators with him as the only people who could understand Reglaon were the Eldorans, Aaron and Petra.

The delegation boarded the Krell Flagship and, as she had successfully transited the portal, Petra was given the Captain's chair. She moved the large vessel out to the five hundred thousand kilometre mark, giving an order for the navigator to plot the course and enter the displacement settings she had given him. Unfortunately he seemed to have a problem taking orders from a human female and deferred to Kaddin, only to be rebuffed and relieved from his post – his replacement had no such problems.

Finally Petra seemed satisfied with everything. 'Engage main drive,' Petra commanded and the huge ship began accelerating. 'Make your speed point three of light'.

At 100,000 kilometres from the portal, the navigator initialised the drive and, at 50,000 kilometres, Petra gave the order to energise the displacement field. Instantly, the huge ship was surrounded by a soft blue haze as the field initiated. The worm hole it created intersected with the portal field and flared to a brilliant white then, just as quickly, everything went dark. An almost plaintive cry came from one of the sensor operators.

'Captain, we have lost all sensors... our ship is blind!'

'Don't worry, nothing's wrong... sensors don't work here in sub space... it is a bit scary though,' Petra replied reassuringly.

Kaddin bent low and spoke quietly in her ear, 'It actually scares the shit out of me... are you sure this is normal?'

'To be honest Captain,' she whispered back, 'we have no idea of what is normal here, but our Eldoran friends don't seem to be worried and they have been doing this sort of thing for eons.' Then she added aloud, 'I don't know how long we will be in this transit, but we survived it in our small ship, so I don't think this behemoth will have any trouble.' Her words had the effect she was hoping, everyone was reassured and the tension on the bridge began to dissipate. It took exactly seventeen minutes for the transit; at this point the drive shut down and they re-inserted into normal space in the Tenth Realm.

The first thing they saw was the large ovoid shape of an Eldoran ship. Eldrac-Tar hailed them and greeted them to the realm. He transmitted the co-ordinates for Reglaos and they set off in formation, with four Reglaon cruisers bringing up the rear. Two hours transit time saw them all on the surface, in the royal audience chamber with the Mother Queen resplendent on her throne.

Seated to the left of the Mother Queen was President Malik with Grainger and Dokad to her right. Ranged behind and to each side were the Eldoran Ruling Council members. Thankfully, the Mother Queen had an intense dislike for long pompous speeches and quickly and graciously thanked everyone for their assistance and pledged Reglaos to friendship and cooperation with all. She then handed proceedings over to Eldrac-Tar who now had the hardest task. His speech was also brief and to the point.

'My friends, I also want to give my thanks to all of you for your efforts in defeating this most ambitious, and insidious plan. While you were preparing to transit the portal, I was able to have discussions with the Mother Queen and the leaders of the Twelfth Realm. While some may hold different views, we have reached agreement. We all feel it is time to open up honest relations between realms.

'Too long have we Eldorans controlled inter-realm travel and trade. In fact, our isolationist ideals have stifled any development of relationships which this venture has shown can be fruitful and beneficial to all... for this we apologise. The agreement we have forged with the major parties is modest. We accept that inter-realm travel will bring much needed opportunities for us all but it must be managed with great care, lest we end up with another debacle like we have just experienced.' He paused as if to gauge the mood of the room.

'So, to facilitate a smooth transition and ongoing management of the transit lane, we all agree that the portal here in the Tenth Realm should be managed and operated by Reglaos and ask that the portal in the Twelfth Realm be controlled by Freebooters.

'We also accept that there will be some commercial needs. This is something that Eldorans must become reacquainted with, and these needs will be monitored by a committee made up of representatives from the twelfth and tenth realms, with others to be considered as time progresses. So far, we have agreement from the Earth Coalition and Reglaos, how say the Krell and Freebooter representatives?'

Emperor Dokad stood and faced the throne. 'Your Highness, Mr President and members of the Eldoran council, as Leader of the Krell Empire I believe this is the wisest course for this project. We agree.'

Dokad resumed his seat and Allen Grainger stood. 'As Prime of the Freebooters, I concur with this plan also. We will take our responsibility seriously and strive to open free and equitable trade with all, but I have one request. A project such as this will require an overreaching management and I ask the assembled representatives that we give that responsibility to Aaron Abraham. He alone has the contacts and experience to carry out this task.'

There was a general murmur of agreement. 'Would all in favour please indicate by raising their hand, or other appendage?' Almost as one, all hands and other appendages rose, resulting in Aaron now being in charge of the portal project.

With the formalities over, everyone broke and moved towards the huge dining hall behind the reception room. Now was the time for real business: greeting, mingling and the usual diplomatic posturing that passes for dialogue. Thankfully, Tocmal had sent the specs of the translator to his engineers and now everyone had one attached to their auditory organs – ear pieces for Human and Krell, medallions for Reglaons and a myriad of other variants for the other races.

All delegates from the Twelfth Realm were stunned by the species variations in the inner realms. The Twelfth Realm was predominantly humanoid – with a few exceptions. The inner realms were different. Life had taken many forms: humanoid; reptilian; and others that defied human description were accepted as equals. Even many of the Humanoid races were substantially different from Human Beings, something that would challenge many in the Twelfth Realm.

Grainger came over to Aaron and Petra, bearing three glasses of deep green liquid. 'I am told this a wonderful wine... here, try some.'

'It is, but go easy… it has a huge kick. By the way, thanks for dropping me in at the deep end,' Aaron said.

'No need to thank me, it's logical. You know all the players, you have the commercial acumen and you are acceptable to all parties – ergo, you're the best one for the job,' Grainger explained. 'Now, I must go and meet the Mother Queen, any suggestions?'

'Be careful, she is very astute and can pick bullshit at a hundred paces,' Aaron advised Grainger.

As Grainger left, Tocmal took his place. 'Congratulations A-Bra-Ham, I believe we will all work well together. This function will go on for at least two days and I have a feeling that you would rather be somewhere a little more private?' He paused allowing his suggestion to sink in. They both smiled. 'I thought so… come with me.'

He turned and led them past the gathering throng, out a discrete side door and down two flights of stairs to a secluded landing pad. There before them was a small shuttle. 'I have a small domicile far from here, as you may recall. I have pre-programmed the flight path for you. All you have to do is board the shuttle and it will take you there. If you are back in two full cycles, no-one will have missed you.'

He turned to leave, but hesitated. 'You have both taken huge risks in this venture and it almost had a fatal outcome. Now it is time for you… please, go and enjoy.' He gave what passed as a chuckle and left.

Petra turned to Aaron. 'Time to relax and unwind… sounds like just the ticket.' Neither of them had the energy for two days of politicking – time away from all this was desperately needed. Aaron smiled his agreement and they boarded the shuttle. As soon as they were settled it lifted off, and turned away from the city.

Tocmal went back definitely not looking forward to the next few days – he knew these would be filled with political bullshit and posturing. As he entered the room, one of the Mother Queen's aides came to him.

'Our Mother Queen wants to meet with A-Bra-Ham... do you know where he is?'

'He is currently on a mission for me. Please inform our Regent that he will return in two cycles,' he moved closer in a conspiratorial manner. 'Their assistance in this matter is of the utmost importance and the information must be handled with great care.' Tocmal was pleased with himself – maybe he was finally learning how politics worked. The aide, now believing he was in possession of important and classified information, nodded and returned to the royal party. Suddenly Tocmal noticed Sam Grogan by his side.

'Admiral Grogan!' he clicked. 'I am looking forward to working with you in the future.'

'I agree, Admiral Tocmal, but what was that crock you just told the aide?' Grogan asked.

'I needed A-Bra-Ham's input into something, so I asked him to do some research for me... they will return soon,' Tocmal replied.

'Good, now where can two old warhorses go and have a quiet drink? Grogan asked. All this political crap is giving me a headache,' Tocmal gently took Grogan's arm and guided him to a side door.

'Just follow me, nobody will notice our departure.' Tocmal led the way through the door.

***

As the shuttle settled into cruise mode, Aaron and Petra relaxed into the large leather seats, 'Tocmal has thought of everything,' Petra whispered as she located a bottle of Champagne in a cooler beside her seat. 'He must have liberated this from your stocks.'

'I must thank him,' Aaron replied as he opened the bottle with the customary pop of the cork. He poured two glasses and they settled back to sip their drinks.

Petra accepted the glass. 'Finally time to ourselves; all we had to do was save the universe, kill the bad guys and avoid our own deaths in the process.' She smiled and raised her glass in a mock toast.

The shuttle was taking the scenic route and both Aaron and Petra were amazed by the natural beauty of Reglaos; there was little actual evidence that an advanced and very populous culture lived here. Although there were a few large cities, most of the planet was green and lush; rivers and seas were pristine – evidence that the Reglaons were living in harmony with their planet.

'We could learn a lot from our new friends... let's hope we do.' He settled back into his seat and noticed that Petra was already asleep; he smiled and reclined his position and was soon asleep himself.

Four hours later they woke. The shuttle had landed but had not shut down. As if sensing their awakening, the airlock door opened and the gangway extended. They walked out of the shuttle and into bright sunshine.

The pad was on an elevated platform in the middle of a clearing, with forest surrounding it on three sides and a sheer cliff to the south. Aaron saw the entrance first; to a casual glance it could have been a cave except that, on closer examination, a clear door could be seen. As they approached, the door slid open. Inside, the cave was light and very large, with doorways leading off the central passage way. They had just entered when a view screen nearby activated and Tocmal's image appeared.

'Welcome, my friends. I will be brief. These screens can direct you to the various areas of the domicile, some of which are new and designed for human guests. My mate decided we needed to redesign to accommodate new friends. Food and beverages have been placed in the new preparation area so please enjoy. Oh, just a word of warning again... do not swim in the stream... we have some large and very hungry predators... there is a pool on the upper level I think you will enjoy.' The image faded and was replaced with a map of the domicile.

Petra traced the path to the food area and grabbed Aaron by the hand,

'I'm starving... time for you to seduce me with your culinary expertise.' She giggled as she tugged on his arm.

'Hang on, what's this?' He was looking at what seemed to be a small pool of some sort, the glyphs of Reglaon writing still unintelligible to him. He touched the screen and a voice responded informing him the area of interest was a hot spring bath. 'I have a better idea... how about a nice long soak, a massage and then dinner? I don't know about you but I ache all over.' Petra agreed enthusiastically and they began following the directions to the pool.

The pool was large, easily able to hold a dozen people or more, and it was cut out of natural rock. The hot spring that fed it gushed up through the bottom with a combination of water pressure and bubbles. Petra dipped her hand into the water, and let out a squeal of delight. 'It's perfect... I'd say about thirty seven degrees.' Neither wasted time in throwing their clothes off and quickly lowering themselves into the effervescent water.

'God that feels good,' Aaron exclaimed as he sank below the surface. The water seemed to be more buoyant than normal so they both floated freely, allowing the jets of water and air to gently massage away the aches in their bodies. Aaron relaxed completely, just his nose and mouth above the water. No sounds, except the muffled rush of the spring reaching his consciousness. He drifted, both mind and body relaxing, allowing the pent up adrenalin residue to be expelled from his body by the gentle but incessant vibrations of the spring.

Time disappeared, he had no idea how long he had been floating until he felt something brush against him. Aaron opened his eyes to see Petra floating beside him, also in an almost trance like state. Gently he moved closer, reached out and stroked her arm. She responded, turning to face him, her face a mask of serenity. She opened her eyes and smiled, gently pushing toward the side of the pool – Aaron followed.

'This pool is amazing, I feel totally rejuvenated,' she announced as Aaron leaned on the ledge beside her. 'It's hard to take in what's happened isn't it?'

'What do you mean?' Aaron asked. He gazed at her floating naked beside him, her breasts and nipples demanding attention. He reached out, but Petra's hand intercepted his.

'It's only a few weeks since we met and in that time, you've reconciled with your family, we've discovered that our universe is not alone, we've been involved in an interdimensional war… ' Petra paused and looked deeply into Arron's eyes. 'What will we do in a few years?' She giggled as Aaron pulled her close. He kissed her, Petra responded with enthusiasm. She straddled him crushing herself into him, grinding their hips together. He lifted her gently, taking her left nipple into his mouth, teasing it and nipping it. Petra groaned her appreciation then she pulled away and floated free. Aaron followed as she climbed out of the pool.

They found a soft grass like area and lay down, gazing longingly in to each other's eyes. Petra leaned over and gently kissed all around Aaron's face — she loved every beautiful detail — then continued down his neck, while gently tweaking his nipples. Aaron sighed with delight.

She followed the hairline from his belly button with a soft touch of her finger down towards his now risen cock. Aaron grabbed her hand and kissed her fingers then along her arm up to her neck. He covered her mouth with his lips and passionately kissed her while caressing her breasts. He stroked her inner thighs and she moaned with anticipation. She slowly rolled over and moved down his body again, her lips tantalising everywhere she touched. She reached his throbbing member, taking it into her mouth and, slowly at first, she began to rhythmically move it in and out; Aaron's groans of pleasure coaxing her on. Suddenly she stopped and pushed him back on the lounge, straddling his chest.

'My turn,' she said, her voice deep and husky. She moved till she was positioned where he could reach her most sensitive parts. Aaron took to the task with great enthusiasm, his tongue flashing over her pleasure bud. He savoured her musky scent as it drove his desire to new heights.

'Slowly, we're in no rush,' she whispered. Aaron responded as Petra rocked and groaned in time to his tongue's attention. Petra broke contact, moved down his body till she was straddling his hips. She reached for his cock, placing it where she wanted it. 'Now for the main course,' she moaned as she dropped down, impaling herself on him. She started grinding her hips against his, slowly at first but then getting faster till she was in a frenzied motion, pushing him as deep into her as she could. Aaron reached up and grabbed her breasts, holding them and caressing her nipples as he did. Petra let out a startled cry, her orgasm taking her by surprise, but she didn't stop. She wanted more; she kept grinding and thrusting, Aaron matching every movement. Again Petra cried and this time Aaron's climax matched hers.

Finally sated, Petra collapsed and dropped onto Aaron's chest. They were both covered in sweat and breathing hard, but satisfied as never felt before; a total satisfaction of body and spirit.

As their breathing slowly returned to normal, Petra disentangled herself from Aaron and slowly and seductively slid back into the pool. Aaron followed her, but with much less grace. Once again they floated, allowing the waters to reinvigorate their bodies.

Petra moved to Aaron. 'As I recall, Aaron Abraham, you were going to seduce me with your culinary expertise. Now, get your arse out of this pool and do just that!' She smiled as he reluctantly complied, climbing out of the pool and taking one of the large towels hanging close to the edge and wrapping it around his waist.

'Boy, it's a tall order after that little session, but I'll do my best!' Aaron left for the kitchen and wasted no time, deciding on a simple meal of rib steak seared to a rare finish, accompanied by a whisky cream sauce with sautéed mushrooms and baby carrots. The contents of the stasis larder were unbelievable. How Tocmal had arranged this

Aaron had no idea, but he was very glad he had.

Aaron set about his task with vigour and half an hour later, just as he was serving the meal, Petra appeared in the doorway. She was dressed in a flowing white gown that did very little to hide her nakedness, instead it enhanced and emphasised her curves. She stood there, gazing appreciatively at Aaron's appearance. Except for an apron, he was naked. 'I do hope this is how you're going to cook and serve all our meals.'

'This is going to be one short meal,' Aaron said as he placed a glass of red wine in front of Petra.

'Steady, stud, we have plenty of time and I told you... I want a marathon, not a sprint.'

The steak was perfect and they talked through recent events. Finally, as she finished her meal, Petra made an observation. 'One thing puzzles me, did you see any cattle?'

Aaron shook his head as he studied the piece of steak on his fork. 'No, but it looks like steak, smells like steak and it tastes as good as any I have ever had, so don't ask questions, just enjoy.' As they finished, Aaron moved to Petra and scooped her into his arms, her breasts pressing against his chest.

'Well, now that you've been fed, let's move onto something else.' His lips again met hers.

Petra broke free. 'I agree... didn't you promise me a massage?'

Aaron groaned softly. 'Yes, I do recall something like that.'

Petra stood, offered her hand and coaxed him away from the table. As he passed her she gave him a playful slap on the backside. 'Yes, you really do have a cute arse.'

Aaron had learnt a couple of massage techniques back in his Krell academy days; sport and physical training were mandatory and because Krell sports were more like combat, knowing how to ease muscle pain was a must. Petra initially purred under his skilled fingers, but eventually fell into a deep sleep. Aaron stopped and lay down beside her on the bed, his own fatigue capturing him as he also fell into a deep sleep.

Several hours later they both woke, slowly returning to reality. They lay quietly for a few minutes before Aaron rose on his elbow and lay there gazing at her.

'Petra, I think I love you,' he said.

'You think? I know I love you Captain Abraham,' she said with mock dismay. 'So, what do we do about it?'

'Well, I am afraid my family is very traditional. They will demand you make an honest man of me, especially considering you've had your wicked way with me,' he retorted.

'Wicked way... you call that entree my wicked way?' she teased. 'Your memory is bad... remember I told you before... when I've had my wicked way with you, you won't have enough strength to walk.' She smiled as she pushed him onto his back and jumped on top of him. They continued to play and make love for the rest of the day and finally, Aaron had to admit, she was right. He was exhausted, but extremely content.

They spent the next day and a half exploring their location and enjoying the time together; away from the madness of the previous days. Finally they rose early on the last day to Tocmal's hail. It seemed that they would be required for the final reception in the afternoon so they had breakfast, cleaned the kitchen and returned to the bedroom.

To their surprise, there were two dress uniforms laid out on the freshly made bed. This made no sense, as they had never seen any staff or even a robot that would explain how things seemed to magically get done or just appear. Once dressed, they returned to the shuttle, the engines starting as soon as they were seated. They relaxed and watched as the beauty of Reglaos flashed past them.

Thirty minutes later, they were back in the city disembarking. The final reception was more of a farewell ceremony, everyone now eager to return to their own world. Agreements had been forged and treaties signed but one issue remained.

No race, or species, could operate a portal that was powered by Trisidium, so a decision to shut down the systems while new MAM reactors were installed was taken. A time frame of one hundred and twenty days was agreed and designs were exchanged. The final plan would be decided within ten days at which time both portals would be shut down for the conversion. At the conclusion of the short ceremony, each went to their respective ships for the journey home.

***

Now back in the Twelfth Realm, Aaron was happy to see that repairs to Condor had been made and his ship was again ready for service. He left Petra to inspect the work, saying he had some urgent business to attend to. He locked himself in his office and placed a secure call to Henry back on Earth. He was there for three hours before he finally finished and returned to the bridge. As per his earlier instructions, they were already on course for Earth. Petra was in the command chair as he entered.

'Status report Number One?' he asked.

Petra replied. 'On course for Earth, displacement seven... we should arrive in ten hours... all systems are nominal, Sir.'

JT joined them on the bridge with Valiant now secured in the hold.

'Captain, may I have a minute in your ready room?' he asked Aaron.

Aaron agreed and they left the bridge. JT could hardly contain himself. 'Aaron, I've had a call from David... the bunker... they've opened level seven, the garage level. He says there are hundreds of old vehicles... trucks, cranes, all sorts of things! Maybe we can find The Second's car collection down there. I thought we could take a few days and explore ourselves.'

Aaron stopped, the faint possibility of there actually being some substance to the family myth, pricking his interest. 'Great, sounds like a plan... I'm in!' Aaron replied enthusiastically. 'I have a few things to attend to first, though. By the way, what day is it?'

'Friday, Earth time Sir,' JT answered.

'Wow... all this took less than a week... Sunday sounds good.' Aaron smiled. It'd be good to spend some quality time with his nephew. After thirty years absence, he really needed to get to know the man JT had become.

Even though they were travelling with three other ships, none were visible, each of their companions now secure in their own worm hole. All three arrived in the Solar System within minutes of each other and headed to their respective berths. Aaron had elected to take Condor to Perth space port as Henry had arranged for a ground inspection. Once they landed, Aaron again gave his crew the opportunity to complete their leave that had been rudely interrupted and, once the ship was secure, everyone was quick to depart.

Aaron asked Petra to take JT to Orange as he had business to attend to. They took the yacht and left, with Petra wondering what he was up to.

Aaron watched as the yacht left the space port; he then made a call to the number Henry had given him, arranging to meet the person on the other end in fifteen minutes. He left and took a ground taxi into the heart of the city, arriving at the address he had been given ten minutes later. He arranged for the taxi to wait and entered the building, then took an elevator to the twentieth floor. The elevator door opened onto a nondescript reception area, not at all what he was expecting.

There was an annunciator panel on the wall beside the only door in the corridor so he pressed the button and introduced himself. A small thin man gave him access and led Aaron to a large office and closed the door. Thirty minutes later Aaron shook the small man's hand, thanking him for his service, left the building and took the waiting taxi to the Abracorp office building. This time he paid the driver and went inside where his brother was waiting for him.

'Welcome back... seems congratulations are in order,' Jeff smiled as he shook his brother's hand. 'Come on, we don't want to be late for dinner.' They took an express elevator to the roof where Jeff's shuttle was waiting.

During the two hour flight to Orange, Jeff and Aaron discussed the new power system to be constructed and the possible opportunities arising from inter realm trade. Aaron seemed a little distracted and Jeff put this down to what he had just experienced. He decided a weekend at the family compound was just what everyone needed and let the matter drop.

They passed over the Great Australian Bight and sped towards Adelaide. Aaron loved this part of the flight – the wild rugged coastline, the power and majesty of the sea – it both calmed and enlivened his soul. Once there, they made a course correction for a direct path home. Thirty minutes after they left Adelaide, Jeff alerted the landing field of their imminent arrival, set the shuttle into a shallow dive and began the landing cycle.

The shuttle flared and slowly descended vertically toward the main landing pad. The sight of the compound awash with light welcomed them, filling both with a feeling of safety. They were surprised to see two shuttles already sitting in the parking bay – one belonging to Silas Greenbach, the other showing the ensign of the Fleet Admiral. A sense of foreboding crept into the cockpit, but neither brother commented.

They took the pod to the house and were greeted by Sonia and Petra.

'We have guests?' Jeff asked.

'Yes. Your father, the Admiral, and Silas are huddled in your study, very cloak and dagger. They've been there for the last hour without emerging,' Sonia remarked.

'We'll probably need more scotch if they have been in there that long,' Jeff snorted. At the same time, the study door opened and Jason poked his head through, looking very serious.

'Jeff, I think you and Aaron should come in,' both his sons acquiesced and went into the room. Inside the mood was even more sombre and, to Jeff's surprise, his whisky decanter was still full. He scanned the faces of the men;

going to the sideboard he poured each person a large measure of whisky before he spoke.

'Ok, why is everyone so glum?' he asked.

Grogan spoke. 'We have pieced together what happened; it turns out that Allan Dean was the traitor. He was the one who set up the attempt on the President and who fed all the intel to Sarclan; his DNA was found in what was left of the Frigate in the Tenth Realm. Crompton and his goons have scoured everything on Dean. Evidently, he was part of a small group that sympathised with Sarclan. After the incident at Zyralin 4, he went off the rails, blamed JT for everything and was out for revenge.'

Aaron interrupted. 'This Zyralin 4 thing; everyone mentions it but I still have no idea what it was about. I know JT disobeyed orders but in the end he saved the day, and that's where the so called Zyralin manoeuvre comes from. What has it got to do with Dean?'

Grogan looked up, and drained his glass. 'Maybe we should all have another... this could take a while.'

When everyone had a fresh glass of whisky, Grogan began.

'Dean's career had stalled, and he considered he was stuck in logistics. Although he had completed all the command schools – and with good results as well – he had never actually commanded a group. Somehow he convinced Morris to allow him to do that, thus improving his chances of promotion. He was given command of the recon force that went to the Zyralin system... there had been reports of Raider incursions. While they were at Zyralin 4, three KL10n cruisers approached.

'The rules of engagement stipulate that until any approaching ship has been identified, all Coalition ships shall maintain a full shield protection. Dean thought better and ordered shields to be dropped... after all, these were Krell ships and we are all friends.

'JT thought otherwise and kept his shields at maximum. The KL10ns were renegade ships; they opened fire and Dean's and the other ship were severely damaged in the first volley. From there, JT took control of the battle and ended up defeating all three enemy ships.'

'What! One old Vigilant class took out three KL10n cruisers?' Aaron interjected. 'They weren't manned by Krell officers if that's the case. Hell, if the odds were the other way, the Krell would probably win.'

'Agreed, he was very lucky, and that's what led us to believe they were just being ferried with a minimal crew,' Grogan added. 'We believe they were on their way to Sarclan. In any case, JT disobeyed Dean's orders and saved the day. Dean brought charges... he swore that JT had fired first and caused the whole thing.

'Unfortunately for him, the ship's log said different. Since then, he's been on a mission to get back at JT for destroying his career. For the last six months, he's been feeding information to Sarclan and doing his bidding here. Now he's dead and so is Sarclan... that's at least some good news.' Grogan stopped and sipped his drink.

'But that's not why you were all so glum when we walked in,' Jeff said pointedly.

'No, we can't find the two ships that came through the portal. It's like they just vanished... that can't be good and we can't consider this attack over until we find them.' Grogan turned to Aaron. 'Your friend, Jok-Tar is being very helpful. He's furnished us with basic information on the jump drive you have; not enough to be able to build it but enough for our engineers to verify its capability. It seems that the two ships we are looking for may have a similar system; this will make it extremely difficult to find them. Add to that the capability of their weapon systems, and we have two very dangerous vessels operating in our realm.'

Aaron thought for a few seconds. 'Admiral, there may be a way to track them. One of my junior engineers has developed a system that may help. Tomorrow, I'll get him to join with Jok-Tar and see if they can make it work.' He was thinking of Harper's system that allowed them to track cloaked Krell vessels only a few days ago. 'But I get the feeling that this isn't all you are concerned about.'

'No, it isn't,' said Silas now joining the conversation. 'This business of supposedly having killed Eugene twice is a bit worrying. I believe that between Greenbach Technologies and Abracorp, we should have a DNA profile of him so our people are searching old records as we speak. Hopefully we can sort this out tomorrow as well. Jason and I are the only two we know of that have met Eugene... at least the only ones alive. Very soon, we will have to formally identify the bodies... if we can.'

'Well, that's it,' Aaron said. 'Obviously, there's nothing more we can do tonight so let's drop the long faces and enjoy dinner... I'm sure Sonia and Mother have rustled up something special.' He stood and went to the door. 'I'll see you there.' Nobody actually took any notice of how quickly he departed, even leaving his drink untouched.

He found Petra sitting on the back porch watching the full moon's light dance over the lake, with Prince curled up on her lap.

'I see that I have been replaced.' Aaron quipped as he

approached her. 'I thought he would have deserted us for my mother… I know how she spoils her cats.'

'No. As soon as I walked into the house, he came running up and hasn't left my side since, I think he's trying to tell me something.' Petra smiled as Aaron bent to kiss her.

'I told you, he has impeccable taste,' he replied. 'But I agree that he wants you around, seems he's gotten used to you.' He paused and reached into his jacket pocket. 'Actually, he's not the only one.'

He knelt down beside the lounge. 'I know the reality of all this… we only met a few weeks ago, but it seems like we have known each other forever and, as I told you, my family is very traditional. So, will you make an honest man out of me… will you marry me?' Aaron almost blurted the last few words out as he opened the small package in his hand.

Inside was an engagement ring consisting of a large Tellurian firestone nestled into a circle of Tellurian diamonds. The firestone is harder and more brilliant than diamonds and extremely rare. At its centre it glowed, a brilliant red, and as it moved, the light seemed to flow through it like flames.

Petra was silent. She just stared as Aaron took the ring from the package. He took her left hand and looked into her eyes. 'May I?'

She looked at the stunning ring and back to Aaron, tears welling in her eyes. 'Yes,' she whispered, 'Of course yes!' Aaron placed the ring on her finger and the full moon light caught the stone, causing it to flash brilliantly. Aaron reached out, pulled her close and kissed her.

'This is the most beautiful thing I have ever seen,' Petra said softly.

'No, it is just a lump of rock... you are the most beautiful thing I've ever seen,' Aaron replied. As if to emphasise the comment, the cat took that moment to try to catch the flashing lights on Petra's hand. They held each other for a long time until Petra spoke.

'I suppose I really should go and ask your mother for your hand, if they are that traditional.' She laughed as they stood and went back into the house with Prince trotting happily behind.

Dinner should have been a quiet affair except that Amanda noticed the ring as soon as Petra entered the dining room. In her usual exuberance, she congratulated the both of them, enveloping Petra in one of her famous *mother hugs*. Jason congratulated his son in his usual gruff tone mumbling that it was about time as Aaron wasn't getting any younger – and from Jason Abraham, that was an emotional response. As was the tradition in the Abraham family, much champagne flowed and the women started making plans for the wedding.

***

Aaron and Petra didn't arrive for breakfast until after nine; Prince had deserted them at five thirty seeking easier targets. Amanda let him into her rooms and gave him the treats he was now used to, while Jason showered and dressed. He was in a very sombre mood, even though he was very happy for his younger son. Today he had a grim task to perform. During the night the record search had proved fruitful.

For many years, all humans had been DNA tested at birth and this information was on public record. Unfortunately, this had become law after Eugene Sarclan was born. Thankfully, Jason's father had instituted this protocol as a requirement for Abracorp employment, the main reason being for the benefit of identification as the company was involved in a number of dangerous industries. The search had located the results for Sarclan and these were now sitting on Jason's data pad. He came into the living room, scooped up the pad and turned to Amanda.

'I really wish this wasn't necessary. You know I always believed in Eugene. He was one of the brightest minds I have ever known.' His voice was edged with sadness.

'I know darling. But that doesn't change what he has done and we need to sort this mess out.' Amanda hugged her husband and for the first time in their life she really didn't know what to say. Jason broke away and left the room. Amanda picked up Prince and now comforted by his loud purring, went back to bed.

Aaron was surprised to see his mother just sitting down to breakfast. Normally she rose with Jason at five thirty as they had done all their lives.

He smiled as he enquired, 'Champagne a little too strong last night?'

Petra gave him a playful punch in the side. 'Don't be cheeky to your mother,' she chided.

'Not too strong, but a little too much maybe,' his mother admitted. 'What do you two have planned today?'

'Nothing much, I have a little work to do this morning and JT asked me to have a look through the garage, in the bunker later,' Aaron answered.

'Oh good... you boys go and play with your toys. We have work to do, don't we Petra?' Amanda replied. 'We have a wedding to plan!'

Petra seemed taken back but quickly recovered. 'Yes, I

suppose we do.' She realised that she was not alone in the planning of her wedding.

'Now Mother… this will be Petra's day… don't railroad her into anything… ok?' Aaron advised sternly.

'Just finish your breakfast and go and play… we girls will be fine.' Amanda dismissed Aaron's comment with a rueful smile.

After breakfast, Aaron went to Jeff's study and contacted Harper who agreed to work with Jok-Tar. He then contacted Jok-Tar and arranged for him to collect Harper and start work on the detection system. After that, he called Henry to discuss the plan he was working on for the new venture. Henry informed him that he was already formulating something and it should be ready in a couple of days.

Aaron sat back with a sigh of relief. Now at a loose end, he called JT and found he had already gone to the garage. Aaron used the old elevator in Jeff's office to follow, looking forward to the chance to finally see what his ancestor had preserved for posterity.

The elevator stopped on the foyer level.

Aaron exited and was met by a site safety officer, taken to an office, and given the necessary equipment. Once he had donned the gear, the safety officer escorted him to another office where he met JT and the Project Manager, Graham Rogers.

'There's a slight problem on level seven at the moment so I thought you might like to see some of the progress we have made… we'll be able to enter the garage area later this morning,' Graham proposed. Aaron agreed and the three started a tour of some of the lower levels that were so far unknown to JT.

Level nine proved to be fascinating; it was the armoury. The plans showed each level was staged so that no two levels were actually directly above the other. Level nine was entirely dissimilar; it had been extended out so far that it was totally isolated, spatially, from all other levels.

'This is an example of just how well the bunker was designed,' Graham explained. 'This level was one of the most dangerous – with the quantity of munitions being stored here – so the Second simply put it way out from the rest of the structure. It has its own vent and exhaust systems. In the event of an explosion, this level would be lost but all others would be secure… brilliant engineering!.'

JT and Aaron nodded, looking suitably impressed.

They continued down the levels, each giving up secrets and aspects of the planning that had gone into the design, Aaron now seeing his ancestor in a whole new light. Finally Rogers received a call from the team in the garage level giving them the all clear to open it up.

Aaron watched JT with some amusement, remembering him as a small boy, excited about something new and unknown. Finally the elevator deposited them at the correct level, JT impatient to get moving. 'This corridor is huge, why so large?' JT mused, aloud.

Rogers replied in a matter of fact way. 'This is where they were to store all their heavy equipment – even aircraft of the day. It has its own access drift, and that's intact and still ready to use.' They continued along the corridor and, as they rounded a curve, there before them was the survey team standing in front of a huge set of doors.

The team leader came up to Rogers and they discussed the doors and their operation, finally agreeing that they were safe to open. Rogers moved to an access panel and opened it to reveal a small control board. There was a keyed master switch. Rogers took a bunch of keys out of his satchel and worked through them. He found one that had the same code number on it and inserted it into the master switch.

He paused and turned to JT. 'Would you like to do the honours?'

JT wasted no time in turning the switch. Immediately, lights on the panel illuminated and the sound of an old electric motor starting was heard. The control panel held two buttons and a code board. Rogers pulled out a data pad and began interrogating it.

'On that code panel, enter this: four, seven, eight, nine, two, zero.'

JT complied and a small display activated with the words *code accepted*.

'Now press the green button,' Rogers instructed. Again, JT followed his instructions. Nothing seemed to happen and JT looked to Rogers for an answer.

'Wait... just wait,' he re-assured. 'We have found that many of these sealed areas were filled with inert gas, like nitrogen. It takes a bit of time for the old systems to remove that and replace it with air.'

The time passed quickly and it wasn't long before the sound of the door mechanism operating was heard. Slowly the doors began sliding sideways, taking another five minutes to fully open and overhead lights to activate.

They stood, speechless, as they saw before them row after row of vehicles from small utility type vehicles, to large transport prime movers, cranes and flatbeds. Slowly, almost as if in a trance, the three moved through the doors. They walked down the row immediately to their left, JT recognising some of the ancient brand names on the vehicles: Mack; MAN; and his childhood favourite; Kenworth. He stopped, gazing at the large prime mover before him.

'I've only ever seen vids or old pictures of these... never one in the flesh.' JT was enthralled with the sight. They walked down the rows of trucks finally coming to an area where old aircraft were stored. 'What was the Second thinking? There's enough here to supply a small nation.'

'He was a visionary. Things were bad back then... maybe he was preparing for just that. Maybe he was looking at the possibility that he may need to restart the whole country,' Aaron mused as he gazed at the find. Just ahead was another set of doors, smaller than the first set but obviously locked. 'Graham, see that?' he asked.

Graham, moving ahead, saw the doors that Aaron had indicated together with the access panel beside it. Once again, he reached for the key ring as he opened the access door and noted the code on the master switch. He rifled through his keys until he found the corresponding one and inserted it into the master switch, turned it and waited for the prompt on the screen. Once he had this he called up the information on the data pad and entered another code. His code was accepted and he pressed the green button.

The system cycled through the atmospheric purge process and then the door began to open. Slowly it moved to their left. As it passed the half way point, overhead light panels came on and before them were rows of ancient automobiles of all types. Graham looked at JT.

'You share more than a name with your ancestor. What did they call him? Yes... a mad petrol head.'

John just stood and stared, unable to speak or move. Before him was the greatest treasure he could ever have wished for: old cars, internal combustion engines, rubber tyres, and, except for a layer of dust, they looked in perfect condition.

It was well known in the family that John Thomas Abraham the Second had a major vice — he collected old cars. This collection, or obsession, was a thing of rumours and debate, and had remained so, having never been found — until now. Here before them was the evidence.

'Looks like there are about a thousand of them,' Graham

said. 'Like most of the areas we have opened, this garage was sealed and de oxygenated... there's no corrosion. In fact, if you look at all the vehicles and aircraft, they all look brand new.' He turned and looked back into the main garage area.

JT and Aaron slowly moved forward into the garage, their shared love of the ancient things drawing them like a moth to a flame. Aaron stopped at one, a low slung sports model, its curves and shape marking it. 'I don't believe it,' he said as he moved around the vehicle, 'Where would he have found this... and in this condition?'

JT joined him and together they stared at the car. He gently tapped the front fender and it gave a metallic sound. 'Fuck, its original!' he swore in astonishment. 'I thought it could only be one of the replicas I've read about.' But there was no doubt; what they saw in front of them was a genuine Cobra 427.

Graham watched the pair – they were like devout pilgrims on a religious retreat. He smiled to himself having no idea why anyone would want these old things.

'Well JT, I'll always know where to find you now,' Aaron chuckled. 'And I think I might have to spend quite a bit of time here as well.'

EPILOGUE

Bureaucrats can be so frustrating.

Although Jason had provided Sarclan's DNA records to the administration, bureaucracy had taken over and red tape started to back up, frustrating Jason no end. It had been a month now since the decisive battles both here and in the Tenth Realm had put an end to the threat of Sedition domination. In that month, Sam Grogan never had more than a few hours each day to relax, let alone sleep. He was tired – bone weary – but the results were starting to show.

The search for the two warships that had come through the portal from the Tenth Realm was painfully slow but there had been a few solid leads to follow up. On a more positive note, the final version of Harper's new sensor program had shown great promise; it was now up to commercial agreements to finalise the use of it.

The Cordoba Corporation had been indicted as an accomplice in the Sedition rebellion. The head of the corporation, Luigi Cordoba, had mysteriously disappeared, leaving his son Antonio to face the music. The fallout from this would take years to sort out.

Sam smiled. *Only fitting... you wake the tiger, you're bound to be bitten* he thought. His musings were interrupted by the intercom on his desk announcing another arrival. He sighed and touched an icon on his console, 'Yes, Lieutenant?'

'Admiral, Silas Greenbach is here to see you,' the young Lieutenant replied.

Sam had been waiting for this meeting for the past three weeks

'Send him in.'

The door opened and Silas walked in. Sam stood and went to greet him. 'Welcome, Silas, thanks for coming.' The two men shook hands. 'No matter how many times I see you, you never look any different.'

'Now, Sam, no flattery. It's good to catch up again after all that has happened,' Silas replied.

'How's the new power system for the portal coming?' Sam asked

Silas smiled and shook his head. 'Sam, don't bullshit a bullshitter. You know very well how it's doing, but since you ask, we are very pleased with the progress. Now, what did you really get me in here for?'

The two men had known each other for many years. In fact, they had met on Sam's thirtieth birthday and that was two hundred and sixty years past. In all that time, Silas had never seemed to age, unlike Sam who was now showing his advancing years. He nodded and motioned for Silas to take a seat in one of the large Chesterfield arm chairs, while he busied himself pouring each of them a good three fingers of whisky before taking the seat opposite his old friend.

'Silas, we have a small dilemma and you may be the only person alive who can solve it. But first, I must ask you some awkward questions. Any answers are strictly between us... the room is secure.' Sam paused allowing Silas to appreciate his words. Silas nodded his acceptance and Sam continued.

'We have known each other for over two and a half centuries and today you still look the same as you did the day I met you.'

Silas began to speak but Sam waved him to silence. 'Please, old friend, allow me to finish. There are many who suggest that you have cloned yourself a number of times and that you are actually the same Silas Greenbach – albeit cloned – who founded the company, and not his descendant. Some say that is why Greenbach Technologies purchased Clotech so many years ago.' Sam stopped, giving Silas the chance to respond.

Silas drained his glass and held it out for a refill. 'We may need a couple of these.' Sam took the glass and refilled his as well. When he was comfortably in his seat, Silas continued. 'You know me as Silas Greenbach the fourth but, unlike anybody else who has a number after his name; mine refers to the version of the same person, not just the generational number. The rumours are partially correct so let me explain.

'Greenbach Tech started funding cloning – as a silent partner in Clotech – back in the twenty two hundreds, mainly to find better ways to produce crops and food. In twenty three ninety, my ancestor, Silas the first, came across a young scientist, Eugene Sarclan.

'His work in cloning was far more advanced than anything else at the time. He was an amazing young man, with drive and determination to match his intellect. His research was so far advanced, especially in the area of memory recording and transference, that the original Silas poured massive amounts of money into his work.

'Eugene believed that not only could we clone people, we could also transfer their complete consciousness... but more importantly, their subconscious. Thus, he believed we could live forever without reproducing, just replacing those who, in his mind, were worthy.

'This is where he and Silas disagreed. Silas saw it as a vehicle to help those who had suffered life changing injuries, but Eugene convinced him to continue the funding and the research grew further.

'Eugene would often say he wanted a few more of himself as he would be able to work on the same project, but from different angles, thus utilising the one mind set covering all possible research streams at the one time but, with a common goal.

'He believed that this was the key to much greater discoveries, and he may have been correct. We know, now, that he did create at least two versions of himself. You can imagine the opposition we would have had in those days if this had become common knowledge. Every religious nutter would be screaming for our heads, so this research was done secretly.' He paused as they both took a sip from their glass.

'The twenty fourth and fifth centuries were a mess, population rising, people living twice as long as they did previously and the planet's eco system starting to shut down. The human race had finally ended religious wars that had plagued it for centuries, but so much of the planet was decimated. For the next hundred years, Eugene continued his research and later, in twenty five twenty five, the partnership between Greenbach Technologies and Abracorp was struck... Eugene was part of that. None of us knew, at that point, anything of his extracurricular activities.

'It was around this time when I had that accident. I was visiting one of the manufacturing facilities... I can't even remember which one... when there was an explosion. I suffered horrific burns and other injuries. All the doctors gave me only days to live, but Eugene decided otherwise.

'Somehow, he forged documents that stated my need to die at home. I never had any such wish, but he compelled the doctors to honour my wishes and had me transferred to his research station.

'This is where I was first cloned. Eugene worked night and day to build me a new body. At the same time, he was recording my entire brain and mind: memories; ideas; everything. When the body achieved maturity... it actually only took around ten weeks... he transferred my... essence I suppose is the word, into this new host and Silas Greenbach the second was born, complete with all the knowledge and experiences of his predecessor. I was later told that it took seven attempts before Eugene had complete success and I survived. I subsequently funded more research to perfect the technology. The rest I believe you know.' Silas took another swig and waited for Sam to digest the story.

'So, how many times have you,' he paused looking for the right words, 'regenerated?'

'If we take the first attempts out, four times. When I *die* and my *son* takes over, we use the number, but in reality, Silas Greenbach the Fourth is, mostly, the same as the original. There are some differences but, to date, there has been negligible degradation from my original self. The only down side is that I am unable to father children... a legacy from the first attempt. So you see, cloning is my only avenue to procreation.'

Silas again paused, as if unwilling to dig deeper. 'Sam, I don't understand why you couldn't have asked this before, and why you needed me to come here to tell you. We have been friends for so long and I would have trusted you with this. Hell, I trusted you with my life a number of times, so what gives?'

Sam gave his friend a long and enquiring gaze. 'When we took Cordoba Blue down here and defeated Dean and his cohorts that had escaped to the Tenth Realm, we were left with two bodies... two bodies of the same person. Jason furnished us with the DNA records from Abracorp and, after much red tape we now have the results. Both bodies are an almost perfect match for Eugene Sarclan.'

Silas shook his head. 'I always thought this would be the outcome. Eugene was totally convinced that if he had more of himself, he could achieve more. I think we should bring Jason in on this, after all, he did know Eugene briefly. He worked with him when he was a young man.'

Two hours later, Jason Abraham arrived at Space Corps HQ. On landing, he was quickly ushered to Sam's office where the situation of two bodies of the same person was fully explained. Jason had already agreed to help with the identification months ago, so his agreement today was tinged with a sarcastic remark about the red tape delay. The three took a secure elevator down to the bowels of the building and climbed into a transport pod for the trip to the secure facility.

Fifteen minutes later, the pod stopped and they were met by four heavily armed guards. Their escort guided them through three security check points to their destination. They stood before two huge blast doors as Sam entered a code and the doors slid open.

The room was huge and well lit. It was also empty except for two stasis pods in the centre, around twenty metres from them. They were totally silent as they approached the pods, so many memories and emotions now entering their thoughts.

For all his faults, Eugene Sarclan had, at one time, been friend and saviour for Silas and gifted employee and friend to Jason. He was also one of the greatest intellects ever to grace the human race.

Sam broke the silence. 'Prepare yourselves. There is significant damage to this body, but his face is recognisable… the other is undamaged.' He entered another code into the panel on the side of the first pod and the top cover changed from opaque to transparent. There before them was the body. Both men studied it for a few minutes before turning to Sam.

'That is Eugene Sarclan,' Jason said solemnly.

'I agree,' Silas added.

Sam repeated the process on the second pod. Again both Silas and Jason agreed that this was also Eugene Sarclan.

Sam seemed relieved. 'Thank you, now we can put this whole episode behind us.' He touched the pad on the pod and the cover was again opaque. 'With Sarclan gone, we have complete closure and we can move forward. Such a shame that a man who was so brilliant, could turn on humanity; there is so much he could have contributed to our species. Thank you both for this.' He turned to leave but Silas and Jason hung back, deep in thought. Sam stopped. 'What's up?'

It was Jason who spoke first. 'We have only identified two Eugene Sarclan bodies, but is this all that's left of him?'

Silas added, 'Remember our discussion, Sam. What if Eugene has done what he wanted? What if these are only *two* copies of Eugene Sarclan… what if he has created multiple versions of himself? If that's the case, we haven't cut the head off the Hydra, only a couple of the snakes.' His words hit Sam like a hammer blow. If this was true, then they had only won the first battle.

'So what do you suggest?' Sam asked.

Jason replied. 'I think the Corps has had the answer, or at least the path to the answer, all along. You need to trace this back to the beginning, to when Sarclan obtained the material and expertise he needed to start his project.'

'What do you mean?' Sam was sure he wasn't going to like the answer.

It was Silas, who answered this time,

'You've got to find Baleraphon.'

Thanks for purchasing this book; I hope you enjoyed the adventure.

To keep up with my latest news about upcoming books and events:

www.gregmutton.com

Facebook and Instagram @gregmuttonauthor.

Book 3

**The Hunt for Balerophon –
due for release July 2020**